RUTH PRAWER JHABVALA

Ruth Prawer Jhabvala was born in Germany of Polish parents and came to England in 1939 at the age of twelve. She graduated from Queen Mary College, London University, and married the Indian architect C.S.H. Jhabvala. They lived in Delhi from 1951 to 1975. Since then they have divided their time between Delhi, New York and London.

As well as her numerous novels and short stories, in collaboration with James Ivory and Ismail Merchant Ruth Prawer Jhabvala has written scripts for film and television, including *A Room with a View* and *Howards End*, both of which are Academy Award winners. She won the Booker Prize for *Heat and Dust* in 1975, the Neil Gunn International Fellowship in 1978, the MacArthur Foundation Fellowship in 1984 and was made a CBE in the 1998 New Year's Honours List.

Also by the author

Novels

To Whom She Will (*US title* Amrita)
The Nature of Passion
Esmond in India
The Householder
Get Ready for Battle
A New Dominion (*US title* Travelers)
Heat and Dust
In Search of Love and Beauty
Three Continents
Poet and Dancer
Shards of Memory
My Nine Lives

Short stories

Like Birds, Like Fishes
A Stronger Climate
An Experience of India
How I Became a Holy Mother
East into Upper East
Out of India: Selected Stories

RUTH PRAWER JHABVALA

———————

A BACKWARD PLACE

JOHN MURRAY

© Ruth Prawer Jhabvala

First published in Great Britain in 1965 by John Murray (Publishers)
A division of Hodder Headline

This paperback edition published 2005

The right of Ruth Prawer Jhabvala to be identified as the Author of the Work
has been asserted by her in accordance with the Copyright, Designs and Patents
Act 1988.

1 3 5 7 9 10 8 6 4 2

A CIP catalogue record for this title is available from the British Library

ISBN 0 7195 6195 7

Typeset in Times

Printed and bound by
Clays Ltd, St Ives plc

Hodder Headline policy is to use papers that are natural, renewable and recyclable
products and made from wood grown in sustainable forests. The logging and
manufacturing processes are expected to conform to the environmental
regulations of the country of origin.

John Murray (Publishers)
338 Euston Road
London NW1 3BH

A Backward Place

1

Etta was propped up on pillows in her bed. She was having an elegant breakfast from a tray. She held a cream cracker between thumb and forefinger and, before taking a bite, said to Judy, 'You ought to leave him, really you ought.'

Judy was thrilled. She had no intentions of leaving her husband, but it made her feel worldly to hear Etta talking about it.

'It's very bourgeois of you to keep going,' Etta said. She pronounced bourgeois with a very French accent, though she herself was Hungarian and her intonation, in spite of the English drawl she cultivated, was basically central European. 'Petit bourgeois,' she added, even more crisply French. 'Marriages, my dear, are made to be broken, that's one of the rules of modern civilization. Just because we happen to have landed ourselves in this primitive society, that's no reason why we should submit to their primitive morality.' She made a face and delicately dusted crumbs from her fingers, as if she were dusting off all that primitiveness she spoke of. 'My dear Judy, you've made a mistake – it could happen as they say to anyone – but if you would only face up to it and get out before it's too late, too *late*, Judy.'

Judy was tempted to say that it was already too late (after all, she had been here nearly ten years now and had two children) but she refrained, because she knew Etta didn't care to have her assertions contradicted. And anyway, as far as Judy was concerned, the discussion was purely theoretical, so she didn't much mind what was said.

'You've got such a terribly phlegmatic nature,' Etta said, closing her eyes in exasperation on the word phlegmatic. 'You just will not realize that life is something to be seized and struggled with, the way Jacob struggled with the Angel. Oh my God, what am I coming to, making Biblical allusions! It's your frightful puritan influence, Judy.'

Judy laughed: she loved such sophisticated talk.

'No, but I'm not, not joking, I'm absolutely entirely terribly terribly serious, Judy. You must leave him and get out. You're just rotting here. Look at you in that *thing*' – Judy looked down at herself, at the sari which she mostly wore nowadays (it saved so much trouble) – 'and your hair too and – ugh, you're awful. You've let yourself *go*. And not only physically, let me tell you as a friend – ' she put down her coffee cup with an angry little clatter and called, 'Run my bath now!'

Here one might have expected a neat maid in black dress and white apron to appear, but instead, her summons was answered by the usual kind of tattered hill-boy servant. Before he could go to the bathroom, Etta hissed at him, 'First the tray, take away the tray, will you never learn.' He bent over her bed to remove her breakfast tray and, as he did so, grinning widely, peered down into her apricot-coloured night-dress with its nylon lace trimmings.

While Etta was in her bath, Judy wandered round the flat. She loved it here. Everything was so elegant, so continental, in such good taste: just like Etta herself. There was a white rug on the stone floor in the sitting-room, and a low divan done up in pearl grey and covered with an array of amusing cushions. The raw silk lampshades matched the curtains, and sophisticated black and white prints hung on the walls. There were two flowers each in two tiny delicate vases. Several gay record-sleeves were scattered on top of the radiogram; a French fashion magazine lay open on the divan. One might have been in Europe.

And it was only when one stepped out of the living-room of this top-floor flat on to the terrace (as Judy now did, for Etta was being a long time in her bath) and looked over the parapet, that it became very clear that this was not Europe. The houses, true enough, were built from jazzy pictures in European or American magazines, but the surrounding landscape was not really consonant with anything those magazines might know of. Vast barren spaces, full of dust and bits of litter, flowed around and between the smart new houses; there was not a tree in sight, and the only growth to spring spontaneously out of this soil was, here and there, little huts patched together out of mud and old boards and pieces of sacking. The whole area was inter-sected by a railway line for goods trains, and there were two prominent landmarks: an old mausoleum of blackened stone and no archi-tectural value (but with a curious air of permanence about it: one felt that when all the pretty houses and all the makeshift huts had gone, this at any rate would still be here), and an enormous brightly coloured advertisement hoarding for rubber tyres. Most prominent of all was the sky, which covered and dwarfed everything, was electric blue and had black kites wheeling slowly round and round against it.

6

'Where are you?' Etta called from inside the bedroom. Judy hurried in, for she didn't want to miss any part of Etta's toilette she might be allowed to witness. She found her sitting at her dressing-table, in front of all her jars and bottles and lipsticks, her negligée slung about her shoulders with her brittle blonde hair hanging loose. She was patting something into her face, leaning forward into the mirror in order to watch herself doing it. She smelled of soap and talcum powder and some sort of delicious bath oil.

'Did you go out in the sun?' she asked Judy. 'That's of course the best way of ruining one's complexion. Don't you know that the Indian sun has been put specially into the sky to ruin our complexions?' She patted more fiercely, as if daring any agent of ruination to come near her. 'It's nothing to smile at,' she said, hawk-eyed in the mirror. 'It might all sound terribly trivial to you but, believe me, it's on these trivial things that one's life depends. You must learn that, you simply must.'

She got up, shrugged off her negligée which fell to the floor (Judy obsequiously picked it up) and revealed herself to be wearing a black nylon slip with a lace top. She reached over to her bedside table, picked a cigarette from her box and lit it, while Judy admired her. True, Etta's flesh, now so frankly revealed (all her shoulders, her arms, her legs) did not look young – it was very pallid and shook a little – but she had kept her figure, and her hair, by whatever means, *was* blonde, and who else could stand there like that in the middle of the morning wearing black underwear and smoking oval cigarettes?

'There is absolutely no reason,' she said, 'when in Rome to do as Rome does. Or rather, there may be every reason in Rome, but certainly, certainly none in Delhi. It's no use sinking down to anyone's level, Judy, we must always try to raise them up to ours. Oh God, now you're making me sound like something colonial, but it's true, it really is *true*. Here, hold' – and she held out her cigarette which Judy, content to play ashtray, reverently took, while Etta scanned her wardrobe with cunning eyes to choose a suitable dress.

'I hate to see you going on and on like this. Married to that awful – well, he *is* awful, don't expect me to mince words. I never, never mince words, you know that.' Judy did. 'If at least he were earning decently and could make some sort of a life for you here, but not even that! It's you who have to go out to work –'

'But I like it,' Judy said.

'That's not the point at all, how stupid of you. That you should *have* to go whether you like it or not – good heavens, what are men for, let alone husbands?' There was some more, but it couldn't be heard because she was pulling her dress over her head. When she emerged, her hair ruffled and her face red (it was a tight-fitting dress), she was saying '... no use going on only for the sake of going on. Give me back my cigarette and zip me up at the back, but careful, hm? I don't want my skin caught.'

Judy did it very carefully. She loved the way the dress clung tight to Etta's waist and over her hips; she also loved being so near to Etta and within her aura of cosmetics and carefully bathed and powdered flesh.

'Why do you stick on like that, why why why? It's so ridiculous.' She fixed a jewelled brooch on her dress, just under her left shoulder. 'It's stupid. It's *mad*. Really, I don't know how you expect me to be patient with you.'

She stood in her tight, pale-green dress with the brooch glittering under her shoulder, and now she was fixing her ear-rings which matched the brooch. Judy looked at her and said, 'How nice you look.'

Judy's home was very different from Etta's. It was in a side-street leading off from a road of shops. At the corner of this side-street was a cloth-shop, then came a brick wall with old posters stuck over it and a wooden door set into it. The door was often open, so that anyone passing could look into Judy's courtyard. There was nothing interesting to see, though – it was like every other courtyard in that area, with a few old string cots, and some washing strung up, and a battered water-container – and even if one could have seen farther, into the rooms leading off the courtyard, it still wouldn't have been interesting or unusual. One room was a bedroom for Judy, her husband and their two children, the other had been made into a kind of sitting-room, and the storeroom didn't hold the trunks and other household objects it had been intended for, but instead had become a room for their old aunt, Bhuaji. There was also a sort of cooking-shed, covered with an asbestos roof, and a very small bathroom with only one tap in it, and an even smaller WC. Out of the courtyard rose a flight of stone steps which led to the upstairs part of the house; here Judy's elder brother-in-law lived with his family.

The original idea had been for the two households to be quite separate. It had been Mukand's, the elder brother's idea: he said he wanted no part in the usual kind of Hindu joint family, which he maintained – and Judy's husband, Bal, agreed with him, not out of any intense conviction but because he felt it to be liberal and forward-looking – was a seed-bed of ill-will and strife. However, somehow or other, the two households had run together and had not proved a seed-bed of ill-will and strife. There was, everyone soon realized, really no point in cooking upstairs as well as downstairs, especially as the children of both households took it for granted that both parts of the house were theirs, to eat, play and sleep at will in either.

Judy was trying to do something about the sitting-room. She often, after having been to Etta's flat, tried to do something about the sitting-room, but never with any success. Now she was holding one of the two cane chairs and looking round for a suitable place to put it. She chose first one, then another, but neither was to her satisfaction, so she finally put it back where it had been before. Then she picked up the other chair and held that and bit her lip and looked round speculatively.

Bhuaji came in and asked her what she was doing. 'Don't strain yourself,' she added. She always said that, whenever she saw Judy carrying anything; it was left over from the times when Judy had been pregnant.

Judy put down the second chair as well. She realized it was not the position of the chairs that needed changing, but the chairs themselves.

'Children have gone to play opposite,' Bhuaji said. 'How quiet it is without them. A house needs children . . . You know what our Prithvi said to me this morning, God bless him? "Bhuaji," he said, "when are you going to get new teeth?"' She cackled with delight. '"Bhuaji, when are you going to get new teeth?" Just like that he said. Now what are you doing?' For Judy was stripping the covering sheet and the mattress off what constituted their sofa and looking despondently at their trunks underneath.

'Do you think one day we'll be able to afford a real sofa?'

'Why not?' Bhuaji said. 'God gives, and gives with both hands.'

Judy sighed and covered up the trunks again. There was no more furniture to think of re-arranging, so her gaze strayed round the whitewashed walls instead. These held two framed certificates, both of them belonging to Judy's husband. One was his BA certificate, the other had a ribbon and seal and said that he had attended a Conference of International Youth in London as an Indian delegate. There was also a picture of him at the airport, going off to this conference with the other delegates, all of them wearing garlands and tight new suits made by their local tailors.

Judy said, 'Do you think it looks all right to have certificates on your wall?'

'Of course,' Bhuaji said and sat down comfortably on the floor. 'Then everyone who comes knows at once what sort of a person you are.'

Judy said, 'What sort of person will people think Bal is, then?'

'They will know he is an educated boy – a B A – '

Judy laughed. She too had been impressed by the BA when she had first heard of it, but later she found that very many people had it and, as far as she could judge, they did not seem any the more learned for it.

'And also that he has been outside, a travelled, educated man – '

'Goodness,' said Judy, and laughed again to think of her Bal as a travelled, educated man. But then she looked round the room and shook her head. 'This is no place for a posh person like him. We must get some furniture – '

'Some nice chairs,' said Bhuaji comfortably from the floor.

'And a sofa – and curtains – and new pictures – and a coffee-table with an ashtray on it.' But even while she was saying it, she was losing interest. She was lying face down on what was now their sofa, and found it really quite comfortable; what more should one want?

Bhuaji, who never sat on a chair and didn't even care to own a bed to sleep on, said sympathetically, 'In your home in London you must have had all these things?'

'Oh lots of things,' said Judy without passion. Too many, actually, she thought: her mother had liked to pick up bargains in basement sales and these were displayed all over their small semi-detached – fire-tongs, novelty ashtrays (though no one in the house smoked), china cats and dogs, plastic doileys, rexine calendars, the statue of the boy taking a thorn out of his foot. All these objects required a lot of cleaning and dusting, so her mother was always busy; not only with the cleaning and dusting but also with keeping a sharp watch over others to see they didn't spoil them, like Judy and her father touching things and leaving fingerprints, or the milkman who had once been caught wiping his feet on the new 'Welcome and Cheerio' coir mat. Judy didn't know what had happened to all these objects now, but she presumed that, after her mother's death, her aunt Agnes had gone round the house, fastidiously picking out what she favoured for herself and sending the rest for sale at the local junk-shop.

Judy never cared to think much of home nowadays (whenever memories of it came up, she did her best to think of something else), so she was glad when, just at this moment, her sister-in-law Shanti came from upstairs and asked her at once: 'What happened today?' Shanti asked this every day. She was fascinated by Judy's office and the fact that Judy went out every day, and was keen to hear of any adventures that might have befallen her.

Judy thought for a moment but had to say, 'Nothing much,' – reluctantly, for she knew Shanti would be disappointed.

And indeed, Shanti's round homely face at once looked disappointed. 'There must have been *something*.'

Judy thought hard. At last she came up with, 'When I was standing at the bus-stop a huge big car passed and at the back – such a sight! A woman with blue hair – '

'Blue hair!' Shanti cried in delight.

'Well sort of mauve really – you'd have laughed – and she was holding a tiny little dog all curled and combed and making it look out the window as if it was a baby she was trying to amuse. Honestly, some people – '

Shanti was fully satisfied. She clapped her hands together and laughed and made Judy repeat everything she had said and go into the minutest detail. Finally she said, 'How lucky you are.' This too she said every day; she envied and admired Judy tremendously for the exciting life she imagined her to be leading outside the house. Shanti herself hardly ever went out: where should she go to?

Judy yawned. She didn't feel herself to be so very lucky; she was always happiest when she had got back home. But there was no point, she knew, in explaining this to Shanti. For Shanti the outside world was so totally unknown a quantity that she had no trouble at all in peopling it with wild and beautiful imaginings. She had been married for sixteen years, had four children and she looked matronly enough, being plump with a round housewife face from which all bloom of youth had long departed; she always dressed in cotten printed saris and had her head decorously covered. But this appearance of hers was misleading, for at heart she was not a matron at all and had not changed in the least from what she had been as a girl before her marriage. In fact, as she had once confessed to Judy, sometimes she thought she would wake up and find that these sixteen years had not taken place, and there was no husband, no children, only herself still living in her father's house and playing games with her sisters.

'One day we shall change places, and you will stay at home and I shall go to your office,' Shanti said, and mischievously bit her tongue.

'Okay,' Judy said and yawned again; she undid her hair and tousled it with her fingers. 'Needs washing,' she commented.

'Should I do it now?' Shanti said. They always washed one another's hair and, while they were doing it, had a lot of fun and confidences together. Altogether they got on very well and had done so even before they could properly communicate together – that is, before Judy had learned any Hindustani. Nowadays, of course, Judy spoke fluently (though with an appalling accent) and she and Shanti could easily exchange their deepest thoughts, whenever they had any.

Shanti lifted Judy's long strands of blonde hair – because she wanted as much as possible (and it wasn't very possible) to look like everybody else, Judy had grown her hair since she had come out here and wore it in a bun – and then massaged her scalp affectionately. While she was doing this, she said, 'Then tomorrow shall I go to your office?'

'Why not.'

Shanti giggled. 'Can you see me?' Then she cried, 'Oh I would never dare, not in one hundred years!' The next moment she looked sad and, still massaging Judy's head, she said, 'With us it's like that. Only to sit at home day and night, cooking and cleaning and looking after children.'

Judy said, 'I wouldn't mind.' She had enjoyed the years she had spent at home with Shanti and Bhuaji and the children, and went to work not out of choice but necessity.

'How you talk!' Shanti reprimanded her. 'If you had to do it, you would know. Never see anyone or anything interesting and nothing going on – '

'But nothing goes on in the office either.'

Shanti looked at her reproachfully.

'What about Bhuaji?' Judy said. They both looked at her sitting peacefully with her eyes shut and her lips moving, probably in prayer. 'She meets lots more people than I do.' Bhuaji went out frequently to neighbouring houses, into the bazaar, to the temple, to the river.

'Only ordinary people,' Shanti said.

'But everybody's ordinary!'

'Even women with blue hair?' Shanti cried, and then she was giggling and light-hearted again.

They talked a bit more – about a sweater that Shanti was knitting and the funeral of a saint which Bhuaji had attended the week before – till it got dark, and then the children came home from playing. Everyone went to sleep early: Shanti upstairs (where her husband, who got very tired in his office, was already asleep), Bhuaji on the mat, spread out in her little room that should have been the trunk-room, Judy and her two children in their bedroom. Bal did not get home till some hours afterwards; no one heard him, for he was very careful and walked on tiptoe. He was always considerate.

*

12

Judy had had a job for the past five years. First she had worked with a motor-car agency which belonged to one of Etta's admirers, but after he had ceased to be an admirer, Judy's job was no longer quite secure; so she was not really surprised when one day she was told that they were cutting down on staff and her services would no longer be required. Later she found out that the proprietor had wanted her job for a nephew of his income tax inspector, and though she did not bear a grudge about this – she was worldly enough to know that income tax inspectors had to be obliged – her dismissal came at a bad time for her. Bal was away in Bombay, chasing after some film job he had been vaguely promised, and was not in a position to send money home as regularly as they had hoped. For a time she had had to rely on her brother-in-law Mukand, who lived upstairs, and though he considered it his duty, in a resigned sort of way, to stand by her, she did not relish her dependence. She knew that Mukand's salary (he worked as accountant in a small manufacturing business) was enough to provide for one family, and that his own, but not for two; and besides, she had not in England grown up with the idea that other people were there to provide one with a living, even if they were – one might even stretch a point and say especially if they were – one's relatives. As her father often said, 'Never be under an obligation to any of them bastards' (them bastards being the world in general), while her mother's way of putting it was, 'Shut the door and don't trust no one.' Judy had a more open and trusting nature than either of her parents, but the conviction that the world didn't owe her a living was as strong in her as it had been in them.

She had spent her days going from person to person, searching for a job, and come home tired and defeated at night. Those had been terrible times for her; but even they came to an end when some friends of hers called the Hochstadts told her of an organization called the Cultural Dais, which was in need of an assistant. They introduced her to the Honorary Secretary, a Mrs Kaul, who had interviewed her and offered her a very small salary which Judy, amazed at her own aud-acity but quite determined not to be got for less than she and the children and Bhuaji could live on, had tried to make her raise. They had bargained to and fro for quite a while, sitting there in Mrs Kaul's exquisitely appointed drawing-room, both of them with the sharp looks on their faces they wore when they haggled with shopkeepers in the bazaar.

She was appointed as assistant to the General Secretary, a young man called Sudhir Bannerjee, who had not welcomed her. He said there was little enough for him to do all day as it was, and now she

had come to take away half. But they got on well together and were
pleasant company for each other during the long hours in which there
was nothing to do. In the original scheme of things, the Dais was to
have hummed with intellectual activity all day long, people coming in
to use the library and engaging in on-the-spot discussion, but this had
not happened. Apart from preparing for and conducting the lectures
and meetings, and bringing out reports and a little monthly news-
sheet, there was nothing much going on. So it was that Sudhir and
Judy carried on long, idle conversations during which they found out
quite a lot about each other.

There were two small wooden tables in the office, one for Sudhir and
one for Judy, and they sat with their backs to each other. She would
often hear him grumbling to himself and jabbing viciously at the keys
of the typewriter. She always guessed then that soon his breaking-
point would come and he would turn round and speak contemptuously
of the Dais and their work there. He thoroughly despised his job.

So it was nothing unusual when, that morning, he suddenly gave a
loud snort, stopped typing and read out loud: 'A member of the
public then got up and asked, "Could the speaker kindly point out
some lessons that the Medieval Traders Guild of Europe hold for the
India of today?" And what is more, can you believe it, he actually
pointed out these lessons – here they are, four of them: *a, b, c, d*.'

Judy didn't answer; she knew there was never any necessity for
adding fuel to his fire. And indeed, the next moment he had jumped
up, pushing back his chair so hard that it fell over. He was very tall,
with long limbs. He started pacing up and down the office and, when
he found this cramping, he went through the partition into the library.
She listened to him rummaging in there. She knew he couldn't possibly be looking for a book, for he had long since read everything
worth reading there. Certainly the choice was very limited. There
were stacks of government publications on the distribution of the
canal waters and such-like topics, and a number of somewhat tattered
volumes which had been donated at various times and were of a
mixed order and quality (Tolstoy: *What Then Must We Do?* J. S. Mill:
On Liberty. Samuel Smiles: *Thrift*. An Observer: *Whither India?* R.
Rolland: *Life of Vivekananda*).

He folded back the partition, the way they did when they had a
meeting, so that library and office became one long hall. He stood at
the end opposite to Judy, before a little table and with his back to the
library bookcase, just as their speakers always did. With one hand he
supported himself on the table, the other held an imaginary lapel; his

14

feet were crossed at the ankle. 'It is worth bearing in mind,' he said in a nasal voice, 'that under such conditions cultural themes develop their own criteria so that it might develop under scrutiny that Huguenot poetry of the seventh century is not absolutely incompatible with Hottentot poetry of the ninth.'

'Very funny,' said Judy.

He came out from behind the table and looked gloomy again. He really disliked his job, and her one fear was that one day he would give it up and go back to Calcutta, and then someone else would come to be General Secretary. She didn't want anyone else; she had got used to Sudhir and liked him. He was, as she often said, a real card.

She went back to addressing envelopes for the next meeting (a talk on Indo-Dutch relations from the fifteenth century to the present day). She did it very slowly and carefully, in her best handwriting, because there was no other work and she didn't want to sit around bored and maybe get on Sudhir's nerves. She took particular pleasure in addressing envelopes to the President, the Vice-President, the Prime Minister and members of the Cabinet. None of these people ever came, but Mrs Kaul, the Honorary Secretary, said it was important to send them invitations so that they could keep abreast of the work being done at the Cultural Dais.

The telephone rang and Judy picked it up. She put her hand over the mouthpiece and said in a low, worried voice, 'It's Mrs Kaul for you.'

'I'm not here,' Sudhir said.

Judy transmitted this message, and then had to listen patiently for a long time while Mrs Kaul delivered herself of some harangue at the other end. When at last she was able to replace the receiver, she said with a sigh, 'She wants the report on Cultural Background to International Relations.'

'Does she indeed,' Sudhir said pleasantly.

Just then their landlord appeared and said in an accusing voice, 'One of you has been in my kitchen.'

'A thousand pardons, dear Doctor!' cried Sudhir, bending his head and touching his hand penitently to his forehead.

Their landlord really was a doctor, and there was even a board outside at the gate, giving his name, qualifications and consulting hours. However, no patients ever came to avail themselves of his skills, which indeed he had long since ceased to practise.

'It is not,' he said, in a milder tone than that in which he had started off, 'that I grudge the use of my kitchen to you, but you see a landlord has his responsibilities.'

Sudhir nodded so gravely and listened so attentively that the Doctor felt prompted to expand on his theme. 'Imagine now if I allowed you to make use of my kitchen whenever you pleased. There would be inconvenience to me, but this of course I would be willing to overlook. But then also, how could I say no to that one?' And he jerked his head contemptuously towards the back, where there was another room which he had let out to a young government clerk at what he now considered a shamefully low rent. 'He too would put claim on my kitchen and would come in and have his food cooked there. Chi,' said the Doctor in disgust both at the clerk and at his food before continuing in a different tone: 'There is also the legal aspect. I am the landlord and you are my tenants. We have entered into contract to effect that you have use of this spacious hall but not of what lies beyond it. These terms must be honoured by both sides, otherwise to what purpose are contracts and legal ties?'

While he was talking, he walked round the room, tapping the walls, trying the windows to see they opened and shut properly, with the concerned and important air of proprietorship. This house was his largest, indeed his only stake in life. It was a handsome house, though not quite on as grand a scale as the huge portico in front might have led one to believe. It had been built by the Doctor's father, a rich merchant who had earned a lot of money and had been more concerned with making some show of it rather than building himself a really comfortable place to live in. He had had the portico constructed leading to the large hall with high ceiling and marble floor which was now the office of the Cultural Dais; but beyond that he had given up and built three poky rooms and a kitchen which he had considered good enough for his family's everyday living.

'What would you say,' inquired the Doctor, with quiet satisfaction, 'is the value of this property today?' and he went on to speculate on this pleasing problem at some length. Judy continued to address envelopes and Sudhir to type his report. They did not feel disturbed by the Doctor's presence or conversation. He often came and usually talked about the same thing, so there was no strain of either listening or replying. It was rather pleasant in the office at such times. The office itself was bare, with only the two tables and a stack of collapsible chairs and, on the wall, a photograph of Tagore and another of Dr Radhakrishnan, but when they looked out of the windows, they could see the trees along the road, all heavy with yellow blossoms.

Etta entered the restaurant and stood poised within the door. She

16

saw Clarissa immediately, but nevertheless hovered there a moment longer and pretended to be searching round. She liked entering restaurants and having everyone look at her. And everyone did look at her, and eyes followed her as she tripped smartly on her high heels, head held high and slim hips swinging, to the table where Clarissa sat waiting for her.

Clarissa was sprawled on a velvet sofa, with her things – her sketching-pad, a few grubby parcels, the big checked cloth bag which served her permanently as handbag and shopping-bag – scattered round her. 'Late as usual,' said Clarissa.

Etta sat down and began smoking cigarettes immediately. She looked round the restaurant from under half-closed lids to see if there was anyone interesting. There was not, but she was gratified to note that the ripples created by her entrance had not yet subsided and people were still looking at her. She put a careless hand to her blonde hair and ordered coffee.

'You're looking tired,' Clarissa said. 'There are bags under your eyes.'

Etta smiled pleasantly. There was much she could have retaliated with, but Clarissa looked such a frump anyway, it was hardly necessary to stress the point. Her wispy hair, which she had attempted to build into a top-knot, had most of it come down. She wore her usual Rajasthani peasant skirt – this one in green and orange – and a blouse of thick handspun cloth, printed over with scenes from Indian village life.

'You're probably run down,' Clarissa said. 'You need a holiday.'

'But I always need a holiday.'

'I might be going up to Naini Tal next week. I'm longing to see my mountains again.'

'Who are you staying with?'

'The Kapurs, I expect.'

Etta made no comment but had a few hard thoughts. The Kapurs were a wealthy family, with a beautiful house in Delhi and another beautiful one in the hills. Etta herself had gone to stay with them several times, but she found it distasteful the way Clarissa sponged on them. Clarissa was like that, she imposed on people.

'Mira keeps asking when am I coming to stay with them, so I thought I might as well go. You can't keep saying no to people.'

Etta took a sip from her coffee and then beckoned to the waiter: 'I asked for coffee.' He stared at her. 'This isn't coffee,' said Etta. 'It's yesterday's gravy.' He went on staring in incomprehension and she said wearily, 'The man is stupid. Call the manager.'

'I don't know why you must always fuss so,' Clarissa said. 'I've drunk two cups of it and it's quite all right.'

'The manager,' Etta repeated to the waiter in a quiet but meaningful voice.

The manager was a beautifully groomed young man with a black bow-tie and a ring on his finger and wavy, oiled hair. He was a nephew of the proprietor and very concerned to hear about Etta's coffee. He spoke angrily to the waiter.

'I hope it's not too much of a nuisance . . .?' Etta said, looking up at him with her head a little to one side and making big green eyes.

The young man adjusted his bow-tie. Then he barked again at the waiter. Soon Etta had new coffee in front of her which she sipped with a demure air of righteousness.

'It's nothing to you, I suppose,' said Clarissa, 'that you got that poor bearer into trouble.'

'Don't be silly.' Actually she said 'thilly', for sometimes, when she wanted to be either particularly appealing or particularly exasperating, she affected a lisp.

'You've got no sense of human dignity, that's what's wrong with you, Etta.'

'How terribly wrong you are. It's because I've got so much sense of human dignity that I refuse, but absolutely and entirely refuse, to drink bad coffee.' She took her powder compact out of her bag and looked into its mirror. 'Let alone pay for it,' she added, as she dabbed some powder on her nose.

Clarissa gave a snort of disgust. 'Don't you go playing the spoiled darling with me. I've known you much too long.'

Etta said, 'How right you are. *Much* too long.' She shut her compact with a little click and dropped it back into her handbag. 'Look, Clarissa dear, are we going to quarrel *all* morning? Just give me notice so I can get into the right frame of mind.'

Clarissa's expression changed at once. She stopped looking angry and instead became tender. She laid her hand on Etta's. 'You know I don't want to quarrel with you.' She spoke in a low voice and looked at Etta with sincere eyes. 'We're friends.'

Etta tried to accept this gracefully, though at the same time she manoeuvred to get her hand out from under Clarissa's. She hated physical contact and Clarissa's hand, being slightly damp, was particularly distasteful to her.

Suddenly Clarissa snatched up her sketchbook and thrust it at Etta as a peace offering. 'Here, just see what I did the other day. I went down to Mehrauli and found the most thrilling types. Look at this old man, isn't he the most marvellous character you've ever seen? What nobility.'

Etta looked, and looked away again. She took out her handkerchief and wiped the feel of Clarissa's hand from her own.

'I love these simple, earthy types,' Clarissa said. 'Every line on their face tells a story. It's so inspiring for an artist.' One leg of hers, ending in a big foot on a big flat sandal, came up on the sofa and she supported her sketchbook on it the better to admire her drawing. 'Doesn't he remind you of one of those Russian peasants you get in Tolstoy? The same strength and earthiness. Only of course the Indian peasant has a sort of spiritual quality about him, a divine yearning which raises him – don't you feel that? – above his own earthiness.'

Etta lifted her nose in the air and sniffed. 'I think this place has a nasty smell.' Clarissa looked at her in disgust. 'Well it has,' Etta said, 'I can't help it.' And indeed it had: it was one of the best restaurants in town, but the smell of yesterday's food, and that of the day before, clung to and seeped out from the velvet draperies, the deep red carpet, the black and gold mouldings on the walls.

'And I think there's a spot of tomato ketchup on the tablecloth,' Etta said, pointing to it with a fastidious finger.

Clarissa angrily tossed aside her sketchbook. 'It wasn't me who suggested we should meet here! It's you who're so fond of these fancy places!'

'But how was I to know,' Etta wailed, 'that there was going to be horrid tomato ketchup on the tablecloth?'

'You know very well I can't stand these kind of places. I find them completely stifling. Suffocating!' she cried and tugged at the neck of her blouse. 'I'd be much happier if we met somewhere outside, in the fresh and open air, simply under a tree.'

'Under a tree,' echoed Etta in amused distaste. 'How droll.'

'And don't try to be so English. I for one like your Hungarian accent, I think it's quite attractive, and I don't see why you should go to such trouble to put on a phoney haw-haw English accent.' Clarissa herself was a genuine product of the British Isles although, after so many years in India, this was no longer as obvious as it once might have been. Her accent had lost some of its local colour and idiom, and her complexion, once probably rosy and redolent of English skies, had taken on the withered pallor of all Western women too long in the East.

'Clarissa dear, I think we're quarrelling again.'

Just then the manager came up to ask whether the coffee was now to Etta's satisfaction. She gave him a dazzling smile (her teeth were still good though somewhat yellow) and said, 'Absolutely perfect, thank you,' so that he once more adjusted his bow-tie and, not content with that, wriggled his shoulders so that the pads of his coat fell into better position.

'I hate to see you flirting like that; it's awful at your age,' Clarissa said, but immediately afterwards she changed her mood, threw up her arms above her head and cried, 'How sick and tired I am of all this sophisticated town life! I've got to get away, away!' People at adjoining tables looked at her in astonishment, but she was too passionate to care. 'Back to my beloved mountains – Nature, the simple life, that's what I need desperately.'

Etta said, 'At the Kapurs?' She smiled. 'All those lovely servants cooking and serving all those lovely meals all day long; I quite desperately need a bit of that kind of simple life myself.'

'I've said it before and I'll say it again,' Clarissa said fiercely, 'people like you shouldn't be in this country. You don't belong.'

'No, thank God.'

'I came here out of conviction and idealism, not like you, who just came out on a chance marriage – '

'Don't remind me, please, of that chance marriage, not so early in the morning.' Etta's first marriage, more years ago than she ever allowed anyone to remember, had been to an Indian student whom she had met in Vienna: the handsomest, most cultured, charming boy one could imagine. Who would ever have thought that, once back in India, he would turn out to be so very much attached to his most uncultured family and, moreover, altogether so different from the gay youth with whom she had gone dancing in all the nicest cafés?

'If you'd had any guts you would have tried to adapt yourself. To fit in. Look at someone like Judy – '

'Yes, poor Judy.'

'Not poor Judy at all! She's doing very nicely. She had the good sense to realize that the only way to live here was to turn herself into a real Indian wife – '

At that point the band started. It was a very loud band, consisting of four lusty young Goans with white teeth and a lot of energy. They strummed and drummed and sang, they puffed out their cheeks, their feet in tight nylon socks went up and down on pedals. Etta held her head and groaned.

'One either merges with Hindu civilization or is drowned by it!' Clarissa shouted above the noise.

'Oh I'm one of the drowned ones, most definitely definitely one or the drowned ones,' Etta said, still holding her head in agony.

Judy's little boy, Prithvi, had had fever all day. She didn't go to the office but stayed with him to soothe him, sponge him and put ice on his head. By evening the fever came down and he lay on his bed, looking pinchèd and worn and with his eyes much too big. Judy also felt exhausted, after the anxiety and nursing, and she lay on her string cot next to him. It had been a hot and trying day.

Bal came home late in the evening, only to change for he had to go out again almost immediately. Meanwhile though, while he was changing his clothes, he was very nice to Prithvi and did his best to entertain and amuse him. Judy watched Bal dressing. He wore a finely starched muslin kurta and pyjama, which had come back from the washerman only that morning, and black slippers with little coloured flowers embroidered on them.

Prithvi said weakly from his bed, 'Why do you have to go out? Stay with me.'

Bal, who had been carefully combing his hair with oil in front of the oval mirror that hung from a nail on the wall, stopped doing so and turned round to Prithvi with a tender, loving smile. 'Of course I want to stay with you but, oh it is so awful, Papa has to go out to work.'

'Who works at night? People go to office only in the day.'

Bal said radiantly, 'Isn't he clever, Judy? My God, we have a clever son. A sweet sweet, good good, clever clever son.' He went back to combing his hair in the mirror, scrutinizing himself very carefully as he did so. With his back to them he said, 'You see, Papa's work is different. Papa is an artiste and that is why he has to work at night.'

Bal always called himself an artiste. He was a very small-time actor. He had had bit parts in a few films and he hung around the radio station to get any parts that were going there, and sometimes he participated in stage productions where he was lucky if he recovered his travelling expenses. His international début had been some ten years before, at the age of twenty, when he had managed to get himself chosen a delegate to a Youth Conference in London, and had taken part in a little Indian playlet that was put on at Friends House for the entertainment of the various delegations.

Judy said, 'I didn't know you had a broadcast tonight.'

'Not a broadcast – Kishan Kumar has come to Delhi for his premiere and he has called me.'

'Don't go,' Prithvi said in a pampered, sick-child voice.

'How I would love to stay with you, but you see how it is, poor Papa has to go and earn lots of money so that he can buy his children nice food and toys and clothes, and medicines too when the poor darlings are sick.'

Judy was feeling hot, tired and irritable. She had once met Kishan Kumar and had not liked him. He was a successful young film star and was always surrounded by hangers on, of whom Bal was one. She said crossly, 'Kishan Kumar is not work.' She too wished Bal would stay at home just for this evening.

'He is an important contact for me,' Bal said. He had finished combing his hair and was now inspecting the result. 'Probably we shall talk business together tonight.'

Judy could guess how they would talk business. They would all crowd into Kishan Kumar's plush hotel suite, and Kishan Kumar would sprawl on a sofa with the others on chairs and on the floor round him, drinking his whisky and laughing at the schoolboy jokes he made; or, if he wasn't in the mood to make any, they would strain every nerve to entertain him, rivalling each other as to who could do it the best.

She said bitterly, 'What do you think you can ever get out of him?'

Bal was amazed; he stared at Judy with open mouth and Prithvi took advantage of this moment of speechlessness to whine faintly, 'Stay and play with me.'

'But, Judy, he has so much influence! He is an important person in the film industry and he can be very useful to me. Already he has put a lot of work in my way.'

'Like what?'

'In *Mere Dil Men Rehta Pyar* – '

'You appeared for one minute and said two words.'

'You don't understand. It is not for how long you appear on the screen or how much you say – '

'I know: when they saw you in *Mere Dil Men,* all the biggest producers shouted "Who's that wonderful man? Sign him up immediately!" '

'It is not impossible,' Bal said, primping himself a bit more before the mirror. He was, it was true, very handsome; he had a beautiful profile and large black eyes and white teeth and a lot of thick black hair. After such a wonderful head, his figure came as something of a disappointment, for he was short and tended to be stocky. 'This is how discoveries are made. All the biggest stars started with very small roles

– Kishan Kumar himself also. Govind!' he shouted for the servant, and gave him a rupee and said 'A packet of "Panama", and be quick about it.' Now he stepped back from the mirror and tried to see himself full length, but of course it was impossible because there was not enough space to step back into. He only took two steps and was stopped short by one of the beds. There were four beds in the small room – two real beds, with mattresses, one for Prithvi and the other for Gita, and two string cots for Bal and Judy. The only other piece of furniture was an old-fashioned wardrobe, with a carved top and ornate legs, into which as many as possible of the family's belongings were stuffed. There was also a cupboard built into the whitewashed wall, and this too was full to overflowing with clothes, toys and old crockery. The rest of their things they kept in suitcases piled up against the only remaining piece of empty wall space.

'How do you think I got that part in *Gharonda*? Only through Kishan Kumar of course.'

'Have they paid you for that yet?'

'That is quite by the way. Really, Judy, it is no use arguing with you, you always start talking about something that is nothing to do with the argument.'

'I was only asking.' And while she was about it, she would have liked to ask some more: when were they going to pay him? And when would he be able to give her some money? It was quite an urgent problem for it was getting towards the end of the month and her salary from the Cultural Dais was almost spent. However, she repressed the desire to mention this because she knew that, whenever she brought up the topic of money, he tended to become evasive and, at the same time, to look ashamed.

'The important thing for someone in my position,' he said, dabbing a little khas scent behind his ears, 'is to keep up my contacts. That is the only way to get the big chance I am waiting for. You didn't go to the office today?'

'How could I?'

'Of ourse – poor Prithvi. But it makes a bad impression to miss days at the office.' When she had first got a job, it was Bal who had made the most fuss. He said it was humiliating for him that his wife should go out to work, and he even said – though he knew he didn't mean it – that he would not allow her. For the first few days of her job (this was when she was with the motor-car agency) he made many scenes, sometimes acting great anger and sometimes great sorrow, and once he even cried. Judy was sorry to see him like that but she took as

23

little notice as possible and only hoped he would get over it. This he did quite quickly, and indeed his whole attitude changed so completely that only a week or two later he was extolling the virtues of female independence and what a wholesome advance it was to see women going out into the world and taking their place side by side with men.

'I think he is better now,' Bal said, blowing a quick smile and kiss at Prithvi. 'Tomorrow you can go. You see, it is the same as with our broadcasts and shooting schedules. We have to be there, we can't make excuses – my child is not well, I have a stomach ache, my cousin is getting married – oh no,' he said, and shook his head in a worldly-wise way, 'at such a rate we wouldn't keep our job for long.'

Gita, their daughter, barefoot and rather dirty, with her hair all undone, came rushing in to retrieve an ancient toy out of the wall cupboard. Prithvi asked in a weak voice for water.

'Water?' Bal said. 'Of course he shall have water. Pour it for him, darling,' he told Gita who, however, had found her toy and rushed out with it to where her companions could be heard playing games. Bal poured it himself out of the earthenware water-container which stood on the floor by the bed. But Prithvi said, 'With ice in it.'

Bal looked at Judy, who said 'There isn't any.' They had bought some earlier in the day and kept it in a basin, but it had all melted away.

'With ice,' Prithvi said again.

'Govind!' Bal called in a loud voice.

'He's gone for your cigarettes,' Judy pointed out.

'How long he is taking. It is no use sending him anywhere.' He had a final look at himself and seemed satisfied. 'As soon as he comes back, he must go for the ice.' He made a pursed kissing mouth at Prithvi and said, 'Good-bye, darling.'

'I'm thirsty,' Prithvi said in a tearful voice.

'As soon as Govind comes back, at once he will fetch ice for you.'

'I want it now. Now.'

Judy stayed lying on her bed and told Bal from there, 'You'd better go and get it.'

Bal didn't have a watch – he had pawned it some years ago – but all the same he flicked out his wrist and frowned at it. 'It is getting very late. They must all be waiting for me.'

Judy had another vision of Kishan Kumar's hotel suite and of Kishan Kumar himself sprawled there in splendour. She said, 'First get the ice.'

Bal pretended he hadn't heard. He went out quickly, through the courtyard and into the street. He had got almost to the end of the brick wall and was by the cloth-store at the corner, when Judy caught up with him. She held on to the sleeve of his kurta. Her face had turned pink and her eyes, looking at him directly, were stark blue and angry. 'Get the ice,' she said.

'Let go.'

There were people in the street. Judy didn't care, but Bal was very much embarrassed. He turned and saw the shop-man sitting inside his cloth-store staring at them. Bal waved and smiled to him – 'Hallo there, Mohanji, how are you today!' – and then walked back with Judy. When they were inside their courtyard, she let go of his sleeve and he indignantly brushed at it to get out the creases she had made. 'All those people saw us,' he said. Gita and her friends were playing dolls' wedding in the courtyard, but took no notice of Bal and Judy.

'I'm not going out for my own pleasure,' Bal said, giving a last soothing flick at his sleeve and blowing on it. 'In film work – you don't know how it is, we have to be alert all the time and look for our opportunity.'

'Get the ice,' she said. Prithvi obligingly started to cry for it from the bedroom.

'It is very important for me to keep up my contacts. Without contacts you can't succeed in my line.'

'Are you getting it or not?'

He hesitated very briefly. 'All right,' he said, and hesitated once again but for a different reason. For an awful moment she thought he was going to ask her for the money. But he changed his mind and went off groping for coins in his own pocket.

She was not happy with her victory, though. In fact, she felt mean for the rest of the evening, especially when she thought of him with Kishan Kumar. She imagined him before the bored gaze of the successful film star, dancing, singing, jumping, looking as eager as Prithvi, his ears pink with effort, and hope glowing in him that it would all somehow lead to his big chance.

The next time Etta and Judy met it was at the Hochstadts. Etta was a frequent visitor there, and Judy dropped in whenever she had the time. It was very pleasant at the Hochstadts. They were a German couple who had been settled in England for many, many years and liked to think of themselves as English: which was, however, difficult, for they still spoke the language with a strong German accent, and besides, they looked so very central European. Dr Franz Hochstadt had rimless spectacles and grey hair cropped close to the skull, while Mrs Frieda was solid and matronly and wore tastefully low-cut, two-piece dresses with a lace front let in at the bosom. Dr Franz was an economist of some standing, who had been called out to India on a two-year appointment as an exchange professor at the University.

Etta sat in an arm-chair with her legs crossed and smoking her usual oval cigarettes. She had already half filled an ashtray which was balanced on the arm of her chair. She was being amusing. She was telling them something that had happened to her in the post office in the morning: 'He kept me waiting fifteen minutes and then he weighed – he actually actually *weighed* – my letter, and then you know what he told me?' Here she tried, with scant success, to reproduce an Indian clerk's accent: ' "Excuse, madam, this is wrong counter." Can you believe it? After all that?' She gave a laugh; she was inclined today to see the incident in a humorous light, though in some other mood it might have driven her into a frenzy of irritation. 'Is there anywhere else in the world where such priceless fantasies happen daily?' And she gave a shrug, a throwaway gesture of the hand and another laugh.

Mrs Hochstadt smiled with her. 'It is one of the many charms the country has for us.'

'Charms!' Etta exclaimed and cast appalled eyes to the ceiling. 'That's not exactly the word you'd use if you wanted to get something done.'

'Life plays itself out to a different rhythm here,' said Dr Hochstadt. 'It is fatal to come to India and expect to be able to live to a Western rhythm.'

'Well, Franz,' Etta said, 'then all I can say is the sooner they change their tune the better.'

'The West pushes forward in staccato rhythm,' said Dr Hochstadt, 'the East repeats the same note over and over – dom, dom, dom' – he sang this in a deep voice, giving force to it with his fist – 'over and over, and again and again, reaching not forward but down, down into depth.'

Judy didn't have much of an idea what they were talking about, but she was used to having the conversation at the Hochstadts pass over her head. She liked being there, all the same. The place had a very comfortable European atmosphere. The Hochstadts lived in a suite of rooms in a government hostel full of MPs and high-ranking civil servants. Even the furniture was provided by the government, but somehow the Hochstadts had managed to put their own touch on everything. There were lace tablecloths, some abstruse objets d'art (unattractive collectors' pieces), many heavily bound books on economics, philosophy, art and religion; over all this hung the smell of Dr Hochstadt's cigars and of the coffee which Mrs Hochstadt brewed on a little electric ring specially bought for the purpose (she had nothing but contempt for the coffee sent up by the caterer from the kitchens below).

'Believe me,' said Etta, 'if you had to live here for long, you'd soon lose the taste for that dom, dom, dom.'

'The echo of the Marabar caves,' said Mrs Hochstadt. They were cultured people and had of course prepared themselves thoroughly before coming out to India. 'How does it go – boum, boum – '

'To a confirmed European like myself,' said Dr Hochstadt, 'the sound is of course strange but also often sweet.' He turned to Judy. 'And what does our other little expatriate have to say?'

'Oh I don't know much about music really,' Judy said.

'Leave her alone,' Etta said wearily. 'She doesn't know what you're talking about. She doesn't understand civilized language. She's busy proving that it's possible for a nice healthy English girl to be an Indian wife in an Indian slum –'

'It's not a slum,' Judy mildly protested. It wasn't: it was a middle-class district, where shopkeepers, income tax inspectors and unsuccessful advocates lived in crowded but respectable circumstances.

'Don't quibble. What I saw, on that unfortunate occasion when I made the mistake of looking you up in your native habitat, was near enough to a slum not to matter.' It had indeed been an unfortunate occasion. Etta hadn't liked the smell, the noise, the rooms, the children, Bhuaji, and had not hesitated to make this very clear.

'It often strikes me,' said Dr Hochstadt, leaning back in his chair, putting his finger-tips together and displaying the thoughtful little smile with which he sometimes accompanied his reflections, 'that we transitory visitors, however much we may read and discuss and observe, can never have that understanding of India in all her depths which comes to those who are in touch with the humbler people of this land.'

'You sound like Clarissa,' Etta said. 'She's always on about the wretched people in their wretched villages or wherever they hide out.'

'There is to be found the real India,' said Mrs Hochstadt with enthusiasm.

'Well if it is, Clarissa isn't looking very hard. You may have noticed that she takes good care to get in with people who don't live in villages and who aren't in the least bit humble. She likes her comforts, does our Clarissa. Not that I blame her, I'm very keen on them myself, but what I can't stand is all that hypocrisy about the simple life and the true values, that just makes me sick. I'm smoking too much,' she added, as she lit another cigarette with slightly agitated fingers.

Dr Hochstadt endeavoured to bring the discussion back to the impersonal level on which it had begun: 'For the new-comer in India perhaps one of the most interesting aspects is the correlation – and here I have in mind not only physical facts but also intellectual and spiritual ones – the correlation of the old and the new, of what has been and what is –²

'Oh do stop it, Franz!' Etta interrupted. 'India, India, India, all the time, as if there was anything interesting to be said! One has the misfortune to be here, well all right, let's leave it at that, but why do we have to keep on torturing ourselves by talking about it?'

Dr Hochstadt and his wife exchanged a brief glance of understanding. 'All right,' said good-humoured Dr Hochstadt, spreading his arms wide in a gesture indicating total submission, 'we will talk about what ever you like. What is it to be? I am ready.'

'I also,' said Mrs Hochstadt, folding her hands in her lap and looking at Etta with a merry twinkle.

'I wish you two wouldn't try to show a sense of humour. It doesn't suit you at all.' She turned to Judy. 'How is Culture thriving at your Dais? Tell us what's going on in those glittering circles.'

'Oh gosh,' said Judy.

'I do so admire your superb gift of self-expression. Heavens, I'm so tired of you all, I think I'll go home.' She opened her handbag and began to touch up her face. This, at any rate, in spite of her impatient mood, she did with care and love. 'I shall put on some of my French records, my darling Sablon and my dearest Piaf, and then I can forget you all and how dreadfully you bore me. Good-bye Franz, and au revoir, Frieda dear, and next time I come I hope you're going to be a lot more entertaining. Don't bother to call on me or ring me or anything,' she told Judy. 'I mean it. I've given you up.' She rose from her chair and looked over her shoulder to make sure her dress wasn't wrinkled at the back.

'Wait a minute,' Judy said. 'I'm coming with you.'

'Oh no, you're not. You're not going to share my taxi and have me drop you at one of your sordid little bus-stops.' Just before she went out, she said, 'The coffee was nice, Frieda dear. Thanks for that, anyway.'

The Hochstadts looked at one another, and at Judy, and smiled. Judy didn't smile with them, but pretended interest in a dull-looking intellectual weekly. She knew the Hochstadts were now going to discuss Etta. This they did, in the nicest possible way. They were wise and understanding about her, and had many interesting things to say about the effect India has on a certain type of European. Judy was certain that everything they said was true – they were, after all, intelligent, cultured people, with a wide knowledge of life and psychology – but she didn't care for them to say it. It was too easy for them. They were going back, they had their flat and Dr Hochstadt's job waiting for them in London. As far as they were concerned, everything here was only an awfully pleasant interlude. It was different for Etta.

When the Cultural Dais office closed in the evenings, Judy would rush to the bus-stop. She was always in a hurry to get home, but Sudhir lingered a bit. He had nowhere very much to go. He lived in a place called the Royal Hotel, which was near the station and was occupied mainly by young men like himself, who were far away from their homes and families and did not have a very grand salary. He had a shabby little room on an upper floor, leading off an open space round which were grouped other identical shabby little rooms. He did not much care for these lodgings but, nevertheless, spent a great deal of his free time in them, for he had nowhere else to go. From time to time he made forays to the pavement booksellers and came back with an armful of paperbacks and read his way through them. He thus came into contact with a great variety of reading matter, ranging from the *Origin of Species* to last year's best-seller. Sometimes he read so much that he became confused and could no longer distinguish between things, and everything seemed to him not to have advanced very far beyond words and certainly had no connection with anything he knew or had experienced.

Sudhir came from one of those genteel Calcutta families whose present fortunes were low but whose past it was always a pleasure for them to recall. His great-grandfather had been a famous educationist and a leader of the Brahmo Samas movement; his grandfather had been a distinguished professor at the University; his father, however, a sickly and ineffective man, could do no better than a small job at the National Library which he got and maintained not so much through his own abilities as through the respect still accorded to his family name. Sudhir himself had studied history at the University, and one did not need to be told that he had been a brilliant student. He still looked, more than anything, like a brilliant student – the sort who, without even trying, is the leader of opinion among his fellows and the shining hope of his professors, and who, at the end, out of some cussedness or as a grandiloquent gesture against the system of education, fails in his exams. Sudhir, however, did not fail in his exams; he passed them in the first division, and then spent two years looking for a job. He looked in Calcutta, Delhi, Bombay, Poona, Patna and many other places, but found that no one was interested in an ex-brilliant student whose family may have had connections in the past but had none in the present. These were two very bad years. At the end of them, his father died and left Sudhir to look after a mother and two sisters. This forced him to change his tactics, and he began to spend patient hours outside great men's offices, finally to be rewarded with a job in a newly-founded college in some very remote district of Orissa. Here he stayed till his department was shut down for lack of funds, whereupon he returned to Calcutta and began to look for another job. All other attempts failing, he had to return to what he had hoped never to have to do again, and take chits of recommendation from one great man to the other. He must have done it very ungraciously for he came up with nothing better than a part-time teaching job at an evening college. He supplemented this with writing articles for papers which paid him Rs.25 for 2,000 words; and after a while fell in with some people in advertising who offered him a job at a salary some four times any he had commanded before. He was very happy to accept but after a few months, for reasons he never explained, returned to the evening college. He continued to write a great many articles, and managed to get both his sisters nicely married, one to an engineer in Jamshedpur and the other to a doctor in Asansol. When his mother died, there was nothing to keep him in Calcutta, and he began to look round for somewhere else. This time he was lucky and did not have to wait for long. One of the Ministers on whom he had so unprofitably danced attendance a few years earlier, and who had been a pupil of Sudhir's grandfather, had since had the good fortune to be promoted to the central Cabinet in Delhi. On one of his visits to Calcutta, he had been invited to grace a function at the evening college at which Sudhir taught; and catching sight of Sudhir (whom he remembered not so much as his petitioner but as the grandson of a distinguished grandfather), he did him the honour of falling into conversation with him, in the course of which he asked him to come to Delhi and help to build up a new cultural centre which had just been founded. At the Minister's invitation, Sudhir went to see him the next day, and to his surprise – for he had thought it was made only in the warmth of the particular moment and for want of anything really cordial to say – found the offer was repeated. 'We want some of our own Bengali boys up there in the capital,' said the Minister with a chuckle; which Sudhir at once recognized as an attitude of rank communal favouritism, but because he was heartily tired of Calcutta, of the evening college, and of being very poor, he didn't so much mind just then to have it operating in his favour.

When he was in the mood and was with someone he trusted, Sudhir could be very loquacious, and it was in these moments, during their long boring office hours, that Judy learned all this about him. She thought it was a sad story, especially the years he spent looking for employment, and she could imagine him tramping from place to place and being kept waiting and the bitter, disgusted expression he must have worn. So she said, 'What a shame,' over and over, while she listened to him, with such true feeling that he laughed and became frivolous and made light of it all. 'It's an old story,' he said, 'from log cabin to White House,' and he waved his hand round the office to indicate the White House. But she said no, it was sad, to think of him after all that studying he had to do and then not get a decent job, it wasn't right, she said. She didn't think it could happen in England – though she was vague about it. She was vague about everything to do with England. Perhaps she had forgotten, or perhaps she only didn't want to remember.

Yet it wasn't, as far as Sudhir could see, as if she had had an unhappy childhood or anything like that. There were just the three of them – herself, her mother and father. Grandparents? They were dead before Judy was born (her parents had married late). Uncles, cousins, aunts? No, said Judy. Sudhir shook his head: you English are strange. Stung, Judy admitted that there was one aunt Agnes, her father's sister. She didn't say much about her, though; she didn't evidently care for her Aunt Agnes. Well go on, Sudhir said. But what was there to tell. They hadn't led a very interesting life. 'We were just ordinary people,' she said. Her father had made precision instruments in a factory; her mother cooked and cleaned and kept Judy away from strangers. Her mother didn't trust strangers; these included the neighbours. You were safest if you kept yourself to yourself. So they did, just the three of them, in that tight little house, with the doors and curtains firmly shut to keep the cold and the strangers out.

Both her parents had been alive when Judy had married Bal and gone away with him to India. Bal had promised them that he would send her home every summer – but of course there never had been the money. Now both her parents were dead. The father died of lung cancer ('he'd never smoked in his life,' Judy said, bitterly, as if she thought it unfair). So the mother was left alone in her clean house with the household bargains and the closed doors. Then she died too. Judy didn't tell how she died, not till later. Not till one day when she felt she liked Sudhir very much and wanted him to know what up till now only Bal and Bhuaji had known. Judy's mother had killed herself; hanged herself in the lavatory (where there had been, for some unknown reason, a hook in the ceiling – Judy remembered looking up at it daily and vaguely wondering why ever it should be there). Judy didn't know who had found her, or how long after. All she got was a reproving letter from her Aunt Agnes: 'hung herself in the lav', Aunt Agnes had written and Judy could just see her writing it, straight-backed in her chair, peering severely over her bosom. It had been a great trouble and embarrassment to Aunt Agnes.

Sudhir had always been very nice to Judy, and after that he was even nicer. He had a sort of instinctive chivalry in him, which prompted him to feel that women, especially when they were like Judy, were entitled to quite a lot of masculine shelter and protection. He knew Bal and, though he liked him, was sorry that Judy did not have a husband who could support her. It seemed wrong to him that she should have to go out to work; and he felt that, as a foreigner, a stranger, she had enough difficulties without having to cope with financial ones as well.

She spoke to him about money quite often, in a completely frank way. She told him how hard it was for them to manage and how, at the end of the month, they always had to ask for credit from the little shops in the bazaar. But at the same time she told him, with pride, that she was saving. As soon as she got her salary, she took twenty-five rupees out of it and put it in a fixed deposit account. She had almost five hundred rupees now, she told him: she was never going to be caught without any savings, the way she had been when she lost her last job and had desperately had to run round to people. Supposing, she said, one of them – the children, or Bal, or she herself – was to fall sick: then what? And she looked at him shrewdly and he could only shake his head and she said there you are, triumphantly. It just showed, she said, that you had to be ready for any emergency, and she, with her nearly five hundred rupees, was. Oh yes, she had learned a lot and was very wise and provident now. And mean, she said: he didn't know how mean she was, she told him. Never, not for anything, except for the emergency she was always expecting, would she break into that precious hoard of hers. Bal often wanted her to – there were so many things he could have done with a nice lump sum like that – but she had always refused to give him a single rupee out of it. Yes indeed, she was a proper miser now.

Sudhir's salary was small but he often had money to spare nowadays – his mother was dead, his two sisters married, and there was no one dependent on him – and he would very much have liked to offer her some of it. But he never did. He felt shy and even ashamed to do so. He thought that perhaps she wouldn't say anything but she would pretend to be busy with something on her table and probably she would blush (she often blushed). And afterwards she would possibly not talk to him so freely about her home affairs again. So he did not offer.

No one quite knew how Etta made a living. It was generally supposed that she had a few securities tucked away, for she had been married several times and she was not the type to emerge from such a circumstance without some fairly solid compensation to show for it. But she had never been married to a really or even moderately rich man, so whatever she may have garnered from that source (though three-fold) could not be all-sufficient to provide for the comforts – more, the luxuries – she so deeply needed and which no one had ever known her to deny herself.

She did occasional, very high-class jobs. Never as jobs, of course, but always as favours, for very high-class people, and when she took her (never inconsiderable) fee afterwards, she always did so with a careless laugh and a why-do-you-bother shrug, while it was they who thanked her profusely. Thus, she had given German lessons to a leading industrialist with business interests in Germany and English lessons to a backward maharani who wished to enter society. Similarly, she had acted as interpreter to a group of Hungarian judges, had taken several parties of American tourists on shopping tours round New Delhi, and accompanied three young princesses from Nepal on a flight to Agra to see the Taj by moonlight. She never seemed to exert herself to get these assignments, but somehow they drifted quite naturally her way.

In addition, she had her admirers. She had given up on husbands long ago for, after three attempts made rapidly in succession and all of them with handsome, educated young Indians, she had come to the conclusion that, while she had no objections to the institution of marriage as such, a more flexible arrangement was better suited to her particular temperament. In her twenties and thirties she had had no difficulty in finding enough admirers to amuse and entertain her and see to it that she had her supply of necessary luxuries. There had been an occasional – strangely enough, mostly elderly – European among these admirers, but her greatest success had always been with Indians.

She was so blonde and so sophisticated, so apparently conversant with the ways of smart Western worlds, they could not resist her. She made them feel as if they were not in dull, homely, backward Delhi at all, but in places they dreamed of – Paris, Vienna, Berlin, where the women were all beautiful and accessible and knowledgeable, and one drank wine out of long-stemmed glasses and made husky conversation against a background of waltzes played on the violin. Etta also taught them what shirts and ties to wear, to stand up when ladies came into a room, to draw out chairs and light cigarettes, and her expositions on the backwardness of India in general and Indian men in particular made them eager to prove to her that they, at any rate, were different, and subscribed to those finer values of which she herself was the embodiment.

All good things, however, come to an end, and now here was Etta in her (though who would dare to say it) middle forties. She was still the same – her hair as blonde, her manner as lively – but the admirers were fewer, and fatter, and less ardent. There were no more elderly Europeans, and now it was the Indians who were, if not exactly elderly, then at least of a certain comfortable middle age. They were, as men of that age tend to be, less inclined to put themselves out, so that Etta found more and more that now it was not they who strove to please her but, on the contrary, she who had to do so for them.

For some time past she had been friendly with one Mr Gupta, who was rather typical of the sort of admirer she had been having in these latter years. He was a hotel owner, a rich but self-made man, a vigorous fifty. He had married all his daughters and settled his sons, his business was doing well, and there was time now, as there had never been before, for a little relaxation. Etta was this relaxation. She was feminine, sprightly, spoiled and kittenish for him, and he indulged her with the good humour of one playing a game he had not played before but of which the rules were easy and pleasant to follow. Gup, she called him, or Guppy, to rhyme with puppy; nobody had ever called him anything like that before.

'Guppy,' she said, from where she lay on her sofa, 'be a darling and get my fags from the bedroom.'

And he went, laughing good-naturedly (he who was used at home to be served by his women hand and foot), and came back not only with her cigarettes but with her sleeping pills as well. 'Why do you take these? It is so unhealthy.'

'Because I have to sleep. You wouldn't like to see me with big black nasty rings under my eyes, would you, Gup?'

'You must take exercise. Go for long walks, lead a good healthy life with big meals and plenty of milk and butter-milk.'

'And become fat like you.'

But he wasn't fat; he was large and strong and well set-up. His hair, hardly greying yet, was still very thick, and even on days when he shaved twice, his cheeks and chin were still darkly shadowed. When Etta had first met him, he had tended to be overdressed, with too many rings and too large a gold watch, but not now. She had seen to that. Now one could be proud to be escorted by Guppy.

'Where are you taking me for dinner?'

'Yes, you can come to the hotel. I will ring up and tell them to lay the table in my suite.' His hand was already on the telephone; he liked telephoning, and spent a good deal of his day doing it.

'Oh no,' she said and wrinkled her nose, 'not your boring old hotel again.'

He patiently replaced the receiver: 'Then I can send for something to be brought here.'

She groaned and stretched herself out flat on the sofa, turning her face to the wall. 'How *boring* it all is,' she said in a voice fatigued to the point of desperation.

He kept silent. It was an old battle. He did not care to take her to places where they could be seen: he was a man of standing in his community, a husband, father, grandfather even, he gave to charity and provided for poor relations and made generous monetary contributions to the political party of his allegiance. Everyone probably knew about himself and Etta, but there was no need to flaunt the fact in public. He was a bold and self-willed man, who took everything he wanted, but at the same time he retained an obstinate regard for appearances.

'I want to go somewhere madly gay,' said Etta. She lifted one leg into the air, wriggled the ankle and stretched the toes; she watched herself doing it, and so did Guppy. 'I want to dance till three in the morning and then be waltzed all the way home in my evening gown.'

Guppy laughed dutifully, if a little absently. She could see from his distracted look that he was thinking of something different, some business affairs, and already his hand was hovering over the telephone to make one of his curt, commanding calls.

'Guppy!' she called, and sat up, swinging her legs down from the sofa and stamping a spoiled foot. 'Now make up your mind: what gay and exciting place are you taking me to? Quick now!'

But he took his time. He pulled up one nylon sock and then the other and settled his feet more comfortably in his slip-on crocodile-skin shoes. When he had finished doing this, he said with a slow yawn, 'We could drive down to the *Rangmahal*.'

'Oh *no*!' Etta said, and sank straight back to lie on the sofa. 'I absolutely but entirely refuse to go there again.' The *Rangmahal* was a dull place some fifteen miles away; it had a few bungalows which could be rented by the day or night, and it was here that men like Guppy came to do the relaxing they didn't want to be seen doing in town. They had an unspoken agreement that, if they happened to meet down there – as often occurred – they would fail to recognize one another. 'I'm not,' said Etta, 'not ever again, going to drive all those long, hot, bumpy miles only to hear the jackals scream, eat a horrid boiled chicken supper, and pretend not to see Lala Bhagwan Dass tickling his little secretary. Oh no.'

Guppy took this calmly. He was quite content to let Etta please herself whether they stayed or went. On the other hand, he was not disposed to give her any more alternatives, and as far as he could see, the decision was now made, the topic closed. He went out on to the terrace, not to admire the view but to think over one or two business problems which were on his mind. He walked up and down, with his hands behind his back and never once looking up at the sky, which was a pale pearly grey with one last lilac streak still fading in the west, and was soon so deep in thought that he forgot all about Etta left lying bored on the sofa.

She resigned herself to another dull evening. It was no use, she knew, to be sulky or throw tantrums, or indulge in any other of the spoiled-beauty techniques she had applied so successfully on her other, earlier admirers. Guppy didn't, he really fundamentally and genuinely didn't, understand how women were to be treated, and it would only be a waste of energy to try out any wiles on him. And since she had got herself dressed for him (in an elegant flowered print, green eye-shadow to go with her green eyes, her hair swept up and a new liquid foundation cream she was trying out) and had already made as much sparkling conversation as she judged he could take, she was now in no mood to waste energy, or do anything further than lie on the sofa and wait for their evening together to end. [...] nothing amusing to happen and there was really not much [...] between herself and Guppy; nevertheless she was prepared to be [...] obliging as he might require her to be. Otherwise he might not want to come back again, and that must under no circumstances be allowed to happen. She could no longer afford to lose people – especially not people like Guppy.

But she was glad when there were thumping steps on the stairs and who should burst in at the door – shouting, 'Anyone home?' – but Clarissa, in her peasant skirt and swinging her cloth shoulder-bag with tassels at the end. She gave Etta a quick, shrewd glance (all her glances at Etta were quick and shrewd, as indeed were Etta's at her: they each suspected only too well what the other might be up to), snorted 'Oh, all dolled up, are we?' and then let pale eyes rove round the room, to take in anything else of interest there might be.

Just then Guppy came in, all unsuspecting, from the terrace, and when she saw him, she was transformed. 'Guppy!' she yelled, and hurled herself in his direction, one thin but muscular white arm twined itself around his neck, while her bag, dangling from her shoulder and swinging to and fro in her excitement, banged him in the ribs. 'What a lovely surprise!' she said, and now hugged him with the other arm too, while he smiled sheepishly and tried to push the bag out of the way. She always greeted him with the same exuberance; the first time he had been surprised (he hadn't considered he knew her all that well), but now he had got used to it.

When her excitement had subsided, she divested herself of her bag, put up her hands to her hair as if to arrange it but actually only disarranging it a bit more, and, standing with her legs apart in the middle of the room, loudly demanded, 'A drink someone, quick!'

This display of energy and drive only made Etta more lethargic. She shifted lazily on the sofa and drawled, 'If you want a drink, dear, you'll have to fix it yourself.'

'What a hostess!' said Clarissa, with a big wink at Guppy; but she lost no time in getting to the drinks cabinet, where she mixed three gimlets; it was to be noticed that, though she was a rather clumsy person in most ways, she performed the mixing of drinks with remarkable deftness (long and continuous practice at other people's cocktail cabinets, as Etta had once tartly observed).

Guppy took his gimlet with good-humoured resignation. He didn't really drink – didn't care for the taste of it; food was his weakness – but he knew that, when among sports, one must be a sport. He did

...ep up with them. He had hardly taken a ... ...as already mixing her second; and a short ... ...plaintive wail from the sofa – 'What about ... ... hand, holding her empty glass, could be seen ... the edge.

...ched on a table, girlishly swinging her legs, her ...hed up rather high to her thighs. She concentrated ...ns she possessed on Guppy: though she had never mar-...always been fond of men and considered it their natural righ... ...flattered and made a fuss of. 'Guppy,' she said, 'when are you going to let me paint you?'

He replied with heavy humour, 'Who will want to see my ugly face in picture?'

'Now don't be modest, Gup,' Clarissa warned. 'You've got a very interesting face. Striking,' she said. 'Strong.' She put aside her glass, slid down from the table and came over to where he was sitting. She gripped the top of his head and his chin firmly and turned the head from side to side, looking at it with a speculative artist's eye. 'You've got a superb line from nose to brow, a real conqueror's face, that's what you've got, Guppy. The *veni vidi vici* type. I'd certainly like to have a stab at you.'

At this Etta gave a hoot of lewd laughter from her sofa. Clarissa ignored her; she took a couple of steps backwards and contemplated Guppy very seriously, with one eye shut. She put up her hand too, as if to get him in perspective. 'Wonderful shading,' she said. He looked down at his glass and twirled it in his hand. He was embarrassed, but rather flattered too. Clarissa was not a good artist, but she got a lot of places through what art she had. When she wanted to establish re-lations with someone rich or important or useful, she always com-mented enthusiastically on their fascinating faces and asked to be allowed to sketch them. She had got access in this way to some very prominent people.

'Once more into the breach, my friends!' she said, and snatched Etta's glass out of her hand and refilled it, together with her own. 'What are we sitting in this stuffy room for? Let's get out – fresh air, the sky, the moon, the stars, romance!' She charged out on to the terrace, as if she were leading a battalion, but neither of the two others followed her. They looked at each other and Etta tapped her forehead. This made Guppy, who had a simple sense of humour, laugh a lot.

It was not as nice on the terrace as Clarissa had expected. It was quite dark by now, and there was no moon, and no stars either, only some dim street-lighting below, which was just enough to show up a few depressing little huts out of the waste of darkness. In one of the smart new houses opposite, though, a party was in progress and, exposed under strips of neon lighting, many people, all looking stiff and uneasy and as if they did not have much to say to one another, could be seen standing about in a newly furnished room. There was a nagging smell in the air, which was not easy to identify but seemed a sort of mixture of sewage and jasmine.

Clarissa came back and said, 'You're a fine couple of stick-in-the-muds, I must say.'

Guppy was still laughing, and when he saw Clarissa, he started all over again. She didn't know what the joke was, but all the same she joined in, just to be companionable. This made Etta laugh too. When Clarissa's back was turned, Guppy caught Etta's eye and touched his forehead, in the way she had done before, and laughed uproariously. He felt he was having an enjoyable time.

'Are you chaps giving me dinner or not?' Clarissa demanded.

Etta drained her glass and said, 'The gin's killed my appetite.'

'Not mine,' Clarissa declared emphatically. 'I could eat a horse.'

That too struck Guppy as very funny.

'Hooves, saddle, sweetbreads and all,' Clarissa said, seeing what a success her horse was. But then she caught Etta making a wry face and pounced on her immediately. 'What's the matter with you? Company not good enough for you?'

Etta did not deign to answer; she only raised her eyebrows and looked pained.

That made Clarissa very angry indeed. She shouted, 'You make me sick! With your plucked eyebrows and your dyed hair and all your phoney manners, you just make me sick!' Her cheeks were flushed, and her top-knot had come down and hung like an abandoned bird's nest against her neck.

Etta, still lying on her sofa, looked her up and down with slow, green, insulting eyes; and drawled, 'I think you've drunk too much of my gin.' Her own speech, however, was not quite as clear as it had been an hour before.

'Listen to her,' Clarissa appealed to Guppy. 'First she invites me, then she insults me.' Her voice was trembling and her eyes looked damp.

'Who, pray, invited you?' said Etta, in the pleasantest manner possible.

39

Clarissa pointed a shaking finger in her direction and shouted, 'You hear her?' She stamped her foot in its broad sandal. 'I won't put up with it! I'll slap her insolent face for her!'

'Ladies,' Guppy appealed in a calm and reasonable voice. He judged it wiser to put a stop to this quarrel, though it rather interested him. He had heard plenty of women's quarrels before – he had grown up and lived all his life in a joint family – but this one was different from the ones he was used to. His own women were very much more subtle: generations of purdah living had sharpened their wits and made them adept at insinuation, at neatly turned, finely veiled personal insults. Clarissa and Etta, on the other hand, were crude enough, he felt, to come to blows; and though he would not have minded witnessing such a scene, he feared there might be a disturbance with the people from downstairs running up to see what was happening and then there would be public unpleasantness.

'I shall send for some food,' he said firmly, and firmly he picked up the telephone receiver and gave his orders to the people in his hotel. He grunted at them in monosyllables, which was all that was necessary, for he had been boss for many years now and knew how to command.

Clarissa allowed herself to be checked by his masculine authority. She sank on to a chair and became plaintive instead of quarrelsome. She said, 'Why does she treat me like that when we're such old friends?' and sat there, despondent, with her legs straddled wide.

Etta appeared to be asleep; at least her eyes were shut. It had got very hot in the room, a close, used-up, tired heat, with the fan stirring up stale air.

'It was a misunderstanding,' Guppy said. He found he could look right up Clarissa's skirt, but preferred not to. Clarissa had never been attractive and now she was no longer young.

'I don't want to quarrel with her,' she said. 'She's my oldest friend. I don't quarrel with my friends. I love them.' She got up and walked over to Etta's sofa and kneeled on the floor by her. 'I think you're a wonderful person. We've had some grand old times together, haven't we? Remember when we all went to Sikri and read Shakespeare in the Diwan-i-Am? Biki Sen made such a good King Lear.'

Etta didn't open her eyes, but she said, 'Cut the cackle, please, and get us another drink.'

'I love your hair,' Clarissa said, stroking it. 'It's such a lovely colour. And I like the shape of your eyebrows too.' She scrambled up from the floor and mixed two more drinks. Then she fumbled through Etta's gramophone records and pulled one out (making two or three slide to the floor as she did so) and put it on, humming to herself in anticipation as she did so.

'Come on,' she cried, 'let's be gay!' It was a very gay record, fast and with a lot of rhythm. She had it on much too loud, but she liked that. She balled her fists and thumped them in the air in time to the music and swayed from side to side, standing with her legs apart and her peasant skirt swinging.

'Come on, Guppy, lead me round the floor!'

He enjoyed watching her, but refused to dance. She tried to drag him from his chair but gave up quite soon for she saw he was both too strong and too unwilling. He had never learned to dance and was not prepared to make a fool of himself. Even when he was at his most relaxed, as he was now, he never lost the sense of his own dignity.

'Hey, Etta girl, let's shake a leg!' Clarissa cried, and she began to tickle Etta to make her get up. Etta resisted and fell off the sofa, whereupon Clarissa seized her arm and dragged her for a little way across the floor. Laughing, stirred by alcohol and rhythm, Etta got up and began to dance. It was a hot, new number and neither of them knew the right steps, but they made them up as they went along. Clarissa crouched down and beat her thighs like a wrestler and cried 'Yuppee!' while Etta, with her dress crumpled and turned up at the back danced round and round, holding her cigarette high up in the air. Guppy laughed and applauded them, sitting comfortably in his chair, one foot going up and down to the music.

There was a ring at the door. It was one of Guppy's bearers with the food he had ordered from his hotel. Guppy's foot stopped tapping, and he curtly told the bearer, who carried a tray covered with a starched white cloth on his shoulder, 'Put it down.' The bearer did so, and began to unpack and arrange the dishes, his eyes delicately averted from the dancing memsahibs. Guppy watched him severely.

The music went faster and faster, and the two women, red and perspiring and almost insanely dishevelled by now, tried to keep up with it.

Mrs Kaul, the Honorary Secretary, was always very busy and nervous before the meetings. She bustled up and down and made Judy's life a misery. Now the rows of chairs were not straight enough, now she found a crack in one of the tea-cups, there was dust on the library shelves and a cigarette-butt on the bathroom floor. Both Judy and the bearer, whom Mrs Kaul had brought from home for the occasion, ran hither and thither on her instructions. The bearer was supposed to be cutting sandwiches in the kitchen, but she kept calling him out of there to assign some new task to him. He went round grumbling to himself and telling Judy in an undertone that he had only two hands, and was on this account certainly going to give in his notice so that Mrs Kaul could get someone who perhaps had four or five.

Only Sudhir remained aloof and idle. He had been quite busy before Mrs Kaul came, and in fact had been responsible for getting everything ready, but when she was there, he relaxed rather ostentatiously and sat on one of the chairs reading a book. She threw nervous glances at him every now and again, and appeared to have many things to tell him; but he was completely engrossed in his book. What she would have liked to tell him most was to change his clothes, for he was wearing his usual khaki trousers and white bush-shirt, which was not really suitable attire for the secretary of the Cultural Dais on their formal occasions. However, she had never yet managed to broach the subject to him, though she had taken it up several times with Judy. She had explained to Judy that, on such occasions, the most suitable wear for the General Secretary was a high-collared coat and jodhpurs ('our beautiful national dress', as she said) or, failing that, a suit in the English style might pass. Judy had dutifully passed on this information to Sudhir, who had received it with a few rude comments and continued as before.

Everything now seemed as perfect as could be, and the bearer was back in the kitchen cutting sandwiches, but Mrs Kaul was still peering round with sharp, anxious looks to find something else to put right. She said, 'We need flowers for the speaker's table,' and looked at Judy as if she expected her to produce a bunch immediately.

'Yes, it'd look nice,' said Judy to gain time.

'You can go and get them from the garden.'

Judy went out into the garden. She knew there weren't any flowers there, but she wanted a respite. The garden was out in front (the back was very disappointing, consisting of nothing but a row of tumble-down servants' quarters) and though there was provision for an ample lawn and flowerbeds, the Doctor did not have the means to keep them up and so they had all now disappeared. There were, however, some very pleasant shady trees and under one of them the Doctor was sitting. He was looking earnestly at his house and trying to draw it on a piece of paper.

Judy joined him. She watched him drawing for a while, then looked up at the sky with the top of the house and the trees full of leaves outlined against it.

'I am making a perspective of my house,' the Doctor explained. 'For the house agents.' He was always making grandiose plans to sell or mortgage his house, but they never came to anything on account of his two brothers, who jointly owned the house with him and threatened a lawsuit.

'I'm thinking of building a hotel on this site,' he said. 'There are good profits to be made in the hotel business.'

Two fat blue pigeons were walking on the grass and from somewhere – probably the neighbouring garden – superb smells came wafting, of jasmine and passion flowers. Judy wished she didn't have to go in again.

Inside Mrs Kaul was now conferring with Sudhir. Whenever she talked to Sudhir, she became very coquettish and feminine; she put her head to one side and looked up at him and she even simpered a bit. It was strange that he should have such an effect on her because he was, after all, only the paid secretary whereas she was the honorary one, and if it had been anyone else, she would have seen to it that the distinction was carefully observed. But Sudhir did not behave according to her strict social standards. It was true, he was much poorer and less influential than she was, but he gave no sign of being aware of his inferiority. This threw her out and made her ill at ease with him.

'Of course the chairman will be proposing the vote of thanks,' she said.

When she spoke to him, he stood up. He was polite to her, though always just barely so.

She adjusted her sari over her shoulder and gave a sideways glance up at him. 'I would like the Minister to speak a few words.'

'If he comes,' Sudhir said.

She put her hand to the back of her smartly bobbed hair to smooth it. She was wearing a discreetly expensive sari of shot silk and smelled of some French scent. She was a very well-kept and carefully groomed woman. 'Otherwise perhaps the Director of the Cultural Institute?' she suggested.

'If *he* comes,' Sudhir said.

Judy came back from the garden to say there were no flowers there. Mrs Kaul was severe with her: these were things to be thought of, she told her, not at the last moment but at the very beginning of one's preparations. She compared the meetings to a campaign where everything must be exactly planned and organized in advance. Then she sent her chauffeur to bring flowers from her house.

The first guests to arrive were some of Sudhir's shabby friends.

They came in a group and clustered round Sudhir and talked excitedly in Bengali. Mrs Kaul pretended not to see them; they were not the kind of members she cared to welcome at the Dais. The Dais, it was true, was designed to be a meeting-place for intellectuals, but she could not believe that people like Sudhir's friends could be classed as intellectuals.

Then some of her own friends came, and they were very much more acceptable. They were all well dressed, spoke good English and had been abroad; in short, they were cultured people. There were also some foreigners, like the Hochstadts, and others from missions and embassies who were interested in culture. All these people knew each other and spoke together pleasantly, having often met at cocktail parties and dinners, so that they had many acquaintances in common. Only Sudhir's friends did not know anyone, and were not known, and they stood at the back very much apart; now that there were all these others, they had stopped talking together in Bengali and only stood in a tight group with their hands in their pockets and looking gloomy.

The guest speaker that day was a Polish man of letters, a thin, blond, refined man in a bow-tie. He was introduced to all Mrs Kaul's friends and the foreigners, and every time he was introduced, he joined his hands together in Indian fashion and gave a little bow. It was already some time past the scheduled time, but Mrs Kaul was reluctant to have the lecture begin because neither the Minister nor the Director of the Cultural Institute, nor anyone else important, had yet come.

At last it was decided that they were not going to come, and after some busy consultation, Mrs Kaul announced that the lecture would now begin. Everyone sat down on the collapsible chairs which had been placed in rows all down the room, facing the lecturer's table at which sat the Polish man of letters and Dr Hochstadt, who was the chairman of the meeting.

Dr Hochstadt got up first to introduce the speaker. He spoke for quite some time, mentioning Mickiewicz and Sienkiewicz and expressing his appreciation of the rare privilege they were about to enjoy – namely, of being allowed a glimpse into the Polish literary scene of today. Everyone looked very interested during the first few minutes of his introduction, but afterwards, when he began to draw parallels between a cultural renaissance in Poland and in India, they became restive and the men began to clear their throats and the ladies to look for things in their handbags.

Etta arrived late. She came in tiptoeing ostentatiously and making a strained face to show how quiet and careful she was being. Everyone, however, heard and saw her, especially as she did not choose to sit at the back but tiptoed right to the front of the room. It took her some time to settle down, sitting, then standing up again to smooth her skirt at the back, placing her handbag on the floor, shifting her chair a bit to bring it in line with her neighbours', turning round to wink and smile swiftly at friends. Everyone was now looking at her, except Dr Hochstadt, who had got into the swing of his speech and was quoting Count Keyserling.

When at last it was the guest speaker's turn, it turned out that he spoke in a very faint aesthetic voice which carried no farther than the front three rows. And even these few were not as fortunate as might have been conjectured, for his English, which he had learned in Poland, was not easy to follow. However, they all sat attentively and nodded appreciatively whenever they happened to catch a point. Mrs Kaul, even though she was worrying about the arrangements for the tea which was to follow, managed to look absorbed; and Mrs Hochstadt, who sat right in the front row, sturdy and sensible and with her legs apart, interjected a 'Highly interesting' or 'Very original' from time to time, which was then echoed by one or two others. The Bengalis and others like them at the back (a few underpaid college teachers and out of work graduates) began to be a little restive, but they were kept in check by Mrs Kaul who took it upon herself to turn round and say 'Sh' at them.

A diversion was caused when Mrs Kaul's chauffeur came back with the flowers he had brought from her house. He stood at the door and coughed, and when this brought no result, he called loudly 'Memsahib!' There were protests, and Mrs Kaul had to leave her place and go to the back of the room to reprimand him. He replied sturdily that he had only followed her orders, and they had a somewhat undignified argument to which everyone within earshot tried to listen. The guest speaker was not in the least disturbed but carried on reading from his prepared manuscript: 'Now will we glance briefly at a contemporary cultural phenomenon which is peculiar perhaps not only to the Polish scene but I think also is it to be found in your India of today.' Mrs Kaul handed the flowers over to Judy and went back to her place, with the composed face of the organizer who has just dealt effectively with a difficult organizational problem.

There was no vase and, in any case Judy had no intention of making a spectacle of herself by going up to place flowers on the speaker's table. Instead she slipped out quietly and went to the kitchen to see how Mrs Kaul's bearer was getting on. She found Sudhir had got there before her and was eating sandwiches and having a conversation with the bearer about astrology. It was much more pleasant here than in the lecture room.

She and Sudhir sat on a string cot which stood in the courtyard. Out of this courtyard opened, besides the kitchen, the Doctor's own two rooms and the room which he let out to a clerk in one of the Ministries. It was here, in this closed-in space and not in the grand long hall now let out to the Dais, that, in the Doctor's father's time, the real life of the family had been carried on. The courtyard was paved in black and white marble squares, and out of its centre rose a large tree in which many birds nested.

Sudhir said, 'I've been thinking about teaching again.' Judy knew that whenever he was particularly dissatisfied with the Cultural Dais and its affairs, his thoughts turned to Calcutta and the evening college where he had taught.

'I want to teach,' he said, 'in theory. It's wonderful – in theory. To open your mind, heart, soul and pour out their contents for the benefit of eager young people: that's how you can think of it when you're not actually doing it.' He took off his glasses and wiped them gloomily on the end of his bush-shirt. How much better he looked without his glasses, Judy thought as she did every time he took them off. He had nice eyes (though of course, she added to herself, not as nice as Bal's), dark and shining and intelligent. 'But when you are actually doing it, then it's not like that at all. There are no eager young minds, only students looking for degrees for the sake of jobs. If they could get degrees by standing on their heads, they would practise all day standing on their heads.' He laughed grimly, but then went on, 'And why not, why not? They are right. If you're poor, your thoughts can only be concentrated on how to make yourself a little bit less poor. You should have seen my students at the evening college. They worked all day and then came at night to learn, to educate themselves. You don't do that sort of thing unless you can hope for some very concrete beneficial results from it. So that perhaps one day you can afford to rent a place where your wife won't have to struggle up and down two flights of stairs every time she wants a bucket of water. That's why you study. It's a good reason, isn't it? After all, disinterested learning and pure culture you can safely leave to that lot in there.' He jerked his head towards the lecture hall, while Judy strained her ears to try and make out what was going on inside.

'I think they're on the vote of thanks,' she said.

They crept up to the glass doors and peeped inside. Mrs Kaul was standing up and speaking: since no one important had come, she had to second the vote of thanks herself. The guest speaker looked absolutely exhausted, his bow-tie had come half undone and he had his eyes shut.

Sudhir, Judy and Mrs Kaul's bearer carried the trays of tea and sandwiches and little iced cakes (these latter obtained at a discount from Mrs Kaul's confectioner) round to the front veranda. Soon the doors were opened and everyone came out. The Bengalis and others sitting at the back got to the tea first, but Mrs Kaul, who knew their ways, clapped her hands and made them stand aside while the more important guests were served. There was a little cluster of admirers round the guest speaker, who sipped his tea with an air of exhaustion and smiled and murmured weak thanks to their congratulations.

Everyone broke up into groups, dotted around the veranda and in the garden. It really looked very pleasant, with the trees in the garden and those out in the street a mass of foliage against a sky which was now, in the late evening, a translucent grey with already a delicate silver twist of moon set in it. The groups of figures, clear in outline but blurred in details, looked charming and well composed, the ladies in their coloured dresses and saris, the men all in white. And their conversation too, when one did not hear what was being spoken, sounded lively and blended with the twitterings of the birds which were just settling down to sleep.

Judy passed quietly from group to group with plates of sandwiches and cakes. She threaded her way in and out of various conversations. Here was a Parsi lady who was explaining to Mrs Hochstadt, intent and interested and eating a cake, her feeling for Chopin who aroused very complicated emotions in her. There was Mrs Kaul, detailing the aims of the Cultural Dais to a tall elderly American – 'we wish to draw in the cultural threads of all nations', and she made the motion of drawing them in with her hand and clutching them against her bosom as if she were holding a bunch of balloons on a string. The Doctor, who usually joined them in their teas, had fastened on to an official of the Yugoslav embassy and was questioning him closely on the subject of rents paid out by foreign missions. Etta was entertaining two university professors and could be seen to be very lively, tossing her blonde hair around a lot and swaying on her heels and waving her arms in the air so that her charm bracelet jingled, while they listened to her with ready, flattered smiles.

Judy lingered among the Bengalis with her plates of sandwiches and cakes. They were all helping themselves to large quantities and eating very quickly as if they were afraid someone would stop them. In this they were not wrong, for soon Mrs Kaul called to Judy across the garden and directed her to other groups. She went and proffered to the guest speaker who helped himself with a limp, exhausted hand while listening to Dr Hochstadt on the subject of myth and symbol. Dr Hochstadt pinched Judy's cheek as she passed and said, 'Na, little one.' The Parsi lady talking to Mrs Hochstadt had now got on to Mozart – 'Così fan Tutte!' she exclaimed, shutting raptured eyes – and vivacious Etta had added three more portly middle-aged Indian gentlemen to her circle. Mrs Kaul was ticking off her beautifully manicured finger-tips at the American – 'Artists,' she said, 'writers, scholars, critics, thinkers: all these meet at our Dais and allow their ideas to flow and mingle.' The Doctor was asking the Yugoslav to make a guess at the approximate value of the property on which they were now standing.

Sudhir came up behind Judy and relieved her of the plates she was holding and took them back to offer among the Bengalis. Judy suddenly felt light-hearted and happy, the evening air was balmy and in the next garden she could see people sitting in white wicker arm-chairs and playing with a little dog which had a ribbon tied round its neck. She joined the circle around Etta, which seemed to her the gayest, and found her wittily describing an eccentric Raja's week-end house-party which she had once attended somewhere near Jaipur. Behind them, Mrs Kaul could still be heard talking to the American – 'Perhaps our most valuable contribution is that our work is carried on in a completely informal atmosphere, friends meeting friends – ' and she waved her arm round the garden for him to look, and he did look, and so did Judy, and saw the Bengalis making the most of what was left of the tea.

2

Bal had a brilliant idea. He woke up with it one morning and couldn't wait to tell Judy. Unfortunately she had already left for work – he was always the last to get up, for he got home late at night and liked to make up for it in the morning – so he had to lie there and think about it by himself. He lay for quite a long time, but in the end jumped out of bed for he had got so excited about his idea that he felt he had to share it with someone, even if it was only Bhuaji who wouldn't understand properly. But she had gone out too, and the children were at school, and the servant in the bazaar. The house was still and empty, only from upstairs came the sound of running water.

Bal went upstairs. This was not something he did very often, and he only did it now because he knew his brother Mukand was not there. The relationship between the two brothers was not close. Mukand tended to regard Bal as one of many crosses life had imposed on him, and though he accepted the fact that there was a duty to be done by him and performed it whenever need arose, he did so more in a spirit of moral rectitude than of brotherly love. Bal in return kept as much as possible out of his brother's way.

Upstairs he found Shanti washing clothes in the bathroom. She was squatting by the tap, vigorously slapping and pounding wet clothes on the stone floor, while water ran into a bucket. There wasn't room for two people in the bathroom, so Bal stood outside the door and said, 'I've had a first-class idea.'

Of course she couldn't hear him, because of the water running, but she could see his lips moving and, thinking that he had something important to communicate, she turned off the tap and looked at him expectantly.

'That is what we need so badly: a real professional theatre,' he was saying. 'And why shouldn't Judy's Cultural Dais start it?'

Shanti did not get excited. In fact, she only stared at him in puzzlement.

'Why do you think the Cultural Dais was founded at all? Only to foster the arts. It is their duty.'

Shanti turned on the tap again, and went on pounding clothes. It took up all her energy and attention and her cheeks were puffed out with the strain of it, while her arms went vigorously to and fro. That was what Bal disliked about women, the way they pretended that housework was the most important activity in the world and, when they were engaged upon it, nothing else was of any account. He returned downstairs in disgust.

Soon he was out of the house and on his way to the radio station. He went there at least once a day, to see if any work had cropped up for him in the drama department. He and several other actors and a few writers clutching manuscripts under their arms sat around in one or other of the little cubicles allotted to junior administrators and passed the time away. The junior administrators always seemed to be very busy, making out schedules and answering the telephone and calling loudly for their peons, and they tried to give the impression that it was a nuisance for them to have all these visitors sitting around in their tiny offices; but really it was well known that they liked to have them there and would have felt bored and neglected without them.

Bal lost no time in telling everyone about his idea, but here too he did not meet with the enthusiasm he needed. The trouble was that, among these people, everybody regularly had a different new idea and always one that was sure to change everything and bring fame and fortune to its originator and his friends. And even when an idea caught on – as, for instance, it had done that time when they had all decided to found a film company of their own – it was never long before interest in it fizzled out and after some time nothing more was heard about it. Perhaps this was due to the fact that all their schemes were on rather a grand scale and hence tended to be long-term ones, whereas their lives were organized on a short-term basis: and so it always happened that they were willing to jettison the chance of earning Rs. 10,000 in the future for the sake of a bit of work that might bring them Rs. 100 in the present.

'No but listen, listen!' Bal pleaded. 'This is quite different. You see, my wife has a lot of influence in the Cultural Dais, they will do everything she says.'

The others looked at him dubiously, not quite knowing how much to believe. It might really be true that his wife had a lot of influence – she was, after all, English and knew how to talk to all these people and make contact with foreigners and high officials in embassies. His English wife was Bal's one point of difference from the others, and it gave him in their eyes a kind of exotic background out of which any surprises might spring.

When he felt he had their attention, Bal became important and even a touch official: 'I will tell my wife to lay my whole scheme before the committee and see that it is pushed through at the earliest date.'

But they were not impressed. The idea of Bal being able, through any source, to influence a committee was too unrealistic to be entertained. They had known him too long and were – apart from his English wife – too much like him. They too had gone to colleges and got BA degrees, and after that, like Bal and together with him, had drifted around in search of their great chance. They even tended to look like Bal, for they dressed as he did in fine white lawn kurtas over pyjama trousers, they grew their hair long and oiled it well and wore Indian scents of khas or rose or jasmine. They were all of them fond of jewellery, and some wore rings and some fine gold chains round their necks and one of them even sported a single ear-ring.

The junior administrator behind his desk was drawing up an important schedule. He frowned over it, and sometimes he picked up the telephone to consult with a colleague in another cubicle. Every time he put down the telephone, he sighed as if overwhelmed with all the responsibility he had to bear. His visitors regarded him with a mixture of contempt, envy and hope, and finally one of them asked him, 'How about that part you promised me in the new serial?'

This let loose a flood of inquiries. Apparently all of them had been promised parts and now took the opportunity to press their claims. And not content with pressing their own, they pressed one another's too, each pointing out the other's rights. The administrator joined his hands to them in supplication and said, 'Please please, you know I am doing everything I can for all of you,' which was precisely what they knew he wasn't. He then went on to lay his own difficulties before them, and though they showed no sign of interest, he carried on at length and became quite heated in the process, recounting the intrigues and jealousies of his colleagues, the hidebound conservatism of his superiors, the slackness and stupidity of his inferiors, all of which combined to foil him in the execution of his brilliant plans.

Before he had finished – he was in the middle of a story of how his colleague in the next cubicle had deliberately mislaid a file in order to sabotage a most important programme of his – his visitors agreed with one another to proceed to the coffee-house and rose one by one to leave. 'Yes,' he said bitterly, watching them depart, 'you are lucky, you can go and sit in coffee-house whenever you like, all day if you want' – a remark they ignored with the contempt it deserved. Some years ago he had been one of them and had drifted around with them wherever they went, but after an uncle's influence had placed him in his present job, he began to think of them as a pack of idle loafers who would never come to anything the way he had done; and they, in return, thought of him as one who had sold out and was no longer to be regarded as a friend but only as someone who might be useful to them and whose office was a place to while away their time in.

In the coffee-house they met with others of their kind – aspiring actors, unpublished writers and many other different kinds of unemployed graduates or double graduates – and they all knew each other so well, since they haunted the same places and usually met at least once a day, that there was hardly any need for greeting. One simply strolled in and sat down in one's accustomed place with one's accustomed friends. Even the waiters did not have to be given orders but automatically brought what they knew each person wanted. This made for a very cosy and familiar atmosphere. The coffee-house was a homely place for all of them, and they sat around in easy attitudes, drank coffee and ate potato-chips or nuts dipped in a lot of chutney, read and composed poetry, smoked their own cigarettes or, if they didn't have any, those they could cadge from others, wrote letters, petitions or applications, studied the 'Situations Vacant' columns in the newspapers, gave one another good advice and spoke with confidence about their future plans.

In these congenial surroundings, Bal could be really expansive about his scheme. And here it was always possible to find people to listen to him, and more, to enter into the spirit of the thing, so that soon his scheme took on a kind of reality and became an idea not only in his own mind but in that of others too. They were all glad to have something concrete and hopeful to talk about, and grew so excited that they smoked up all one another's cigarettes. The coffee-house was a very dark place, in which it was difficult to see one another's faces clearly, and it was also hot and close and full of smoke; and here it was easy to talk on and on, amid that hubbub of voices and the familiar faces and the familiar smell of fritters and coffee and yesterday's crumb-chops. Once a topic had really got going, and had thrown a spark into the imagination, it became after a while no longer an abstract topic but something concrete and sure of achievement. All practical difficulties fell away, all those little details of organization seemed trivial and easy, and one's mind could jubilantly soar on the wings of that success which lay ahead. At this point one always

52

ordered another coffee, even though one could not afford it and had sworn not to have any more: but in view of the prosperity that was just round the corner, how foolish and petty it would have been to deny oneself this small gratification for the sake of saving a few paltry coins.

It was only after some hours, when the subject had been thoroughly exhausted, the last cup of coffee drunk, the cigarettes finished, and people slowly drifted off one by one and new ones drifted in and started on new topics, that Bal felt it was time to leave. Outside, however, it was nowhere near as nice as inside. The sun shone down hard and hot and there was a white glare in which everything looked very clear and harsh. Traffic and people thronged the road, and everyone seemed bent on hurrying to some particular business and had no time for anyone else. Bal collided with a large man in a sweat-stained shirt and a panama hat and though Bal stood still and tried to apologize, the man did not seem to have noticed at all but hurried on with a preoccupied look on his face. After walking aimlessly down the road for a while, and wondering where he should go next, Bal decided to visit Judy's office; he was still taken up with his scheme, though he no longer felt as confident and jubilant about it as he had done in the coffee-house.

Judy and Sudhir were in the middle of checking proofs of the Dais' monthly pamphlet and, overwhelmed by the apparent importance of this activity, Bal tiptoed to the library. There he sat humbly waiting on a chair and leafed through the latest report on the canal waters dispute. Judy, however, followed him almost immediately and seemed very pleased that he had come. She even held his ears and kissed him which he liked but which made him look round nervously and say, 'Someone will see.'

'So what,' said Judy and did it again.

He smiled and bloomed under these caresses, and began immediately to unfold his scheme to her. As he spoke, he became more and more enthusiastic and he looked at her with shining eyes and there was a flush in his cheeks. 'It will be so wonderful, Judy,' he said over and over, and when he said wonderful, he expressed everything one could possibly hope and dream for. She loved these enthusiasms of his. He had had them ever since she had known him, and though that was over ten years now and he had reached thirty and nothing, nothing of what he had hoped ever came true, yet all the same his faith was as bright as it had always been. 'Once I get this chance, Judy,' he was saying, 'you will see how nice everything will be for us,' and she said 'Really?' and also looked very pleased, as if she hadn't heard it dozens and dozens of times before, and he cried, 'Oh really, really!' holding her hands and squeezing them between his.

This was exactly how he had persuaded her to marry him and follow him to India. Judy had met Bal at an International Youth social in London. It wasn't the kind of function she would normally have attended – she never attended anything: she only went from the office where she worked to her home and back again, and twice a week to the pictures, and on Saturday afternoons she washed her hair – but, quite by chance, she had met a girl whom she had known at school and who had persuaded her to accompany her to the social. The friend had turned out to be faithless and, having found some boy to dance with, left Judy to her own devices. These consisted of nothing more than sitting on a chair and watching others dance, alternated by frequent trips to the cloakroom to fix her hair and apply new lipstick; not because she needed it but because she felt embarrassed sitting there so long by herself with no one to talk to. It was on her return from one of these trips that she had accidentally collided with Bal, who was carrying a glass of lemonade. Some of the lemonade spilled on to Judy and though actually it was very little and did neither her nor her dress any harm, she and Bal made as much of the incident as possible, for he had no one to talk to and was feeling left out. They spent the rest of the evening together, and after that they met every day. She was seventeen, and he just twenty.

'It will be my big chance,' he now said, ten years and two children later. 'It is everything we have always been waiting for. Judy, just think, what an opportunity! You have so much influence, and what else is a Cultural Dais for if not for culture? You *must* push it through. Let's talk to Sudhir.'

'Not now,' she said quickly.

'Why not now? Strike when the iron is hot. Sudhir will be glad, in fact he will be very happy, I know, it is exactly the sort of scheme he will like.' Bal was already leaving the library to join Sudhir in the general office on the other side of the folding glass doors, but Judy held him back.

'Don't, Bal,' she said.

'But why not? How silly you are. I must have a long talk with him.'

'I'll do it,' she said. 'I'll talk to him about it.' It wasn't that she was afraid Sudhir would sneer at the idea (he wouldn't) or that he would deflate Bal (he might not even do that), but only that she didn't want Bal, so glowing, so full of joy, to lay his hopes before Sudhir. 'Really I will,' she said. 'Promise.'

'How funny you are,' he said, smiling at her and looking into her face. They were almost the same height.

'And you,' she said, and there was a little affectionate byplay, at the end of which Judy pushed Bal out through the side-door, so that he would not have to go through the general office and perhaps be tempted to open his heart to Sudhir after all.

She didn't mention the scheme to Sudhir that day, nor the next, though Bal kept urging her and even phoned the office several times to find out if she had done anything yet. She couldn't quite say what it was that held her back. Perhaps it was the thought of laying Bal's irrepressible optimism open to Sudhir's irrepressible pessimism: the one's enthusiasm to the other's cynicism. Yet Sudhir too, she often felt, had his enthusiasms; and it was perhaps because he had them, and had seen them often disappointed, that he was the way he was. One had with him the sense that it was only because he had such high hopes of how everything could be that he expressed such disgust at how everything was. When he spoke with his friends, he spoke with passion, as did they, but it was a passion they did their best to hide. They tried to give the impression of being detached and, more, unconcerned. Everything was going to the dogs, they suggested, but of course they didn't care, to them it was all merely an amusing spectacle.

Sudhir's best friend was an old man called Jaykar, who had been a revolutionary during the Independence movement and had spent an aggregate of fifteen years in various jails. Now he had a small pension and whiled away his time swearing at the government he had fought so hard to install and writing and publishing a bi-monthly pamphlet called *Second Thoughts*, in which he exposed with relish all the evils of our present day. He and Sudhir sat for many hours discussing with humorous nonchalance such topics as corruption in high places, the inadequacy of defence preparations, the failure of community development schemes and the impossibility of raising the basic wage level. Sometimes they were joined by the Doctor, who always liked, he said, a good discussion, and who would listen to them with growing astonishment, his head spinning from one to the other. By the time they reached the climax of their exposure, his eyes would be quite round and his eyebrows above them stood up in horror; at this point Jaykar would often cry, 'Wait till you hear what I have written in *Second Thoughts*!' And then he would open his frayed old white coat and, fumbling in its inner pocket, come up with that shabby, ill-printed, four page little news-sheet which he launched upon the world once a fortnight. He would take out his spectacles and perch them on the end of his nose, and then looking over the top of them and holding the paper at arm's length he would read: 'What we as a nation want is not words but deeds, not promises but plans, not sentiments but bread!' After which he took off his spectacles, folded the paper back into his pocket and looked challengingly at the Doctor, who expressed admiration of the prose and commendation of the sentiment, only to find Jaykar and Sudhir grinning at him like two satyrs. That would exasperate him and he would cry, 'But you said it is very serious!' Whereupon Sudhir would reply in his most sphinx-like manner, 'An honest man like you, Doctor, what can you know of the dishonesty that prevails in this filthy world we have to live in?'

It was while Jaykar was there that Judy finally mentioned Bal's scheme. She brought it forward tentatively, and as an idea of her own. 'What we need is a professional theatre,' she said, using Bal's words but not the passion and conviction he brought to them. She pointed out how it was just the sort of scheme the Cultural Dais ought to undertake, and tried hard to recall one or two of the other forceful points Bal had expounded to her. When she had finished, Sudhir said 'Bless you,' and there was a longish silence in which Judy felt that she had not stated the case well.

Jaykar and Sudhir were drinking glasses of abominably strong tea. They drank slowly and with a very thoughtful air, but she did not know whether they were being thoughtful about her proposal or just in general. She rather hoped that they would let the topic rest but had her suspicions that she would not now get off so easily.

After a while Jaykar said 'A professional theatre,' as if he were giving the scheme the full benefit of his reasoning capacities. He looked at Judy with mild old eyes and asked in a mild voice, 'What sort of public do you think will come and visit your professional theatre?'

Judy hadn't thought of any; she had naturally assumed, as far as she had assumed anything at all, that once there was a theatre, everybody would want to come to it.

'Were you thinking of the masses?' said Jaykar, and when he said 'masses' he made a face as if he were quoting from a newspaper or a politician he particularly disliked. 'To bring joy and jollity – or perhaps culture and civilization? – into their drab lives?'

Judy was not worried by these questions. The nice thing about Sudhir and all his friends was that, though they were asking searching questions all the time, they were always ready to supply the answers themselves.

'Don't trouble yourself about these masses, please,' Jaykar said. 'I don't think they feel great need of your professional theatre. Do you know, when you don't have enough to eat and no place to live and can't afford to send your children to school, it is a very strange thing, but do you know you don't really feel the need for a professional theatre?' His eyes were no longer mild but glittered with a suppressed fury which, old and dimmed as they were, was very characteristic of them.

Sudhir said in his amused, flippant way, 'Judy was thinking of a better class of people.'

Judy would have liked to disclaim that; it had an unpleasant ring to it. And it wasn't true either – she hadn't been thinking of any class of people, only of Bal.

'Our Cultural Dais crowd, for instance,' Sudhir said. 'Now they need a professional theatre really badly. Think of those delightful first nights – the speeches, the bouquets, the best saris. Mrs Kaul receiving the Prime Minister and leading him up the aisle to usher him into his seat, while the cameras click and the flashlights flash. Marvellous. And meeting friends in the interval – will there be a refreshment bar, Judy? – "hallo there, how are you, why weren't you at the Kuldips on Monday?" '

Jaykar gave a dry, disgusted laugh and looked as if he were thinking out a paragraph on degeneracy for *Second Thoughts*. Sudhir went further into his stride – 'and afterwards there might even be a well-bred little discussion on the merits and demerits of the play, before the mind turns to the all-absorbing problem of where to eat dinner' – but was interrupted by Judy, who cried with unaccustomed vehemence, 'Yes, I know, and all this while millions are starving!'

Both of them looked at her in surprise. They hadn't meant any harm to her and couldn't understand why she should be upset. She didn't really know herself – and it was true; millions *were* starving, she had to admit it – except that she kept thinking of Bal in the library and how eager he had been.

Sudhir and Jaykar became terribly polite and concerned towards her. They dropped the subject of the professional theatre altogether, and now did all they knew to entertain her. Jaykar told a story about a quarrel he had heard on the bus that morning, between a conductor and a swami who claimed to be travelling at God's expense, and Sudhir topped it with one of a swami who was caught stealing sweetmeats and defended himself by saying that it was not he but God who had felt the sudden craving. Before he left, Jaykar presented Judy with one of the peppermints which he always carried around with him to give to any children he might meet on his way.

Judy took the peppermint home and divided it between Gita and Prithvi, who were rather snobbish about it. She wished she could have taken something home for Bal instead, some piece of encouraging news to greet him with when he came back at night. She would probably be asleep by that time, but he would wake her up, as he always did the last few days, to ask 'Did you talk to him? What did he say?' Then she would pretend to be too sleepy to answer him.

Bal decided to use his own contacts. He was a great believer in contacts, and spent a good deal of thought and effort trying to make them. But somehow he found he could never get at the people who really mattered, and though he knew a great number of those on the periphery – sub-editors on newspapers, assistant secretaries to cultural bodies, distant relatives of high-placed personages – these never turned out to be as useful, when it came to any point, as he had hoped and they had promised they would be.

One of Bal's major contacts to social and cultural worlds above him was Clarissa, and he decided to go and see her. He had known her for many years, having made her acquaintance during her theatre phase when she had thrown herself heart and soul into fostering a great Indian dramatic revival. It was, in fact, through Bal's acquaintance with Clarissa that Judy had got to know Etta and the Hochstadts and thence the Cultural Dais circle. Bal himself, though of course he had met all these other people, had never got on to a really intimate footing with any of them, so that Clarissa alone remained his most hopeful contact.

Her enthusiasm for the theatre had long since waned, but she was still enthusiastic about Bal. She was very fond of handsome young Indians and whereas Etta, in her day, had either married or had affairs with them, Clarissa had always had to confine herself to discovering great spiritual and moral qualities in them.

She lived off the main shopping district in a back lane – a central if not a very attractive place. It was not a residential area at all, but one purely confined to business concerns, with wholesale showrooms downstairs and offices upstairs. Many years ago Clarissa had managed to rent a little office room on the second floor, and though in the meantime its rental value had multiplied ten- and twenty-fold, the proprietors of the building found it impossible to dislodge her. Whenever they tried to do so, she went to see some of her friends in high places to whom she gave so piteous a description of her plight that they were always persuaded to exert their influence and put things right for her.

Bal climbed up the stairs to her room and found the door open. He could see her in a grimy housecoat padding around inside; she seemed to be looking for something, for she kept picking objects up and putting them down again, and muttered crossly to herself as she did so. He called out to her from the doorway, and when she saw him, the cross expression on her face was dramatically transformed to one of joy. She flew to meet him and clung to him closely and for rather a long time. Although he did not relish this intimate physical contact, he was so touched by the affection it revealed that he too tried to make some display of pleasure at the encounter by giving loud hearty laughs and thumping her on the back. When all this was over, she took a couple of steps backwards and, holding his hands, said, 'Let me look at you, you lovely boy.'

He smiled bashfully at the inspection and when she said, 'You look more wonderful than ever,' he replied, 'And you also.' But she didn't in fact, she looked awful. She looked a good deal older at home than she did outside. Her cheeks seemed more sunken (had she perhaps, for the sake of home comfort, taken out a few surreptitious back teeth?) and her skin more grey and lined. Her housecoat kept falling open and had to be held together, and she padded around on big, naked, dirty feet.

'I know the place is a mess,' she said, 'but make yourself at home.' She swept a hospitable hand around and gave a bark of laughter. Bal squeezed himself carefully and a trifle fastidiously – he was, after all, wearing nice clean clothes – into one corner of her old sofa; the rest of it was cluttered with pots of dried paints standing on newspapers.

She flung herself on the floor at his feet and propping one elbow on his knee, looked up into his face. 'Now just tell me everything that's happening.'

Bal tried to give a rosy picture of his prospects. He mentioned one or two radio parts and dwelt at length on everything he hoped for from Kishan Kumar and the film world. Clarissa listened ecstatically, so that he became really expansive: it was not often that he had such a listener, for though Judy was mostly sympathetic, she did not really respond with quite that degree of enthusiasm which his own required. But Clarissa did; and, moreover, she evidently took everything he said at absolute sterling value, and believed as implicitly as he did himself in the great future that awaited him.

'That's wonderful,' she said, 'that's absolutely splendid,' and looked up at him from the floor with eyes that, if she had been younger, would have been radiant.

Bal was touched. He felt at that moment that she was his very best friend on earth and, overcome with the strength and beauty of that sentiment, he told her, 'Only you understand me, no one else.'

She laid her hand on top of his and said in a serious voice, 'That's because I have such a real feeling for you.'

He disliked the pressure of her hand, but when he admitted this dislike to himself, he was ashamed of it, especially in view of the nice things she was saying to him and of his own feelings of friendship for her.

'We can only understand people we really feel for,' she continued in the same serious voice. 'It's the old adage again: where there's love there's understanding. *Tout comprende c'est tout pardonner*. No – well of course, *pardonner* doesn't apply, but you know what I mean. Between people like us there's no need for words. There is such a thing as the language of the soul, thank God.'

'Thank God,' Bal echoed. His hand under hers tingled with displeasure but he forbade himself to draw it away.

'Soul cries to soul to become one with it and with the All.' Then she cried, 'Listen to me talking like an old crank!' And, vastly to Bal's relief, she released her elbow from his knee, her hand from his hand and scrambled to her feet like a young hoyden.

'Would you like some coffee? I think I've got some left.' She unscrewed her thermos flask and peered into it. Since she had no cooking facilities in her room, she was in the habit of filling up her thermos every night at some little eating stall with enough coffee to last her till she went out again the next day. 'Not very hot any more, I'm afraid,' she said as she poured into the cup-lid of the flask and handed it to Bal.

He suspected that she had previously drunk out of the cup. He knew Europeans were not fastidious in these matters, but to him it was deeply repugnant to touch his lips to where someone else's had been. So he only held the cup uneasily and watched her while she poured coffee for herself into a grimy glass and drank it off thirstily. Suddenly she jumped up and cried, 'Oh goody, there's some cake!' and, undoing a little newspaper parcel tied with string, held it hospitably under his nose.

'Thank you, I have eaten my breakfast and come,' he said, recoiling a little from the solitary dried up piece of too yellow cake that lay on the Urdu newsprint.

She hooked her foot under a cane stool, drawing it under her, and plumped herself down on it, with her legs apart and the cake in her lap. She ate with appetite. He felt very sad for her. He thought of her solitary days and nights in this bleak untidy room in the office building, feeding herself on scraps of shop-cooked food and growing older and lonelier and dirtier year by year.

But if this was her fate, she seemed to be very cheerful about it. She squatted happily on her stool and wiped crumbs from the paper with the tips of her fingers and licked them.

Bal said, 'Perhaps you should have a servant to look after you.' He spoke with genuine concern and, to set her mind at rest, added, 'Our Indian servants are not very costly.'

'Oh I'm all right. I like a simple life. No fuss, no bother, cut down your worldly necessities to a minimum, you know.' She laughed and, screwing up the piece of newspaper, tossed it into a corner. She really seemed to have cut down her worldly necessities to a minimum. The room was cluttered, but not with anything either beautiful or very useful. There were soiled clothes, old paint pots, a copper jug, an earthenware water-container; the only pieces of furniture were a string cot, a sofa with the springs leaking out from underneath, a wooden kitchen table and two cane stools. She had strung up a folk-art bedcover against the window. 'Anyway, I'm not home much,' she said. 'Always up and about, that's me, wandering the face of the earth like a sadhu.' This was true. Clarissa only kept her room to have somewhere to retreat to when none of her friends wanted her. For the rest of the time, she stayed in various comfortable houses, either in town or up in the hills or indeed anywhere she was invited, ate at other people's tables, took an interest in other people's affairs and made herself a part of other people's families.

'I'm a sort of free-and-easy mixture of sadhu and artist,' she said, and took pins out of her hair which then came thinly drooping to her shoulders. She gave it a toss. 'I'm for the wild life, the free life – ' She stretched her arms up in longing, and when she brought them down again, she said, 'I don't have to tell you, you know it, you're an artist yourself.'

'An artiste,' Bal murmured. He remembered what he had come for and was about to start on it, but she hadn't quite finished yet.

'People like you and me,' she said, 'are too busy chasing after the eternal values to care much about what we eat and where we live.'

'I care only for the theatre, not for my own personal glory,' Bal burst out. 'If they will start this group, I will soon show them what I

61

can do.' He began to outline his scheme to her, while she squatted right in front of him on her haunches and listened, her elbows propped up on her knees, her cheeks between her hands. At one point she laid one hand on his knee and began gently to massage it, but he didn't notice, he was too excited and all his energies were bent on fully convincing her and enlisting her support.

Judy, Shanti and Bhuaji sat in their courtyard. It was late at night and the children had one by one dropped off to sleep. Mukand, Shanti's husband, was also asleep upstairs, and had been so for some hours. But the three women still sat up, as if they were waiting or hoping for something that the day had not yet given them.

They liked sitting together like this. There was not much to say, but their silence was pleasant and companionable. Shanti's youngest child was asleep in her lap, and she rocked her knee a bit up and down from time to time and murmured a snatch of song. Bhuaji clicked the beads of her rosary and said God's name over and over under her breath. The night air was warm, the sky a brilliant silver from a fat, full moon. A tree out in the street reared over the top of the wall enclosing their courtyard, and next to it was a lamp-post which spilled light over one side of its leaves. It was not, however, a quiet night. Many people passed along the street beyond the wall, out for a stroll, talking and laughing, and others had pulled their beds on to the sidewalk, and there was a little cluster of customers at the betel-seller's and another little cluster playing cards under one of the lamp-posts. It was a crowded area without private gardens, so for most people the street was the place in which to spend the pleasant summer nights.

Shanti said, 'What was it he was telling me about starting a theatre? He was so excited.'

Judy smiled. 'He told you also?'

'I was washing clothes and suddenly he came.' She laughed at the recollection. 'How he talked! And looking at me with big big eyes as if it was I who was going to give him the money to start his theatre.' She clasped her hands before her face and rocked herself to and fro in amusement, while the baby slept peacefully in her lap. 'I didn't understand anything of what he said,' she ended up, and that too struck her as funny and she laughed again.

'It's a new scheme,' Judy said.

'Poor boy,' said Bhuaji, affectionately.

'Oh no,' Judy said, 'he enjoys it.'

They were all quiet on that for a while. It was true, Bal seemed to be happy most of the time, running around with his friends, making his contacts, dreaming up his schemes; which was more than could be said for his brother Mukand. Mukand left the house early in the morning on his bicycle, with his tiffin-carrier clattering from the handlebar, and he came home late in the evenings. On Sundays he mostly slept, he was so tired. He had no time or energy to play with his children or talk with his wife, but he did bring home a regular salary for them every month.

'This morning Bal was lying in bed, ten o'clock, eleven, twelve,' Bhuaji said. 'At last I told him, Child, get up, why are you wasting your whole day away? He said please don't disturb me, I am thinking up plans to make three lakhs of rupees so that I can keep you all in luxury as you deserve.' She laughed and cried, 'Bless him!' and then her rosary started clicking and she was saying God's names again.

'If only he would earn something,' Shanti said.

'Sometimes he does,' Judy said earnestly – not by way of defence (there was no need of defending or pretending or any kind of sub-terfuge before Shanti and Bhuaji) but as a statement of fact.

'Only sometimes,' Shanti said. 'What will happen when children grow up – Prithvi's education, Gita's marriage – ' She rocked her knee and made automatic kissing sounds at the baby, which was stirring in its sleep.

'God provides,' Bhuaji said. To this Judy cheerfully assented. She had none of Bhuaji's deep and active belief in such a good God, but for most of the time she did have a kind of easy faith that someone – and she didn't much care who – would provide, and that, when the time came, everything always worked out. Perhaps this was a reaction against her parents who, in their middle age, had spent much time and worry over the problem of how they would manage on the old age pension. And in the end the problem had not arisen.

'When my husband entered into bliss, what did I have? Where could I turn?' said Bhuaji. 'But look at me today – ' and she cackled with pleasure. Bhuaji's husband (a railway inspector) had died some thirty years earlier and had left her both childless and destitute. She had no very close relatives, but the family at large took care of her and she was passed from household to household, wherever it was judged she would be the most useful and the least burdensome. Her demands were few – her diet consisted of bread and a handful of lentils, and she was content to spread her sleeping-mat in any corner allotted to her – but nevertheless most families were not willing to keep her for very long, and she had often to roll up her little bundle of belongings and pass on to whoever would take her next. For the past ten years, however, she had been with Mukand and Bal, and here they were content to keep her.

'Today just look at me,' she said again, quite smugly, so that Judy replied, 'Yes, today you're a bloated plutocrat.'

'God's will,' said Bhuaji, making her favourite gesture of resignation with one upturned hand.

Judy had long since accepted these frequent mentions of the name of God, though in the beginning they had affected her unpleasantly. She had brought with her from England an ingrained mistrust of the pious – 'bloody hypocrites, the lot of them,' as her father so often said – and tended to associate them with Lord's Day Adventists or Salvation Army women in bonnets. The word God on a sober person's lips had always made her want to either squirm or laugh. But these instinctive reactions had undergone some modification – mainly through her contact with Bhuaji who, she observed, said her prayers and made her visits to the temple and took her purificatory dips in the river not only because other people might be looking but more because she liked and needed and derived satisfaction therefrom. And sometimes it even seemed to Judy – for instance, when she went down to the river in the evenings – that perhaps Bhuaji was right and that what she spoke and sang about and prayed to, or something very like it, was really there.

Indeed, at this very moment, sitting with Bhuaji and Shanti and talking in quiet voices, listening to the sounds of people in the street outside, looking up at the sky which was full of moon and thickly sprinkled with stars, she was filled with a sense of trust and happiness that was far beyond any particular cause she could have named. A party of youths passed their brick wall, talking loudly and singing snatches of film song and, in passing, one or two of them banged playfully on their door.

'They've come out from the last show,' said Shanti with a yawn.

'Bal must've missed the last bus again,' Judy said. 'I hope he's got some money left to take a scooter.' Though she knew that, if he hadn't, he would borrow it from his friends. He often borrowed from his friends; they were generous with each other when they had money. Probably that was why Bal's earnings, when he had some, always lasted a remarkably short time.

'Last night he came in a taxi, I heard him,' Shanti said. 'It must have cost him three-four rupees. Where he gets it from –' She shrugged and laughed and shook her head.

64

'God provides,' Judy said in Bhuaji's voice.

Etta was fond of shopping. She liked to enter the smarter shops in town and have salesmen rush forward to serve her (even perhaps neglecting some plainer clients in the process), for though she wasn't a rich customer, she looked and acted like one. She was very particular and would never countenance anything but the best; and even that she had been known to look on with disdain, tilting her nose in the air and suggesting that perhaps for them this might be their best but that still did not make it good enough for her. And then she would walk out, leaving behind her a counter piled with all the goods she had demanded to be displayed to her, a shop assistant awesomely contemplating the whims of the wealthy, and groups of astonished customers who measured her retreating back from head to foot and wondered who she was.

So she progressed from shop to expensive shop, solitary and cocksure, head high, heels tripping, accessories matching, spoke in a wealthy voice to the salesmen, ignored everyone else and seemed oblivious of the attention she was drawing on herself. At the end of her tour she as often as not had bought nothing more weighty than a card of elastic, but this fact did not detract from her sense of achievement and fulfilment, nor from the pleasant feeling of fatigue that made it imperative for her to relax in some air-conditioned restaurant where she could sit and smoke and sip iced coffee and see, and be seen by, interesting people.

That day she went to Guppy's hotel. Here there were more interesting people than in any restaurant, for it was an international hotel and was largely filled with foreign travellers. The clerks at the desk wore black suits and spoke fluent English, and one of them (from Pondicherry) fluent French, and they had suave manners and wonderful memories for guests' names. The two lifts, smartly operated by liftboys in sky-blue uniforms, kept going up and coming down, and here and there stood piles of waiting luggage, new pig-skin cases and calf-leather holdalls with shiny locks and international labels. There were a number of phenomenally expensive shops, displaying ivory chess sets, gold-tissue neckties, handbags set with semi-precious stones, and other wares of such like nature, which no citizen would ever wish to possess but which the guests at the hotel found irresistible. There was also a travel agent's, with colourful posters of Paris and Venice, and Etta strolled in for a moment to flick through the folders advertising Mediterranean cruises and holidays in Spain with a casual, almost bored air, as if in the past she had taken many such trips and might, or might not, as the whim took her, consider taking one again.

She went and sat in the lounge, in one of the huge biscuit-coloured arm-chairs. Guppy had had the interior specially designed by a White Russian lady who lived in Bombay. All the furnishing was biscuit-coloured except the carpet which was pale green; enormous boat-shaped lights floated from the ceiling. Etta sank deep into her chair, crossed her legs, lit a cigarette and took up a magazine; a bearer brought iced coffee for her and a long silver spoon to eat up the cream with. She turned the pages of her magazine and seemed happily settled and quite unaware of the other people sitting around her. But she was watching keenly. Near her sat two foreign ladies, with the bored waiting expression of transit passengers; they carried the whole weight of a highly organized industry in their superbly cut clothes, their smoothly fitted leather shoes, their costume jewellery, their French scent, their cunningly cut and coloured hair – but with such accustomed, casual ease that Etta, who had nothing but a little Muslim tailor, a Chinese shoemaker and her own ingenuity to fall back on, could not help feeling both a little envious and a little shabby. However, she suppressed both these merely personal emotions in order to follow the cool and rational path of knowledge: she studied the two women sharply and in detail, noted the length of skirt, the shape of the shoes, the colour of eye-shadow, the cut of the hair, and stored it all away for her own future reference. She was never too proud to learn, and these transient passengers, these brief emissaries of a Europe she had left over twenty-five years ago but still looked to for everything that was valuable to her, were her only mentors.

Later she went up to Guppy's suite. She found him relaxing on the sofa in his vest and with his shoes off; he must have just had a meal and was picking his teeth after it. She told him at once, 'Don't do that – I've told you millions of times.'

He tossed away the toothpick, not because of her admonition but because he had finished anyway.

She entertained him with her morning's doings. There wasn't much to tell, and he wasn't very interested, but she talked anyway, making it all sound as amusing and interesting as she could. In between he made a few telephone calls, cutting without apology into the middle of her narrative, but she didn't mind for she was used to it with him. When he put down the receiver and said 'Hm', to show her that she again had his attention, she carried on from where she had left off. At one point he dropped off to sleep. He had the enviable habit of taking little cat-naps during lulls in his activities and waking up refreshed and vigorous fifteen minutes later. During those fifteen minutes she too eased herself out of her shoes and relaxed both her body and her face. Now, with the vivacious expression gone, she looked old and tired, the way she did when she was alone at home. She knew it, but she didn't care; she wanted a rest. The room was beautifully air-conditioned, though not very restful in its interior. The White Russian decorator had not been called upon to practise her art on Guppy's suite, so it was his own taste that prevailed here. The sofa set was in electric blue and the curtains in egg-yolk yellow silk; there were a few very shiny coffee-tables in would-be modernistic designs and lamps of red satin plentifully brocaded and fringed. The carpet was expensive and specially made to several Persian designs jumbled together and coarsened to such a degree that they fitted in very well with the rest of the room. Etta had succeeded in changing Guppy's attire, but not, much as she longed to do so, his taste in furnishing. As far as he was concerned, his suite looked nice and, what was more, had been very expensive, and so could not be changed just because it did not suit the whims of one particular woman.

Etta shut her eyes, to shut the ugly room away from her; she tried to rest but couldn't because she felt it necessary to remain alert for his awakening. She thought of those two European ladies in the lounge downstairs, who even in India remained elegant and always amid elegant surroundings, and who would soon be sitting luxuriously in an aeroplane to be flown, cool and in comfort, for ever away from here. And then she thought of herself, sitting in this room, waiting for Guppy to wake up. Fortunately, before she could get any further, he did wake up, and she slipped her feet back into her shoes and her face back into youth and sprightliness, and welcomed him in a cool, amused voice: 'Chivalrous Guppy! I come to see him and what does he do? drops off to sleep, the lamb.' He yawned widely and rubbed his hair with both hands.

'Shall we go and see a film? I want to do something relaxing. What I'd like most is one of those gooey films – you know, lots of lovely lovey-dovey in million dollar apartments – ' She knew he wasn't listening, but she went on all the same. He was having a wash in his marble bathroom, bending over the basin and splashing his face and the back of his neck and cleaning his mouth out with his finger, the way she had seen people do at public hydrants.

'Not – most definitely not – a western,' she was saying. 'All those guns, oh Heavens no, I couldn't – '

'Your friend came,' he said from underneath the towel with which he was rubbing himself dry.

'What's that, dear?'

'Your friend came. What is her name? Clarissa.' And when he said the name, he seemed to visualize her and it made him laugh.

Etta raised her eyebrows and said, 'Oh?'

'Yes, she – ' He was still laughing, and before he could get any further, the telephone rang. All he said down it was 'Hm', 'Hm', in various thoughtful expressions, but when he had finished, his mood was changed and he was no longer thinking of Clarissa.

But she was. 'And what exactly,' she inquired in a distant, disdainful voice, 'was the purpose of this unexpected visit?'

'What?' he said. 'Who?' preoccupied with whatever it was that had been said over the telephone.

'My friend, as you call her. I simply cannot think what earthly reason she could have to come here. Unless of course it was to cadge free drinks and free meals.' She gave a short laugh, which didn't sound in the least amused, and lit a cigarette with quick, jerky movements.

'She wanted to ask me for something,' Guppy said absently.

'Oh, of that I'm sure. She would never, never go anywhere unless it was to *ask* for something.'

He put on his terylene bush shirt, which hung over the back of a chair. 'I must go down to the office.'

'What did she want?' Etta said crisply. 'Money?'

'Why do you think people come to me?' Guppy said, not bitterly but, on the contrary, amused and rather pleased with himself. 'For my handsome face and cultured personality? Ha-ha-ha!' The telephone rang again and he said down it, 'Yes yes, I am just coming.'

'How much did she want?'

'Only one or two lakhs, she was most reasonable.'

Etta stretched her green eyes wide.

'She wants to start – I will tell you some other time. All are waiting for me in the office.'

'Start what?' Etta cried. 'What?'

'A theatre group. For a friend, she says. I will tell you the truth – except for the one or two lakhs, there was not much I understood. Please make yourself quite comfortable and call for anything you like.' For such a large, heavy man he was quick in movement and he was out and the door shut behind him before she could do anything to delay him further.

Etta, left alone, concentrated all her thoughts on Clarissa. They were not pleasant thoughts.

Judy said, 'And what'll happen to me if you go?'

Sudhir was surprised; he said, 'I didn't think you were so selfish.'

'That just shows you don't know me, not after all this time.' She tried to pout but did not succeed. She had a naturally cheerful and serene expression, and neither pouting nor sulking came easy to her. Altogether she was rather deficient in feminine arts.

'Are you suggesting I stay here only to keep you company?'

Judy laughed and said yes. Then she went back to her typing. She could not type well – in fact, only with two, sometimes three, fingers – but it sufficed for the work there was in the Cultural Dais.

After a while Sudhir came and perched on the edge of her desk, with his arms crossed and his long legs sloping out before him. He said, 'How much longer can I stay here? To sit all day and do nothing – terrible, terrible.'   —

Judy thought how it was not Sudhir so much as Bal who did nothing all day; but it never seemed to worry Bal.

Sudhir said, 'You know I envy a person like Jaykar very much. All his waking hours he spends thinking of that paper of his, *Second Thoughts*. When he hears or sees something, whatever it is, at once he thinks, Should I write about it in *Second Thoughts*? And besides that, he runs around from morning till night wheedling people to give him advertisements and collecting subscriptions and quarrelling with his printer.'

He slipped down from the desk and started restlessly pacing, the way he often did. Really, the office seemed to be a cage for him. 'And when I first came here – I'll confess it to you, Judy, because I think you are stupid and won't understand anyway, so it is all right – ' (She didn't stop typing, but tightened her mouth a little bit so that he wouldn't see she was in any way amused.) 'Yes, when I first came here I came, God help me, with such hopes, such ideas in my head of all the wonderful things I was going to do and achieve.' He snorted, then took out a large handkerchief and blew his nose on it. 'That was the sort of fool I was, and still am. If tomorrow now, for instance, someone were to come and say to me, why don't you go to Trichinopoly or Mount Abu or Budge Budge or some such other place, they are starting a great new scheme there for the uplift of the nation – or for a cultural renaissance or for moral training and reform – anything like that, any kind of hollow nonsense, you know that I would run there? I would believe it, and run there.' He strode up and down more rapidly, shaking his head at himself. 'Why are we like that? Always clinging to some big noble abstract and talking about it and hoping for it and letting it grow large and beautiful in the mind, and then in the end, when there is something actually concretely to be put into action, then what do we do? Absolutely nothing. For by that time we are exhausted by thinking so much and talking so much and dwelling up in such high territory; and to come down to earth is always rather disappointing. Are you listening to me?'

'Of course.'

Although it didn't seem to matter much to him whether she was or not. 'Perhaps that is why all our grand-sounding schemes become like – well, like the Cultural Dais. And when they run at all they do so only because some other initiative has taken over – some Mrs Kaul, for instance, whose principles and ideals are much more firmly based. Mrs Kaul, bless her, cares for none of our noble abstracts but, on the contrary, for some very solid concretes: the Cultural Dais for her stands for social advancement, a place where you can meet nice and interesting people and be in touch and be important, also an opportunity perhaps to wangle a trip abroad . . . Are you still listening?'

Judy had finished typing and she pulled the sheet of paper out of the roller and shut the machine. She thought to herself, how he talks! She couldn't imagine English people talking like that. When something had bothered her Dad, he used to sit and stare at the fire and finally spit into it, saying 'It's all a lot of muck.' That seemed to be the sum total of self-expression he needed.

'What is it that has enervated us? Is it heat? Is it two hundred years of slavery? Is it religion? But the curious thing, you know, Judy, the curious thing is that I don't really *feel* enervated at all.'

Suddenly she said, 'If only you'd help me with Bal. It means such a lot to him, he's always on at me about it – '

'What are you talking about?'

So then she had to tell him all over again about the drama group, only this time she didn't pretend it was her own idea but put all the stress on Bal and how much he wanted it.

And Sudhir became very energetic. He at once sat down and began to draft the proposal, with all sorts of proper headings, so that it looked suddenly very plausible and almost as if something could come of it.

Mrs Hochstadt, unlike Etta, was a careful, solid shopper. She did not care for flash and pomp, so she eschewed the fashionable shops and made her way into the narrow lanes of the bazaar where, she had discovered, *real* goods were to be obtained at a *real* price. She was far too sensible a person to be taken in by the blandishments of decorated counters and glass windows and obsequious shop assistants who spoke English, and realized that better bargains were to be struck at some little wooden stall where one negotiated direct with the proprietor across his pile of goods. He might speak no English and she no Hindustani, but this was not to be considered an obstacle. What mattered was the mutual respect that existed on both sides and which was engendered by their instant recognition of each other, one as a genuine serious seller and the other as a genuine serious buyer.

She stood pinching oranges and, while she was doing it, looked up at the shopkeeper with such a wise, not-to-be-taken-in look that he knew this was one customer for whom he would have to take out his special boxes from underneath. They were engaged in this silent act of mutual recognition when suddenly a whirlwind figure came dashing against Mrs Hochstadt, crying, 'Frieda, is that really you!'

'Good morning, Clarissa,' said Mrs Hochstadt, cordial but calm and still pinching oranges.

But Clarissa was very excited, as if meeting Mrs Hochstadt was a piece of good fortune that could not be enthused over enough. 'And just this morning I thought how I must come and see you, there's something we're got to discuss – are you buying oranges? I could do with some for my orange juice. All right,' she cried to the shopman before Mrs Hochstadt could say anything, 'wrap up six for me too!'

He did this rather quickly, before anyone could interpose, dropping them carelessly into a paper bag folded out of newspaper. Clarissa did not have the wits to scrutinize his goods, so he gave her what she deserved.

'Look here, Frieda, I'm in on a biggish and very exciting sort of scheme, I want to tell you all about it. This is one thing we must all pull together on, you and Franz and I and Judy and Etta – well of course Etta, who knows whether Madame will deign to join us. How much?' she asked the shopman, who told her something fairly outrageous but nevertheless she began to fumble in her big cloth bag.

When she came up with her purse, Mrs Hochstadt laid a restraining hand on it. 'Surely they are only three rupees a dozen?' she said, shrewdly eyeing the shopman who gracefully smiled, showing betel-stained teeth.

'Cheats and rogues all,' Clarissa said cheerfully. 'It's a theatre group, Frieda, a real professional theatre group. I had a long chat about it with Bal, you know, Judy's husband, and it really is quite some scheme, I must tell you all about it.'

But one thing at a time, as far as Mrs Hochstadt was concerned. 'Let me see those oranges,' she said, taking Clarissa's bag and, after one practised look at the fruits inside it, she handed them back to the shopman.

'Now I think you want us to come back to your shop one day, don't you?' she told him. He grinned amiably and gave a scratch at his bare thigh where the soiled dhoti had slipped away from it. 'Well then, you must not sell us bad fruits, I think, must you?' She wasn't angry, merely calm and reasoning. She knew that he couldn't follow her words but she also knew that he had no difficulty with their meaning. He poured all the oranges out of the bag back into the box, making a patient, good face as he did so. Then he pulled out the special box, on which he had been sitting.

'Our original idea was to have the scheme sponsored by the Cultural Dais,' Clarissa was saying. 'We must have a long talk with Mrs Kaul about it all. You see, Frieda, there's such a lot of acting talent about and it's a thousand pities to see the way it's being wasted.'

Mrs Hochstadt took Clarissa's purse away from her and counted out the money for Clarissa's oranges. 'If you want good customers,' she told the shopman as a parting homily, 'you must treat them like good customers. Now come along, Clarissa, I want to buy some cashew nuts. Franz and I always like them with our evening beer.'

The two of them continued their progress down the road. It was an extremely narrow road, with a wall on one side into the niches of which shops were fitted and the usual ramshackle wooden stalls on the other. The lane between them was thronged with shoppers and loiterers and a few stray animals, and littered with straw from wooden crates and with discarded peels; there was a smell of urine and ripe fruits. Mrs Hochstadt picked her way with quiet, steadfast competence, as if she had been used all her life to such crowds; whereas Clarissa, who had moved around in these bazaars for years, stumbled and bumped continually into unexpected objects. And of the two, it was Mrs Hochstadt who drew less attention. In her dark two-piece, with her neatly cut short grey hair and her black shoes with thick little heels and straps across the feet, she was a clear and traditional memsahib out shopping in the bazaar. But what was anyone to make of Clarissa? Her clothes were not those of a real memsahib, nor was the untidy structure of hair on her head, nor, least of all, the excited way in which she talked and clung to Mrs Hochstadt's arm. People smiled, nudged each other, and some of them stood still to look; time was not pressing, and in any case, even if it had been, it was not every day that one was vouchsafed a sight like this in one's own neighbourhood bazaar.

'And besides the Cultural Dais, I thought we ought to get in some private enterprise too,' Clarissa was saying. 'As a matter of fact, I've already taken steps.' She kept talking while Mrs Hochstadt negotiated for her cashew nuts. They moved to several stalls, till Mrs Hochstadt found one where she and the shopkeeper could come to a satisfactory agreement on price and quality. A little group of children and other interested parties followed them around, but neither Clarissa nor Mrs Hochstadt paid any attention to them: Clarissa because she was too excited with what she was saying to notice, and Mrs Hochstadt out of deliberate policy. She and Franz had thoroughly discussed the Indian phenomenon of rude staring at foreigners, they had analysed its causes, both psychological and social, and had come to the conclusion that the only thing to be done about it was to ignore it. So ignore it she did and moved from stall to stall, firm of step and dedicated of purpose, with the same ease and aplomb as if she had been shopping in Selfridges.

When her errand was done, she turned and went back down the lane, to regain the main road. Clarissa was still talking, every now and again giving a nervous, excited little hitch to the big cloth bag that she wore slung over her shoulder. 'I told Guppy we need something like a lakh and a half, and I must say this for him, the angel, he was really sympathetic.' Two little boys were treading hard on their heels, whining for money: 'Memsahib!' they appealed. 'Memsahib!' and even brought out a few English words to promote better understanding: 'Yes please good morning, one two three ten.'

'I told him that it's up to private capitalists, just as much as it's up to the government, to foster these cultural schemes, and I think he got the point.' The two small boys were very close and one of them gave an experimental tug at Clarissa's shoulder-bag. She swung round immediately – 'Don't you dare, you little – ! Bhago! Jao!'

Mrs Hochstadt walked on regardless, facing front. 'Take no notice,' she warned Clarissa without turning her head even a fraction of an inch. She and Franz had discussed the problem of beggars too, and had come to the conclusion that it was no use giving any of them anything. If one wished to be charitable, there were certain charitable organizations to whom one could send a cheque at Christmas or

Diwali or some such time of national rejoicing. But to give to anyone and everyone who asked – no, that was, in Franz's picturesque phrase, like pouring water into a bucket that had no bottom to it. So, come lepers in handmade carts, starving mothers and starving babies, crippled children or deformed old men, Frieda hardened her naturally soft heart against them and refused to see or hear.

'All one has to do is to explain to people. Awaken them to their responsibilities. Now Guppy isn't a bad old stick, but you know he simply isn't aware – what again – I'm warning you!' at the little boys who had now tried a tug at the peasant skirt.

'Ignore them,' Mrs Hochstadt counselled. 'Ignore them completely.'

'Memsahib!' they shouted gleefully. 'Memsahib! Only ten paisa to buy bread!'

Mrs Hochstadt determinedly kept the conversation going: 'If there is someone to help finance the scheme, of course it will be easier to interest the Dais – '

One of the boys very daringly bent down and touched Clarissa's bare leg. The sight of that strange white flesh must have been too much for him and he had to know how it felt to the touch. His fingers lingered only for an instant and then he drew them back with a sharp exclamation and shook them in the air as if what he had come into contact with was something either very hot or very cold and certainly weird and unexpected. His companion doubled up with laughter, holding his stomach with one hand and with the other pointing at Clarissa's leg. So that it was he who, as she furiously swung round, caught her attention first and received the sharp clout on the head which she unhesitatingly dealt out. His laughter changed abruptly to a cry not so much of pain as of amazement, which was echoed by his companion. 'Bhago!' cried Clarissa, red with fury. 'Jao!'

The witnesses to this performance, of whom there were more than one would have expected even in that crowded lane, were divided into two camps: one of which maintained that it served the boy right, that he was nothing but a nuisance and a rascal and that another one like that wouldn't do him any harm; whereas the opposing faction urged that, after all, what was he but a child, and should not everything be forgiven to a child?

Mrs Hochstadt had no intentions of staying for the outcome of this colloquy. She firmly grasped Clarissa's arm and guided her to the end of the lane; and the moment they had reached the corner, she began authoritatively to shout and gesticulate for a rickshaw. It was a main road, so it was not long before a motor-cycle rickshaw drew up for them, and Mrs Hochstadt hastily ushered Clarissa into the seat at the back and, with a heave and a groan, climbed up to sit beside her. The vehicle made off at once, with the noise and hurtle of its kind, vigorously shaking the two ladies cooped up in the frail structure attached to the motor-cycle which was driven by an insouciant youth in a flaming turban, who sang songs which fluttered behind him and died on the wind.

Mrs Hochstadt did not speak for some time. She was, for one thing, out of breath from their precipitate flight, and for another, she was upset. It was a policy with her never to speak or pass any comment unless she was in full command of all her faculties; so that it was only when she felt herself truly calm and collected that she ventured to address Clarissa, and then it was on a topic which had nothing to do with what had gone before: 'Franz will be pleased with the cashew nuts!' she said – or rather, shouted, for the motor-cycle was making too much noise for an ordinary conversational tone. Even so, she was not sure whether Clarissa heard, for she gave no sign but sat staring in front of her, clutching her bag and going up and down with the motions of the vehicle.

They skirted round a bus and, coming out at its other end, nearly collided with a taxi and forced a cyclist off his cycle. Mrs Hochstadt clutched at her heart and shouted to the driver 'Not so fast!' He took no notice but went on singing, in the same hearty way as he had done through their near-accident.

'These people are so careless!' she screamed to Clarissa. Both of them were being mercilessly shaken and Mrs Hochstadt struggled against that familiar feeling of hazard and danger that overcame her every time she sat in a motor rickshaw. Nevertheless she always chose this mode of transport: taxis were more expensive and there was absolutely no point, as she often said, in wasting good money.

Suddenly Clarissa clutched her arm and began to say something which Mrs Hochstadt could not hear. She was evidently excited and troubled and was desperately trying to explain something. Mrs Hochstadt shouted, 'What? What?' into the wind, and then she bent her head forward and put her ear to Clarissa's mouth and heard '. . . don't know what came over me . . . I've never hit anyone before, believe me, Frieda, never . . .'

Mrs Hochstadt tried to comfort her. She shouted, 'You were upset! I think perhaps you were hot and tired!'

Clarissa shouted, 'I respect people! From the highest to the lowest, I respect them!'

Their vehicle swerved again and Mrs Hochstadt turned round and firmly dug the driver between the shoulderblades. 'Slow! Slow!' she screamed but he seemed neither to hear nor feel her.

'I'm not that sort of person!' Clarissa cried. 'Etta is that sort of person, not me! I respect people! I'll show you!' she screamed and started tugging her sketchbook from out of her bag. 'You'll see how I draw them, with tenderness and love – '

'Not now!' Mrs Hochstadt cried as Clarissa struggled with her sketchbook, the pages of which fluttered violently in the wind.

'I respect and understand!'

Mrs Hochstadt was terrified that Clarissa, who was very excited, would fall off. She put both her arms round her and held her as tight as she could. Clarissa took this for a sign of affection and comfort and promptly burst into tears, burying her face in her companion's shoulder. Mrs Hochstadt went on holding her and gave a few soothing pats. They continued the rest of their journey in this fashion, clinging together while the vehicle shook them up and down, this way and that, Clarissa still sobbing while Mrs Hochstadt stared stolidly over the head laid on her shoulder and tried to preserve some calm and dignity in this trying situation into which she had been forced.

Bal was at the airport to meet his great patron, Kishan Kumar. Various other of the film star's protégés and admirers were also there. They waited for the plane to land, forming a somewhat uneasy group together for, though they pretended cordiality to one another, each could not help feeling how much better it would be if all the others were not there. But as soon as the plane landed and Kishan Kumar stepped off it, their differences melted away and they became a coherent smiling group, feeling it seemed with but one heart and that heart full to overflowing with the pleasure of seeing their hero again.

He was taller than any of them, handsomer, more charming, more expensively, more beautifully dressed. As a matter of fact, he was more so than anyone in the airport, and indeed more than anyone to be met with in this everyday world: and so he walked as king, knowing he was splendid yet carrying it off with ease and grace. He chatted and laughed with his friends, a trifle too loudly and to all appearances so much engrossed that he was totally unaware of all the looks he drew. When he was asked – as he soon was, by porters, drivers and college boys – for his autograph, he gave it with a kind of professional humility which was rather at odds with the huge portentous squiggle in which he wrote his name on the proffered scraps of paper.

In the hotel room he sprawled in the fattest arm-chair of all and supported his feet on the coffee-table. The others sat jammed together on the sofa and, two each, in the remaining chairs with some more perched on the arms, and for the rest there was the floor where they sat hugging their knees. Drinks and cigarettes were on the house, and though they would appear later in Kishan Kumar's hotel bill, this was not something that bothered him: money for him was there to spend and make a show of, and he was in consequence immensely generous. He urged his friends to drink and smoke and enjoyed watching them glut themselves on things which were common and everyday to him but unwonted luxuries to them. They made the most of the occasion, and while they thus took their ease as temporary gentlemen, their eyes were all the time only on him and, though perhaps the thoughts that went on in each one's head were individual, there was no indication of this from their faces which wore, each one, a smile that showed they were proud of Kishan Kumar and proud of themselves that they were there with him.

He talked. He had a lazy, drawling way of talking and sometimes, when he remembered, he overlaid his St Xavier's school accent with an American one. He often stopped and his attention wandered, or he just lost interest in what he was saying, or he was tired and had to yawn and to stretch, bringing his arms up from his superb shoulders and letting his chest swell in the silk bush shirt. His audience was not one for which he had to take any pains, and besides, his material was so intrinsically interesting that there was no need of any refining arts in the telling. For he spoke of that Bombay film world to which they all aspired, and spoke of it all – the stars, the producers, the shooting schedules, the 'black' money and the 'white' – with such casual familiarity that his listeners felt as if they too were initiates of that great and wonderful world, and they looked forward, even as they eagerly pecked up each crumb of information that he let fall, of retailing it in the same easy insider manner as his in less favoured circles.

So the day wore on and still they sat, drinking, smoking, calling for occasional meals, and all of them – including Kishan Kumar – blissfully secure in the knowledge that this was really living. The ashtrays overflowed and had to be emptied by the bearers, the room was thick with smoke and most of them were beginning to look somewhat bedraggled. No one was actually drunk but they were all in a state of heightened sensibilities which made them feel and even expect that at any moment something else, something even more marvellous, might happen.

Kishan Kumar had another lazy, luxurious stretch and then he said, 'I'm thinking of starting a production unit of my own.'

Suddenly they all stopped lounging and sat up. Bal felt as if his mind had burst into flame and in one superb flash of anticipation he had a vision of his own glorious future that was, from that moment, about to begin.

He started talking and, though he didn't realize it, in the same breath with all the others. The room buzzed with excited questions and everyone was talking so fast and was so taken up with his own ideas that they failed to notice how they were overlapping one on the other with almost identical words.

Kishan Kumar, who up till then had perhaps not had any very firm notions about this production unit nor – beyond a vague speculation as to its pleasant possibilities – given it much of his time or attention, now saw that he was being taken very seriously. This did not displease him, but he felt the need to gain time in order to collect a thought or two. He shot out his hand and pointed it at the ceiling and cried, 'Look, look!' When everybody looked, he laughed uproariously and slapped his hands up and down on his knees. It was the sort of joke he enjoyed.

His companions' echoing laughter was not as hearty as it might at some other time have been, for their minds and hearts were all on the production unit and they wished to return to it as soon as he would allow them.

One of them said – it may have been Bal or it may have been someone else or even several of them together, speaking as with one voice: 'Have you got anything planned for your first production?'

And now Kishan Kumar himself began to get excited. Just as they had their visions, so he had his. Already, under the stimulus of their enthusiasm and admiration coupled with the drinks he had had, he saw himself – no, *was* the great actor-producer, the colossus of the Bombay film world. He took his feet off the coffee-table and leaned forward eagerly. 'There is a script – ' he said. As a matter of fact, there were many scripts – aspiring writers were always sending them to him – but for his present purposes the first in his mind would do. 'Man, wait till you hear it!' He ran his tongue over his lips and began to tell them the story. He looked wonderful. He was really fired now – happiness shone on his face, which was not only superbly handsome but also very young so that it became, now that he was excited and his film star affectations had fallen away, the perfect mirror for the perfect boy's heart.

It was the usual kind of Bombay film story that he told them – pure hero and pure heroine enmeshed in villainous machinations leading to misunderstandings, partings, tears and songs – but to them there was nothing usual about it. They lived every turn of the story as he expounded it, and even more they lived every character he mentioned, trying themselves surreptitiously in every part and posturing silently to themselves as they slipped now into this character and now into that. The part of the hero, of course, they all severely left alone, even in their own minds; for that was Kishan Kumar's. But all the other characters were theirs to hope for. Bal saw himself in turn as the heroine's unscrupulous brother, as a night-club owner, a prosecuting barrister, a rich uncle just returned from East Africa, and knew that he would do full and more than full justice to whichever role he might be called. He overflowed with faith in himself, in Kishan Kumar, in the film industry, in the future. In that moment of happiness it was not only on his own behalf that he exulted but on that of all the others in the room too. Life was beginning for all of them. He had to shut his eyes in pure bliss, and tears, dazzling in the darkness, gathered behind the closed lids and everything swam in silver.

He heard Kishan Kumar call to the bearer: 'Hey, Joseph, you lazy bastard' – Kishan Kumar was always familiar and slangy with servants and in return expected to be and usually was adored – 'how's about some more drinks for the boys?'

Sudhir had typed the whole scheme out in a very professional manner. It looked really impressive now. There was a concise, weighty paragraph about the need for a professional theatre group in the capital, followed by an elaborate scheme of proposed organization and administration, and ending up in an all-comprehensive summary.

'Aren't you clever,' Judy said, several times over, as she studied this document. But she was a bit frightened too; she didn't know she and Bal had started anything so important.

Mrs Kaul also seemed impressed. She took it home to read – 'to study', as she said: she was a very slow reader, she had to put on her reading glasses and her lips moved when she read and she gave herself little nods every now and again to show she had understood – and when she had finished, she rang up Sudhir at the office and asked him to come to her house for a discussion. Sudhir said that he would have to bring Judy with him, to take notes, and this pleased Mrs Kaul (who loved notes, minutes and secretaries) so much that she even sent her car and chauffeur for them.

No need to describe the elegance, indeed luxury, of Mrs Kaul's home surroundings. Suffice it to say that it was a house accustomed to much high-class entertaining, and that it had that very hushed, abnormally orderly air about it characteristic of places in which not very much ordinary living is encouraged to go on. There was even a sense of reverence which had communicated itself (or was it they themselves who exuded it?) to the servants, who glided about with such discretion and good manners that it was hard to grasp that they had perspiring bodies under those starched uniforms or that, like other people's servants, they lived eight to a room in some unsanitary quarter, drowned their troubles in drink and beat their wives.

Mrs Kaul was sitting on a divan, with her shoes off and in an easy attitude. In front of her stood a girl, dressed very neatly and carefully in a yellow sari with yellow ribbons to match in her hair. She held the strings of a plastic grab-bag between her hands which were modestly folded before her and her head was bent and her eyes lowered. She stood there immobile while Mrs Kaul spoke to her in a severe voice.

'Justice has taken its course,' Mrs Kaul said.

The girl shot a look at Sudhir and Judy from under her lowered lids. Then she murmured, 'Only one more chance.'

Mrs Kaul sighed and softly scratched the sole of her foot. She told Sudhir and Judy, 'She was dismissed for slackness in her duties as secretary to the Social Development Board. We cannot allow slackness in our organization, the burden of work is too heavy.' To the girl she said: 'You can go now. There is nothing more to be said.'

The girl stood dumb and sullen, with her handbag dangling in front of her. There was more, much more, to be said as far as she was concerned, so she stood there and waited.

Mrs Kaul turned all her attention to her two other visitors: 'Last year we were in Berlin where Mr Kaul was head of the economic mission at the International Conference of Civil Servants. We were shown many interesting cultural events such as the State Opera and the Berliner Theatre. From there we went to UK and saw *Rosenkavalier* at the Covent Garden Opera House. This too was a beautiful experience. In Moscow we saw the Bolshoi Ballet – oh my own dear Bolshoi Ballet!' she cried and clapped her hands and shut her eyes for joy. When she opened them again, she said, 'In comparison there is very little that we can show our foreign guests. We are lagging behind in this respect.'

The girl moistened her lips with her tongue, which looked very pale in contrast with her lipstick. Without raising her eyes she said in a stubborn voice, 'My mother is a widow.'

'A professional theatre in the capital would fill a gap,' said Mrs Kaul. 'A most definite gap.' Then, with a loud sigh of exasperation, she told the girl, 'We have already advertised your post in the papers and have had many applications.'

'When my father died, my mother was promised a pension from his office. We have written many letters and petitions and twice a week my mother goes to the office, but there is still no pension.'

Just then Mrs Kaul was summoned to the telephone outside. 'Priti!' she could be heard to exclaim in a joyful voice. The conversation that followed was animated and went on for quite some time.

The other three waited for her in silence. The girl had at last sat down, with a defiant look at Sudhir and Judy, as if she wanted to prove to them that she was every bit as good as they were. She made no attempt to get into conversation with them – on the contrary, she was even at some pains to show that she cared nothing for them, and pinched her lips together and gave a little toss to her head which made her ear-rings shudder. When Mrs Kaul came back, she stood up again.

Mrs Kaul was carrying a pile of envelopes. 'Look at these,' she said. 'These are all applications we have received in answer to our advertisements.' She pulled some letters out of their envelopes and read aloud: ' "I beg to state I am BA of Ludhiana College for Girls from very good family, I am married with two children my husband has polio and is not working for past one year – " '

'I have two younger brothers and one sister,' the girl said. 'My uncle sends us some money every month but it is not enough.'

'And here,' Mrs Kaul said. 'This one is even MA – "refugees from Lahore" ' (she screwed up her eyes with effort) ' "my father was killed in . . ." her handwriting is bad.' She made a compassionate face at Sudhir: 'Everyone has hardships and troubles, but what is to be done? Priority must be given to those with best qualifications. The work must on no account suffer.'

The girl blinked her eyes several times. Her body seemed to clench itself and suddenly she broke out, in a completely sincere voice and in a kind of amazement that her very simple point was not being taken – 'But I *need* the money!'

'You can see I am busy,' Mrs Kaul said. 'I am in conference.' To Judy she said 'Be ready to take notes.'

Judy bent her face low over the notebook she had brought with her. She felt herself blushing in embarrassment and some pain. She remembered how she had gone round from place to place, asking for a job, and how humiliated she had felt, and yet she had been ready to endure more humiliation if only she could get a job. Out of the corner of her eye she could see the girl's feet retreating towards the door; they moved slowly and heavily as if waiting and hoping to be called back. Her shoes were rather gay, with high heels and soles painted red and blue. She lingered by the door.

'Our first task is to set up a committee,' Mrs Kaul was saying. Judy wrote this down: also possible patrons – the Prime Minister? the Vice-President? – and who was to inaugurate the first performance of their first venture. When the girl finally went away, Judy found herself listening to the last echo of her shoes clicking on the marble floors. At the same time she continued to take notes. She wrote down everything that Mrs Kaul was saying, even what it was not necessary to take down. She didn't raise her face once, nor made any comment. Sudhir too, she realized after a while, was not making any comment. He sat very still next to her. Perhaps he too was thinking of the times when he had gone round asking for jobs.

Mrs Kaul went on talking on her own; probably she did not notice that she was not getting any response, for she had quite a lot to say and was getting excited. The subject of the professional theatre really stimulated her.

Even Mrs Hochstadt's good coffee did not manage to soothe Etta. She was very indignant, and the more she talked, the more indignant she became.

'How *dare* she? Hasn't she got enough people of her own that she must go and pester *my* friends?'

'It was for a good cause,' Mrs Hochstadt murmured.

'There's only one good cause she knows and that's her own.'

'The theatre – '

'What do you think she cares about the theatre? Not one single dog's turd! No, all it's to her is a good excuse to worm her way in with people – with my friends, behind my back. Of course she didn't get anywhere with Guppy, that I can tell you, but it wasn't, oh it most certainly wasn't, for want of trying.' She huddled herself together to try and light a cigarette in the breeze of the fan, but she was too agitated to get her lighter going and it clicked and clicked and nothing happened. This made her even angrier. She flung the lighter down and, the unlit cigarette hanging between her lips, shouted, 'Just let me once meet her, just let me get her face to face!'

Dr Hochstadt, who was in bed in the next room, called, 'Oh, I'm getting frightened, I have to hear such terrible threats!'

Etta went in there and stood at the foot of his bed. 'It's no joke, Franz.'

'No, it didn't sound like joking,' he said, twinkling behind his rimless glasses. He was sitting upright in bed and on his lap lay a large wooden board carrying papers and books. He wasn't ill; he just liked working in bed and having his meals brought in by Mrs Hochstadt.

'And all the time she's pretending she's my friend! Etta this, Etta that, oh you're so sweet, you look so nice, I like your dress – and the first opportunity she gets she stabs me in the back. She's a snake' – and when she said snake, Etta's eyes grew very green and the skin stretched tight over her fine facial bones.

'Let me see now,' said Dr Hochstadt. 'Do you think snakes can stab in the back, is this a reptile attribute? I would like to brush up my zoology.'

From behind Etta's back Mrs Hochstadt made warning faces at him not to irritate their guest further.

'*Ve*-ry funny,' Etta sneered. She looked him over – he was wearing some quite colourful striped pyjamas out of which his neck stretched grey and goosefleshed with a little tuft of hair peeping out from the chest. 'Why don't you get up? It's awful to see a *man* lounging around in bed like this. You're absolutely spoiling him, Frieda.'

'He's my great big baby,' Mrs Hochstadt said and looked at him with affection and pride.

Etta went back into the other room. She paced up and down in there, with her arms folded over her green silk dress and brooding over the wrong done to her. The Hochstadts had a little whispered confabulation in the bedroom.

'She is so neurotic,' whispered Mrs Hochstadt.

Dr Hochstadt screwed his forefinger against his temple.

'That scene I had with Clarissa the other day . . . And now Etta too.' She sighed. 'One must keep one's head and be calm and reasonable with them, that is the only way.'

'What are you two whispering about in there?' Etta called. 'Are you discussing me?'

With a last significant look at her husband, Mrs Hochstadt went into the other room. 'Now, dear Etta, I think you are getting too suspicious about your friends.'

'Then what *were* you doing? Don't tell me you were having a little matrimonial interlude – Frieda, really. At your age.'

Mrs Hochstadt had absolutely no intention of taking offence. She gave a smile to reassure Etta that she could appreciate, in all objectiveness, the humour of the remark.

'Of course, Guppy just laughed at her, to him she's nothing more than a ridiculous old maid – which she is, Frieda, she is – but that she should try, behind my back, to get herself in with him, that's what makes me so mad I could scream.'

'No please don't do that.' Mrs Hochstadt had decided to try a lighter approach. 'The neighbours will think the Hochstadts are up to something. Instead, now how about another cup of good coffee?'

'That is what I call a logical and positive idea,' said Dr Hochstadt, joining them in his dressing-gown and his leather slippers.

'Not for you, old Franz. You have already heard what Etta has said: I'm spoiling you. From now on a really strict régime.'

'Of course I really oughtn't to be surprised,' Etta said. She had no time to spare for the Hochstadts in their lighter moments. 'She's always been like that. All smiles and friendship to your face, and then slyly creeping round to pick up whatever advantages she can. How do you think she's been living all this time? On her charm and looks? Ha-ha.'

'If you will only be patient and calm for one moment, Etta,' said Mrs Hochstadt. 'I would like so much to tell you about this theatre group. It will be of great interest to you.'

'I want nothing, nothing, nothing whatsoever to do with it!'

Dr Hochstadt was sitting on the sofa, drinking his coffee in peace. When Etta shouted like that, he looked at her very calmly and kindly and said, 'Now you come and sit next to me, young lady.'

On being called young lady, she tossed back her hair and pouted, 'Don't you play the wise old professor with me, Franz.' Nevertheless she went and sat next to him. 'There we are,' he said and patted her knee in a nice fatherly way.

They then proceeded to tell her about the theatre group. She was not interested – she had never been one for causes – but since they spoke to her in a very earnest way, as one person of culture to another, she pretended to be.

'As Europeans,' said Dr Hochstadt, crossing his slippered feet, 'we are in a position to advise our Indian friends on these cultural matters. Not,' he added, 'in so far as the cultural *content* is concerned. Here we may say they have something to teach us for the Indian spirit has in many fields soared far above the European –'

'How often have I thought,' said Mrs Hochstadt, 'that a serious comparative study of Indian and Western spiritual achievements will widen the horizons of both the one and the other.'

'My point now,' Dr Hochstadt went on, 'is that we can be, as I already said, helpful to our friends in the purely organizational aspect of these matters. You now, Etta,' and he pointed at her as if he meant her to stand up and answer questions.

This made her go all languid. She leaned back on the sofa and stretched out her legs and drawled, 'Oh Franz, what earthly good would *I* be? You know how lazy I am.'

'You're a person of international culture,' he told her.

'Oh dear, doesn't that sound grand.' But she smiled a bit and did something to her hair.

'You have seen things. You have been to the opera, the ballet, the theatre. You have lived in cosmopolitan capitals.'

She felt depressingly aware of how far away and long ago those cosmopolitan capitals were. The larger part of her life had been spent in hot, dusty Delhi, where memories of opera, ballet, theatre quickly faded – or perhaps receded so far into the distance that they retained nothing but a vague outline which, for want of anything more real, one had to fill in with as glittering colours as one's imagination could still furnish.

'You have been a member – and, I'm sure, a most receptive and intelligent member' – he made her a little bow, from the neck upwards, which she ironically returned – 'a member of a public which has for generations been entertained by the most highly skilled entertainers and which has, in consequence, accumulated both a great deal of experience and a great deal of discrimination. Now this is what is lacking in India and this is what you, what we, all we Europeans in India, can supply.'

'India gives us so much,' Mrs Hochstadt said. 'What joy to be asked to give a little in return.'

Etta hated to hear Mrs Hochstadt talk like that. It was the way people who were here for only a short time, and had all their comforts and conveniences laid on, so often talked. As if India ever gave anyone anything! (Except of course germs and diseases.) What had it given Etta, after all these years, after taking her youth, her looks, her buoyancy and charm?

'What do you want me to do?' she said irritably. 'Follow in the footsteps of our esteemed Clarissa, who's for ever serving the cause of Mother India? When she can spare the time, that is, from serving her own cause and worming her way in with her friends' friends.'

The Hochstadts exchanged looks: their work they saw was not yet done. Mrs Hochstadt took the sensible view that it was best to ignore the interruption and carry on from where she had left off:

'Already such a nice start has been made with the Cultural Dais where we are allowed to mix freely with the Indian intellectual and learn from him and also – yes, perhaps also teach something to him of our Western values.'

'Don't look at me,' Etta broke in brusquely. 'I'm not prepared to teach him anything. Really not one single little thing.'

'Where we are guests,' Mrs Hochstadt said, 'there we must also try and give some little returns to our host.'

'I'm not a guest,' Etta said. 'I'm a prisoner.' But then she saw how the Hochstadts looked at her with pity and love, so she treated them to a light-hearted laugh and, taking out her lipstick and compact, began to paint her lips with bold, defiant strokes. After that she took out her eyebrow pencil and went to work with that too.

Judy thought Bal would be very pleased when she told him about the progress she and Sudhir had made with Mrs Kaul. But he seemed hardly interested – or only in a somewhat absent-minded way, as he lay on a string cot in the courtyard and looked up at the sky. 'Very good,' he told her. 'That's nice.'

She was astonished; she put her arms akimbo and looked down at him. 'You all right?'

'Please carry on with this good work. It's very necessary, as I have already explained to you, and even if I myself don't have the time perhaps to be very active in this venture – '

She took a deep breath and cried, 'Well!'

He casually lifted his head to ask, 'What's the matter?'

She ran into the bedroom, where she flung off her sari and took out a clean one to wear. While she was dressing, she kept muttering to herself, 'Well, I don't know', and 'This is the end', and 'I'm fed up', and gave short little outraged laughs. She also looked anxiously out of the door to see if he wasn't going to follow her with explanations; but not at all – he lay there on the cot with his hands under his head and gazing up dreamily. Before she was quite ready and with part of her sari trailing behind her on the floor, she went out to him again. 'After all the trouble we took,' she accused him.

He had one eye shut, concentrating on something in the sky with the other. When she spoke to him, he opened it and asked, 'What trouble?'

At this she was speechless, so, lacking her reply, he assumed the subject was finished and immediately started on a new and much more exciting one: 'It is so wonderful, Judy. Kishan Kumar is starting a new production unit and of course I shall have a very important – '

'I don't want to hear!' Judy cried and put her hands over her ears and suddenly burst into tears. This was most uncharacteristic of her, so Bal had a shock and sat bolt upright on the cot. Shanti leaned over the balustrade upstairs and called down to ask what had happened.

'Nothing!' Judy called back and angrily wiped at her eyes with her sari. 'Only I'm sick and tired of your precious brother-in-law, that's all!'

Shanti laughed. She watched them for a while longer and called into the room to let her husband know what was happening.

'Judy, are you ill?' Bal whispered anxiously.

From wiping her eyes she went on to wiping her nose. She did it loudly and roughly, so that she looked like an indignant child. But she was by now indignant with herself as much as with him, for she resented and was ashamed of her tears. Normally she never cried; she had gone to a tough co-ed primary school where she had learned to overcome any such weaknesses which she anyway despised as much as her schoolmates did.

'Would you like to lie down?' said Bal, all sweetness and compassion – which were exactly what she could not bear just now. She hated to see herself softening up and him helping her in the process. So she shook off the tender hand he had laid on her arm and got up and rushed straight out of the courtyard into the street. She had gone for a little way, when she turned back again and reappeared, to his relief, in the courtyard, but only to warn him: 'Don't you follow me!' She just caught the expression of surprise and sorrow on his face, as he sat there on the string cot, and then she was off again.

She had no clear destination, though she walked with a very resolute step, looking neither right nor left. She was the only European living in the neighbourhood, but people had got used to her over all these years, so no one stared at or followed her nor did any children cry 'Mem, mem!' as they had done when she had first come to live here. She walked straight through the street of shops, not lingering a bit (though usually she liked having a look at things and wondering whether she could afford to buy anything and having a word or two with the shopkeepers all of whom knew her very well) and then made in the direction of the temple. She had a vague idea of finding Bhuaji and having a calm, ordinary talk with her about what was to be cooked for tomorrow's food or whether Prithvi needed a haircut, or only to walk home with her and say nothing special.

Bhuaji was just coming out of the temple. She was accompanied by another elderly widow who was telling her about the strength and efficacy of a certain kind of prayer. Gita and Prithvi were with her too, and they were busy choosing sweets from one of the stalls outside the temple. The widow was telling Bhuaji: 'Once my second daughter-in-law was very ill after her delivery. Whole day and night I sat by her bed, chanting and chanting only this prayer, and by next morning, just think, she got up and cooked a dish of rice and cream.' Bhuaji shook her head in admiration and both the old women out of the fullness of their hearts cried out as with one voice the name of the Lord – 'Hari Om!' – and lifted pious eyes to heaven.

Most of the women going in and coming out of the temple were old and most of them wore widow white, though there were a few young married ones, many of them pregnant and reverently carrying fresh green leaves filled with rose petals to offer within. All of them showed great respect to the holy men who sat resting on the steps, or had curled up to sleep in some corner, their heads covered with their orange robes and their staff and begging-bowl laid by their side. A South Indian beggar-woman was also sitting on the steps, together with her child which was of indeterminate age and sex and as filthy and ragged as she was. She was a well-known figure in the area and did quite well in small coins and scraps of food. It was generally suspected that she was of unsound mind though this could never be quite proved, for she spoke some unidentifiable South Indian dialect which made it impossible for anyone to communicate with her.

Judy accompanied Bhuaji down to the river, while Gita and Prithvi walked behind them and ate the somewhat grimy sweets they had bought. There was quite a lot of water in the river, and students sailed up and down in their rickety old college boats. Many people walked or sat on the sandy banks which were, except for the flies, a pleasant and relatively cool place. The sun had just set, leaving a mass of golden clouds over the river; in the distance one could see the big iron bridge with its traffic of buses and lorries and tongas and cycles. Chanting and the sound of cymbals came from the temple.

Bhuaji rested a little on the sand. She chose to sit near a holy man – she loved such company – who lay reclined and at his ease and amused himself with scooping up handfuls of sand and letting it slowly trickle out again through his fist. He did not look particularly holy – he had a crude peasant face with small eyes and a large, spreading, smallpoxed nose – but his orange robe and his air of freedom and leisure were enough to enchant Bhuaji. He also turned out to be pleasantly talkative, and Bhuaji soon managed to draw him out about his experiences. He had been to all the places of pilgrimage, right from Madurai in the South up to the Himalayas – Mahabalipuram, Bhubaneshwar, Puri, he enumerated, Benares, Kurukshetra, Rishikesh, Badrinath; and 'ah!' cried Bhuaji at each name, with such rapture as if she could see and smell the places, and feel the holiness that emanated from them. He had also seen many miracles occur by the goodness of God and the power of faith – at Gwalior an illiterate village girl deaf and dumb from birth had suddenly opened her mouth and recited, in the original Sanskrit, a whole section of the Satapatha-Brahmana; while in Namli, in the district of Ratlam, a rich landlord notorious for his vile ways was carried away never to be seen again on a tongue of flame that had leaped out from the sky.

Judy did not listen to everything – she could not understand too well for he spoke in a very rural Bihari accent – but she heard snatches here and there and these she found interesting. For the rest, she enjoyed being there and watched the boats on the river and Gita and Prithvi playing with some other children on a mound of sand, and people passing and a herd of buffaloes having a bath in the river. Suddenly and for no particular reason she could mention she remembered evenings at home in England: how they sat hunched round the fire muffled in their woollies in their little parlour in their little house with the windows and curtains shut tight against the rain and the neighbours; watching the television while Mum maybe told some indignant tale of a brazen woman at the greengrocer's that morning who had tried to jump the queue. But that was far away, long ago, and now here she was where all was boundless and open in the warm air, the river and the sky and the sand, everything wrapped in a veil of pearl-grey evening light faintly tinged with pink, through which gleamed only the golden clouds and the black bridge with red buses on it. The South Indian beggar-woman had come down from the temple and now she was sitting on the sand and looked at the water, with her dirty matted little child crawling near her playing with stones, and the singing coming from the temple and the birds flying in the sky overhead. The children on the sand-mound were shouting with excitement for they had found a 25-paisa coin buried in the sand, while the holy man was now telling Bhuaji how he had, with his own eyes, seen a child that was a reincarnation of the Lord Krishna (the signs were infallible: bleeding from the knees, a permanent mark on the forehead and the gift of speech at two days old) born to a poor weaver woman in Veerpur, in the district of Morena.

Judy forgot why she had run away in anger from home. She only remembered Bal sitting so sweetly on the string cot and looking after her surprised and sad, and she felt full of love for him and wanted to go home.

She heard Bhuaji say, 'Come, child, take blessing from him,' and found the holy man looking at her with pleasure, his hands already raised to give the blessing. He pursed his mouth affectionately, as to a child, and coaxed her to come nearer.

Judy giggled. She was reluctant to go near the holy man and be touched by those huge, gnarled peasant's hands and she also suspected that his smell would not be nice. Bhuaji whispered to her 'Go, child – you don't know what power these people's blessings have.'

Judy shut her eyes tight as the hands descended on her head. She had been right about his smell. His breath struck hot on her face as he mumbled his holy words, and she couldn't stop giggling to herself. As soon as he had finished, she leaped up and ran off, calling to Gita and Prithvi who came tumbling off their sand-mound after her. She could hear Bhuaji's agitated voice calling after them but she didn't stop or look back, she was in such a hurry to get home again.

3

Clarissa came swinging into the office and shouted, 'Where's Judy?'

'Gone out,' Sudhir said.

She dumped her bag on Judy's table and sank down in the chair, with her legs wide apart and stretched out in front of her. 'Phew,' she said, 'it's hot out.' She took up some sheets of typewritten paper and fanned herself with them.

'Be careful with that,' Sudhir warned her. 'It's our report on "Cultural Trends – East and West". A very valuable document.'

Clarissa glanced at it for a moment and then went on fanning herself with it. 'You do such a lot of splendid work here. I think it's absolutely wonderful. I admire you,' she said and looked him, clear and honest, in the face. She paused a while, in case he might care to take her up on it, but he didn't, so she went on, 'And dear Judy too. It's marvellous to see how fast she's learning. She can't have had much education – she probably went to some elementary school and left school at fifteen – you see,' she said and leaned forward and whispered to him confidentially, 'Judy doesn't come from a very good class. Good heavens,' she shouted, 'as if it mattered! I assure you I couldn't care less about that sort of thing, even though I am English and I do, I must confess, come from a family who are rather sticky about who is who. What nonsense it all is! It's something I've never had any time for. Mother used to be wild with me the way I'd pick up with just simply anyone. I judge people by their worth not by their birth.'

'Just like we do in India,' Sudhir said.

She gave him a look which decided her that he was serious, so she pursued his point: 'Of course you have the caste system but that's something entirely different, isn't it? I'm very very anti-untouchability and all that, I think it's simply horrible, but I can see all the same that there's something beautiful about the caste system. Beautiful and right. Every man in his own rank, doing his own work, there's a divine harmony there which is entirely lacking in the West today. I do enjoy talking to you, Sudhir, you're such an intellectual and you make one really think.'

He wonderd why she had come. He decided that probably she was lonely and spent her time going round to other people's houses and offices just to have someone to talk to, some face to look at.

'Still, we mustn't get carried away!' she cried and snapped out of her intellectual mood with a smile. 'Otherwise we'll be at it till all hours – that's how it is once one gets started on one's ideas and ideals.'

'Did you want to talk to Judy?'

'Yes, and to you. About this theatre project – now, Sudhir, what's that face for? It's a good scheme. You mustn't be so cynical, Sudhir.' She looked at him earnestly and then came over and laid a hand on his shoulder. She was kind and understanding with him. 'I know life isn't always what one expects it to be, but if you use cynicism as a defence you soon lose all sense of true values.'

First he wanted to laugh. Then he wanted to be angry. He resented patronage of any sort, and to be patronized by a foreigner, a European, an Englishwoman of all people, was particularly distasteful. The hand laid on his shoulder seemed to him the pseudo-paternal hand of the British Raj, and his instinctive reaction was to want to shake it off as rudely and violently as possible. But then it struck him how foolish, how out of date this reaction of his was. There wasn't any British Raj any more, and here was only poor Clarissa, all on her own, who wanted nothing more than to have someone to talk to and who liked the company of young men. So he left her hand where it was, and he even bowed his head and looked thoughtful, to show how impressed he was by her words.

She gave him a little tap and said, 'Well don't let's get too serious. Life is a jolly affair, so they tell me, and we have to take it with laughter, laughter all the way. Ugh,' she said and cut a face and staggered a bit from the knees in comic imitation of someone reeling under life's burden.

She began to pace round the office, looking at everything worth looking at (the pictures of Gurudev and Dr Radhakrishnan on the wall, a high-class art calendar depicting some theme of ancient legend and given away free by a firm of paint manufacturers) and then passed through the glass partition into the library. She may have come to talk about the theatre project, but meanwhile she seemed content to pass her time, and Sudhir's, with whatever distraction came her way.

She emerged from the library, holding aloft Rolland's *Life of Vivekananda*: 'Do you know that it was this book that really and truly finally decided me to come to India? I'd wanted to come ever since I was a tot, but it was this – this dear, darling book' – and she kissed it – 'My Bible! My Guru!'

She dropped to the floor where she sat with her knees drawn up and her arms clasped round them and the book lying in her lap; she looked down at it and fondly smiled. 'I can remember so well the first time I read it. Something in me just – oh, I don't know, just snapped, I suppose, and I knew – that's where I belong. I'm going. This is it. Of course the family'd had connections with India for ages and ages – one of my great-uncles was a Supreme Court judge in Calcutta and another was a Chief Commissioner somewhere – all that boring stuffy sort of thing. But that wasn't my India, oh no.'

Just then the Doctor, their landlord, came in. He began to complain about a tap which had been left on in the courtyard by some careless person, but Sudhir held up his hand to check him. 'Can't you see this lady is telling me the story of her life?'

The Doctor gazed at Clarissa in astonishment. She hugged her knees closer and gave out a loud girlish laugh. 'Don't make it sound so solemn, Sudhir! He's teasing,' she told the Doctor, who pulled out one of the office chairs, dusted its seat with his hand and indicated it to her with a courteous, gentlemanly gesture.

Sudhir said, 'Doctor sahib thinks it is not suitable for an English lady like you to sit on the floor.'

'Lady! For heaven's sake, you've got me all wrong! I've done nothing my whole life long but try and get away from being an English lady!' She clasped her knees and rocked herself to and fro with laughter.

'Excuse me,' said the Doctor and, as was usual with him in moments of embarrassment, stroked his hand over his bald head. He did not know what else to tell Clarissa, so instead he turned to Sudhir and said with some energy, 'Why must you make your jokes in front of this lady? You put me in a very bad position.'

She scrambled up from the floor, and her left hand dusting her skirt from behind, she held her right out to the Doctor. 'I'm Clarissa. I know we haven't met before but you don't mind if I'm rather informal, do you? It so happens I'm a very informal person.'

The Doctor shook the proffered hand. He seemed flustered but also rather happy. He kept on shaking her hand and saying he was honoured to meet her, and then he became quite expansive so that it was not long before he was telling her his family history: his father who had made a lot of money in business and built this beautiful house, he himself who had devoted himself to studies, his brothers who were greedy and quarrelsome and harassed him over possession of the house – all this he laid before her with the eagerness of one who has at last found the sympathy and intelligence required of a listener. He also told her about the room he let out to the clerk from a Ministry at such a ridiculously low rent, and then he asked her where she was living and how much rent she was paying.

'Oh *me*,' she said in a voice which made it clear she was a very special case. 'I'm here, there and everywhere. Free as a bird,' and she flung back her head, exposing her throat and her mouth slightly open, which made it look as if she was gulping great draughts of freedom. 'I can't bear to be cooped up. I have to be always on the go and, when I get fed up with the city, I go tramping off into the hills. Oh those hills of mine!'

'Hill stations are to be recommended for the health,' said the Doctor.

'And not only bodily health. Something happens, don't you find? when you get up there in that cool clear crystal air, somehow you find you can really breathe as you were meant to breathe, and something in you unfolds and expands as if it knew at last it was in its true element.' She caught the puzzled look on the Doctor's face and broke off and explained. 'Of course I'm mad, anyone'll tell you I'm completely crackers.'

Sudhir felt sad for her. He imagined how she must have come out to India first, spurred on by Romain Rolland and the Light of Asia and the Everyman edition of the Bhagavad Gita, and intent on a quest in which notions of soul and God played a prominent, if vague part; and how valiantly she had kept up this quest, or at least the pretence of it, though she was getting older year by year, and lonelier, and more ridiculous, and soul and God perhaps no nearer.

'Well, we're a fine trio of chatterboxes! I've come to have a good sensible discussion about our theatre project, and here we are talking philosophy and life and goodness knows what else.'

'I am very fond of philosophical discussion,' the Doctor said.

'And political discussion,' Sudhir said.

'With serious people,' said the Doctor, turning to Clarissa.

She looked at him with her painter's eye. 'Yes, a sensitive face. Maybe I'll sketch you one of these days. You didn't know I was an artist, did you? Artist, philosopher, general lay-about, but above all' – and she stretched up her arms and folded them behind her head and took a deep luxurious breath – 'a free soul.'

'There is very little opportunity to meet people with whom one can have a discussion,' the Doctor said. 'So often I sit in my garden and strange thoughts come to me, on all kinds of subjects, but who is there who is interested in such thoughts? Nowadays people care only for eating and drinking and going to the cinema.'

'You see?' Clarissa cried to Sudhir and pointed at the Doctor. 'There's another one looking for a cause. Oh I've met masses of people, I meet them every day, who're just longing to get involved in something real and dynamic and creative. That's why I put such faith in this theatre project of ours. It'll be a rallying point for all those hundreds – nay thousands – of people who're burning themselves up with their own energy. This country is bursting with energy, I tell you, energy and talent, and all it needs is channelling. Sudhir, I think we're on to something big!'

Sudhir had thought he was interesting himself in the theatre project only for Judy and Bal's sake, but he now saw that there were other people too who expected something from it.

Etta really didn't want to go to the *Rangmahal*, but since Guppy was set on it, she saw how very unwise it would be to refuse. The *Rangmahal* was not a gay place, though it had started off with gay intentions. It had been built, some years ago, as a week-end resort about twenty-five miles out of town in an area which, up till then, had been given over entirely to dust, a few ruins and a great number of jackals. There was a motorable road, but the traffic passing along it consisted as a rule of nothing faster than bullock carts and camels. The advent of the *Rangmahal* was meant to change all that. A number of cottages were built, all with the most modern of conveniences but in what the proprietor liked to call 'our old style' – that is to say, they had little arches and pillars and latticed windows, and were painted in white (to look like marble) with a gold border. There was also a main club house and a swimming-pool which had a dance-floor attached to it and a little dais for the band to sit on. When the *Rangmahal* had first opened, there had been open-air dances, as planned, and people swam in the swimming-pool and the band played and they got out and danced in their swimming-costumes. But very soon the clientele of the place changed. The foreigners and the young people who had swum and danced no longer came, and now it was almost exclusively older men who availed themselves of the facilities of the *Rangmahal*. Their interest was wholly confined to the week-end cottages, so that the management very soon found that it was no longer necessary to clean the swimming-pool very regularly or to engage a band.

Etta and Guppy sat on garden chairs on the veranda of their cottage. Guppy was in a relaxed mood; he loosened his trousers and said, 'I have eaten very well.' His dinner had been the high point of his evening. He had spent much time and trouble in ordering it, a task which he had set himself the moment they arrived and which involved him in lengthy confabulation firstly with the room bearer, then with the head bearer and finally with the assistant manager. In its beginnings the *Rangmahal* had prided itself on its continental cuisine, but since its latter-day clientele went in mainly for hot curries and oven-baked chickens with plenty of pickles, it had changed its policy: which suited Guppy very well, but reduced Etta, who hated Indian food and could not eat it, to a diet consisting of boiled chicken and steamed Victoria pudding.

Such a meal did nothing to lift her spirits. She wished they had not come. It might be dull in her own flat and in Guppy's suite, but here it was both dull and dreary. Nothing was going on anywhere. A few of the other cottages were occupied, but they all had their doors and windows shut and the air-conditioners going. From one of them came the sound of a transistor radio. Beyond the cottages, the countryside stretched far and wide and empty into the darkness. No sound came from it, no smell except of dry dust. The sky seemed equally endless and desolate. There was no moon visible, though it must have been lurking somewhere, for the clouds that drifted slow as ghosts across the sky seemed faintly shadowed with light. This was just sufficient to outline a few ruins that stood far apart on little mounds. Now and again the jackals howled. Etta tried to keep up her spirits by humming the Soldiers' Chorus from *Faust*.

'They make a very good keema curry here,' Guppy said, loosening his trousers a bit more. He sighed with satiety and said, for the third time since they had come, 'It is good to get away sometimes from all the worries.'

'I don't have any worries. I'm just a good-time girl,' said Etta, with an attempt at playfulness, though she didn't feel in the least playful.

It was, however, a success. He gave a little grunt of a laugh and patted her hand. He liked the thought of her decorative idleness in contrast to his own busy, purposeful life.

'Let's go and have a look at the swimming-pool,' she suggested – not because she particularly wanted to but only so as not to have to sit dumbly staring at the desert.

He showed himself reluctant. He felt too contented, had eaten too well, to want to do anything further. But she half coaxed half bullied

96

him, in the most charming way she knew, so that with a groan of good nature he gave in. There was, as a matter of fact, even something pleasing to him in thus giving in: it was an unusual exercise for him and showed him that he was in a holiday mood.

They passed a couple sitting on the veranda of another of the cottages. The man was far back in the shadows, so they could not make out who he was – possibly he was an acquaintance and perhaps even a business associate of Guppy's – but the girl was perched on the steps of the veranda, and while it was too dark to see her clearly, one could just distinguish a slim shape in a short white dress, out of which a great deal of long naked leg protruded. She was talking incessantly in English with an Anglo-Indian lilt to it: 'I'm crazy about dancing and Saturday nights, boy oh boy, you see us beating it up at the Club, one-two one-two fling us the old horseshoe.' Her voice followed them a long way, a very young voice, shrill and piercing in all that silence like the notes of a Goan band.

The swimming-pool was full to the brim with some very brown, turgid water most of which seemed to be rain water. Many dead leaves and dead insects floated on the surface, and one larger shape which may have been a dead bird. It was very dark here. The fairy-lights in the trees were no longer lit, in fact half of them had been dismantled. No one had, however, removed the sign standing on the dais of the band, and though most of the gay paint had crumbled off, it could still clearly be read: 'The Fernandez Frolickers'.

Etta began to laugh. She laughed more and more and even covered her face with her hands in dramatic mirth. Guppy waited patiently for her to finish; he was used to such strange outbursts from her and was not even surprised. He had long ago come to the conclusion that these people – people like Etta, Clarissa, all Europeans – were different from him and his kind: he had nothing against their difference (live and let live) though his tolerance was tinged with a sort of easy, good-natured contempt for them.

'It's so *typical*,' Etta at last brought out, when she had laughed her fill.

He didn't understand, but this mattered very little to him. He knew it was nothing worth making an effort to understand.

'God, oh God,' said Etta, 'how typical.' She covered her face again and sank down to sit on the dais of the bandstand.

'Shall we go back?'

She sat quite still with her face covered. When she uncovered it, there was no trace of laughter left. 'When I was young,' she said, 'very

very young – sixteen, seventeen – I used to go swimming all through the summer. We'd cycle to a place called the Sunshine Swimming Club. Isn't that a nice name? And the sun *was* shining all the time. Not like your sun – a real sun, and one smeared oneself with some delicious smelling oil and there one lay on rugs and got baked the most beautiful beautiful golden brown. I can still smell it all, you know? That oil we put on, and the chlorine in that blue blue swimming-pool water and our lovely healthy skins soaked in sun. Did you know that when one's skin – our skin – becomes sun-tanned, one can see a tiny fluff of hair on the forearms and this hair is all gold, like a gold dust, and you know what it smells like? Like new-mown grass. It really does. Like new-mown grass left out to dry in the sun.'

After a pause Guppy said, 'Whenever I have been in Europe, it has been raining. Pfoo – terrible. Rain rain rain, all day, how can people live like that?'

'It doesn't rain when you're sixteen.' Then she laughed – 'God, isn't it awful, I sound like something out of Chekhov. Oh to go to Moscow!'

'Moscow? There it is very cold. I don't think you would like to be there.'

'Bless you, Guppy.' She reached out her hand for him to help her up. It took some time for him to realize what was required, and when he did, he hoisted her to her feet as if she were some heavy object. He laughed a bit as he did so; it seemed to him so ridiculous that she couldn't get up by herself.

While they were strolling back – past the club-house, which was deserted and only its veranda lit up by a dim bulb under which two bearers silently squatted, waiting for someone to call them – Guppy said, 'Perhaps this time I shall have better luck. Perhaps this time it won't rain.'

'What?' Etta said – not very interested, for she was busy fixing one ear-ring which had come loose.

'Oh I didn't tell you?' he said as if it was something that had slipped his mind. 'Yes, there is a hoteliers' conference in Cannes, in the South of France.'

'Cannes,' she said and stood still.

'Afterwards I shall have to travel round a little. There is the new Hilton in London I shall want to see, and a very interesting experiment in the bed-breakfast system in Rome.'

'Guppy,' she said. She was still standing there and was still holding her ear-ring, which she had forgotten to fix back.

'Come, please walk. I want to lie down on the bed. Oh, I'm tired,' he said and gave a bigger yawn than was strictly necessary.

She walked. Everything was as before – ghostly clouds in a moonless sky, jackals, and now and again the cry of some night-bird – but Etta was no longer depressed. She was excited and all sorts of busy thoughts came and went in her mind.

The girl and her protector were still sitting outside their cottage and the girl was still talking, in the same young, untiring voice – 'So Maggie, my girl friend, the one I told you about who has that nice cushy job with Air India, Maggie told her straight, "Why don't you act your age?" she said, straight out like that if you please . . .'

The room bearer had turned down their bedcovers and Guppy tested the Dunlopillo mattress with his hand and seemed satisfied. He began to undress. Etta sat on the edge of the other bed, her hands in her lap, and making no effort to get ready for bed.

Guppy was already lying down. He felt comfortable and even luxurious, so much so that he wished there was someone to give him massage to enhance the sensation. His wife gave excellent massage: and how she could crack toe-joints!

'Take me with you,' Etta suddenly said. As soon as she had spoken, she heard the much too naked appeal in her own voice, so she quickly tried to cover it up. 'I'll make my hair in a bun and buy a shorthand notebook and I'll be a super super secretary for you' – enabling him, if he so chose, to take it as a joke.

And that was how he did choose to take it. He had a big hearty laugh on it, as if it were a really first-class joke she had made there for his amusement.

The coffee-house was packed tight. The fans spun furiously from the ceiling, without giving much effect, and people who could not find anywhere to sit hung over the back of other people's chairs. Nobody seemed to mind being hot or crowded. Bal and his friends were certainly too deeply engrossed in conversation to mind anything. Bal was telling them about Kishan Kumar's production unit; it was an exciting subject and soon Bal was busy allotting jobs to everyone. They would all move to Bombay and become well-known names in the film world. They had many ideas on how films should be made, and several of them had the most wonderful scenarios all worked out in their heads. The future looked very grand, and how grand it was to talk about it!

However, all good things must come to an end, and it was time for one of them to go and meet a man who had promised him a job, and for another to attend some function at his uncle's house, and a third to take his wife and children to the railway station. Their group split up, and those that were left looked round for other amusement. It was only then that Bal saw Sudhir and Jaykar, though they sat at a table very close to his and had been there for some time.

He got up to join them. He was detained on the way by some acquaintances of his who sat crowded round a table and with whom he had to exchange greetings. One of them asked him whether he would like to buy a fountain-pen and, though he had no need and not much desire for a fountain-pen, he felt it would be impolite not to have a look at it. So he stood by their table and earnestly scrutinized the pen, holding it up to the light with a knowledgeable frown, while a bearer with a full tray and a harried expression, begged 'Please, Babuji,' to be let through.

'So?' he said, in friendly greeting, one arm round Sudhir, the other round Jaykar. He called vaguely over his shoulder 'Bring a chair!' though of course there were no chairs to spare and, even if there had been, the bearers were all too busy to bring him one.

'You were having a very interesting conversation with your friends,' Sudhir said.

'Yes, we were discussing – ' He looked round again for a chair and, since there wasn't one, he shared Sudhir's. He hunched himself eagerly over the table and looked now into Sudhir's face and now into Jaykar's while he told them about the new scheme. He had talked about it all evening, but he still wasn't tired, especially not now that he had the stimulus of a fresh audience.

But this audience was, unlike his previous ones, unresponsive. They heard him in silence and no look kindled in their eyes to answer his. At last Jaykar said, in a quiet voice, 'And what for? Why?'

Bal was surprised. He looked at Jaykar and said 'You don't understand. We shall be a very progressive group and our ideas will revolutionize the film industry.'

Jaykar began to get excited: 'What are all these hare-brain schemes? A healthy young man like you, with all your faculties intact, is there nothing else you can do for a starving country?'

Bal looked hurt. He tried to defend himself, to point out that he was an artiste, but Jaykar was too far gone on his own train of thoughts to have any time for Bal's. He pointed out that first things must come first, and invited Bal to go out and teach or nurse the sick or look after orphans or, if he wasn't capable of any of that, at least to work honestly with his hands and help to lay drains. He got more and more excited and his voice rose and his hands trembled as he fumbled to unbutton his coat and bring out a copy of *Second Thoughts* to quote from. People at neighbouring tables began to get interested and one friend of Bal's tipped back his chair to whisper into Bal's ear, 'Who has bitten the old man?'

Bal laid his hand on his friend's arm and whispered back, 'It is nothing. We are only having a discussion.' While this was going on, Sudhir asked Jaykar not to excite himself any further.

'Who is excited?' Jaykar cried. 'I'm not excited! I'm only explaining to him, for these people must be made to understand!'

Bal said 'I do understand. You are right, quite right, I agree with everything you say. But please also try and understand my point – if you will only listen to me for one moment – '

'Why should I listen to you!' Jaykar cried and struck the table. 'I'm an old man, I have heard enough, more and more than enough nonsense my whole life!' He turned to Sudhir. 'And why do you bring me here to sit here among these' – he waved his hand at all the faces which had turned round to stare and listen and, looking at them, words failed him – 'these – apes! These loafers, these worthless nothings, who sit here chattering like old fishwives while the country is falling in ruins about their ears!'

The apes and loafers thus referred to continued to look at and listen to him with interest. One of them politely asked, 'Excuse me, sir, are you a member of any political party?'

Jaykar got up in disgust. He rapped on the table and called for the bill. When Sudhir tried to pay it, and Bal too fumbled for money, he got angry with both of them; he was a poor but a very proud old man. He slammed the money on top of the bill and told the bearer in a furious voice: 'Don't look for any tips from me. I don't believe in such things. They are only for beggars and for slaves.' He thrust his angry face into the bearer's. 'Are you a beggar or a slave?' he shouted, so that the bearer drew back in fear.

Outside it was much cooler. It was night, and all the shops were shuttered. Even the hawkers who at night spread their wares in the arcades were packing up. Jaykar walked in front and Sudhir and Bal behind him. Bal was trying to explain his position to Sudhir; he was very anxious to defend himself and looked up pleadingly at Sudhir, who strode along with a preoccupied frown which made it difficult to know whether he was listening or not.

'I believe in art,' Bal was saying. 'In art, in culture, in all these matters. I have given over my whole life for them. I don't earn very well but one day I hope, very soon now – Judy also is happy about my new plans. She didn't tell you? Yes, she is very glad.' He gave a nervous laugh.

Jaykar had stood still by a display of paperbacks spread out on the pavement of the arcade. He looked at the lurid titles and the lurid covers, showing naked blonde women lying on tumbled beds, and nodded with satisfaction. He had quite recovered his composure. He patted the bookseller graciously on the shoulder and congratulated him on his choice of stock. 'You have a fine business instinct. How exactly you have gauged the taste of our literary intellectuals! You will go far.' The young man was just packing up, but he courteously stopped doing so to allow them to make their selection.

Bal, seeing Jaykar in such a good mood again, began to explain himself. He said that he did have strong feelings for the poor and that he was often tempted to devote his life and services to their uplift. But what could he do? He was, after all, an artiste, and there was this urge in him for self-expression. Would it be right to suppress this urge? Wasn't it written – and here he appealed to Sudhir to back up the reference – that each man must do according to what was allotted to him? And was it his fault that an artiste's lot had been allotted to him?

Jaykar saw that Bal was hurt and felt sorry. He turned away his head in embarrassment and said it was all right, he had not meant Bal personally.

'He was rehearsing for *Second Thoughts*,' Sudhir said.

'Yes, rehearsing!' Jaykar said, forcing amusement.

But Bal was not satisfied. He began defending himself all over again. A ragged little boy came trailing up behind them with a vast bunch of balloons on a string. 'Only one rupee,' he told them, 'only one rupee for the lot.' His eyes were ringed with fatigue.

Bal laid both hands on his chest as if to demonstrate his sincerity: 'Conditions in our country are terrible, I know it – hunger, disease – terrible, terrible.' He seemed really deeply moved and his voice sounded choked. 'Please don't think for one moment that I –'

'One rupee for the lot!' said the little boy in a tired voice.

Bal put his hand in his pocket. He was excited and it took him some time to disentangle a rupee note from other crumpled papers and a handkerchief. It was evidently his only rupee and he gave it to the little boy and took the balloons.

But standing there, holding this large festive bunch of balloons, he suddenly felt sheepish. He began to fear that his companions might think he was insincere and had only made a gesture to impress them. But he *was* sincere – he felt extremely sorry for the little boy and he meant, he really deeply meant, everything he had been saying. How to convince them of that? He looked at Sudhir, but Sudhir seemed so tall and so remote, and so clever; and Jaykar too was clever and, moreover, old, very old, so he also would not understand. Yet Bal desperately wanted both of them to believe in him and not to have any bad thoughts about him; he ached with the urge to reveal himself fully, to be understood right down to his depths which were surely good and true.

But now all he could think to say was 'Gita and Prithvi will like the balloons.' He turned to Jaykar and began to explain to him, in case he didn't know, who Gita and Prithvi were. He also told him how old they were and where they went to school and dwelt on a few other personal characteristics of theirs which it evidently gave him pleasure to discuss. Both Jaykar and Sudhir liked hearing him talk about his children and they stood for some time in the deserted arcade listening to him, while the bookseller, who had realized they were not serious customers, packed up his stock in cardboard boxes.

Mrs Kaul had convened a meeting. Not an official meeting but a gathering of friends whose opinion she respected. These were all Europeans – to wit, Dr and Mrs Hochstadt, Etta and Clarissa – except for one gentleman, a Mr Jumperwala, who was very interested in cultural matters. They were to discuss the formation of a professional theatre group in an informal way in Mrs Kaul's drawing-room; and to aid this civilized discussion Mrs Kaul had laid on a very civilized tea to which the Hochstadts and Clarissa, all three of whom had very healthy appetites, did fine justice.

Etta's interest in the theatre group was less than burning, but she liked being there. She always enjoyed a visit to Mrs Kaul's house, where everything was so well ordered and expensive, even if perhaps it lacked that certain note of chic which Etta herself would have known to introduce had she had Mrs Kaul's means at her disposal. She also enjoyed the deference Mrs Kaul – who was not by nature or position a deferential person – paid to her opinions. As soon as she came in, she was asked to pronounce on the merits of a new raw silk lampshade Mrs Kaul had acquired, and when a friendly, half-humorous discussion arose in the course of the tea as to whether cake-forks were to be considered quite the thing (Mrs Kaul had brought a charming set with her from Bangkok, but she had heard somewhere that in the best society cake was crumbled with the fingers), it was Etta's ideas on the subject which Mrs Kaul listened to with the most respect. Mr Jumperwala too, a dapper little gentleman in a shantung suit and buckled shoes, showed her marked attention, making her the chief target of his polished English manners and addressing his wittier remarks hopefully in her direction. This put Etta into a special good humour, which even the boisterous presence of Clarissa could not dispel.

So everything was going very well and just as Mrs Kaul had planned it. They touched on various topics of universal interest before finally settling down to the theatre question: and here too they found themselves in the most satisfying agreement, each of them conceding the point that a professional theatre in the capital was a highly desirable objective. They dwelt for some time on the virtues and benefits such a theatre would bring and, to illustrate the thesis, each one brought forward a memorable theatre experience undergone in some foreign land (they were all, of course, well-travelled people). Mr Jumperwala, for instance, recounted the pleasant evenings he had spent in his undergraduate days at the Cambridge Footlights ('in my family,' he explained, 'we are all Cambridge people,' and with a wink at Etta, 'the light blues, you know'), and then, warming to his subject, he told them of week-ends in London where one could always take in a show – his own particular favourites were the musical shows – and round off the evening with a glass of cider in that dear old English institution, the 'pub'.

All this was very well, but Dr Hochstadt – who had himself regaled the company with an account of and comparison between the Salzburg and Glyndebourne festivals – felt it was now time to be practical. He put his finger-tips together and called for a discussion on what he called ways and means.

They discussed ways and means. Of course, a regular committee would have to be formed and a Minister invited to be its Chairman. They themselves would form the nucleus of the committee but many others would have to be co-opted, so that all the various facets of social and cultural life in the capital might be represented (Mrs Kaul shut her eyes for a moment and rapidly counted a few of them off on her fingers – Mrs Mathur, the Hon. Sec. of the PEN Club, Mrs Desai who was the leading spirit behind the Handloom Board, Miss Freni Spencer, the President of the Music Circle ...). And of course the committee would also have to include officials of various Ministries, notably of the Finance Ministry: and at the word finance, they all grew thoughtful and Dr Hochstadt hummed 'Hmmm' and drummed his fingers on the side of his chair, as was his habit when any particularly knotty problem presented itself.

Clarissa said brightly, 'We must rope in some of the big business boys.'

Etta, who had not up till then taken any very active part in the discussion but had contented herself with smoking cigarettes and languidly crossing and uncrossing her legs (an activity which, it had not escaped her notice, was of interest to Mr Jumperwala), suddenly sat up and glared at Clarissa.

'In other countries,' put in Mrs Hochstadt, with speed, 'business interests are often the leaders in the field. In America, for example, they have many different foundations and bequests: Ford, Rockefeller – so many – Fulbright – '

'Who,' said Dr Hochstadt, with a smile which showed he was about to state an interesting and original point, 'could be more generous, more charitable, more all-giving than the Indian millionaire in his old age? After many many years, during which he has thought of nothing but only to increase his wealth, then suddenly at the close of his life he gives it away with the same enthusiasm with which he has first accumulated it. And for what?' said Dr Hochstadt, suddenly impassioned, with rising voice. 'Only for this: for the greater glory of God. Yes, one word from his guru and all will be given for the building of temples, the feeding of Brahmins, the founding of ashrams. For spiritual nourishment. For religion.' He shook his head in admiration. 'A truly fascinating country.'

'Religion is the opium of the people,' said Mr Jumperwala. 'You'll excuse me, I'm a modern man.'

'Not to worry,' said Clarissa. 'We'll find us a couple of modern millionaires.'

'Who exactly did you have in mind?' asked Etta, quite calm and business-like and stubbing out her cigarette in a dragon-shaped ashtray made of blue enamel.

Before the Hochstadts could say or do anything in between, Clarissa blithely replied: 'Matter of fact, I had a word with Guppy about it.'

'Oh you did, did you?'

'Wait,' said Dr Hochstadt. 'First we wish to formulate our general policy, then we shall go on to consider particular ways of approach.'

'He liked the idea awfully,' Clarissa said. 'He promised me a lot of support.'

'Promised *you*!' cried Etta.

'Wait,' Dr Hochstadt said again.

'I'd like to know who you are to go and get promises out of *my* friends!'

Mrs Kaul, who had only just caught up with the general drift of the conversation, said 'I think it is a wonderful idea to get some of our business friends interested in our project.'

Here Mr Jumperwala supported her heartily. 'Get 'em out of the temples,' he said jovially, 'and into the circuses' – and gave a decorous laugh.

'Since when have you been so thick with him?' Etta challenged Clarissa.

Clarissa had by now collected herself sufficiently to do justice to herself: 'I'm *amazed*,' she said, in a very English, vicar's wife voice, 'Even from you I hadn't expected such pettiness.'

'The question here is not one of pettiness, but of plain decency and decorum,' Etta replied.

Mrs Hochstadt turned to Mrs Kaul. 'Although of course our committee must be representative, it should not be so large as to be unwieldy.'

'You're right,' Clarissa said. 'Pettiness is the wrong word. What I mean is plain meanness.'

Etta was busy lighting a new cigarette. Her lighter failed, as it always did in her moments of crisis, and Mr Jumperwala jumped up and said, 'Allow me.' A non-smoker, he was not very expert at it and wasted several matches before he got her alight. This gave Clarissa time to elaborate – 'Meanness and spite,' she said.

'Thank you,' Etta told Mr Jumperwala and gave him a nice smile. She took her first puff, with evident enjoyment; after that she turned to Clarissa. 'Anyway, Guppy and I had a good laugh about it all. He thinks you're *sweet*.'

'We had an absolutely serious talk! He was most impressed!'

'Of course,' said Etta. She turned to Mr Jumperwala. 'I'm afraid it's gone out again. Could you – ' Proudly he jumped up, proudly he lit, and with only two matches this time. 'Thank you *so* much,' said Etta.

He cleared his throat and patted his tie. 'The tobacco gets too damp in this season. If a humble non-smoker may be allowed to venture an opinion.' He gave a smile. 'Yes, I'm afraid I am a confirmed non-smoker. It's the habit of a life-time. How my English friends would rag me! "Dusky," they said – they called me Dusky – "Dusky, if you don't look out you'll be too good for this world." '

He chuckled, and Etta with him before she turned once more to Clarissa. 'I'll tell you how impressed he was. He was so impressed he asked me afterwards if I was sure it was safe to let my friend Clarissa go out alone.'

Clarissa jumped to her feet. Her face was very red. Mrs Kaul looked up at her in surprise and then remembered her duties as a hostess. 'Over there,' she said and pointed to the bathroom door. 'Of course you know the way.'

Mrs Hochstadt followed Clarissa to the bathroom. She found her sitting on the edge of the tub. Mrs Kaul's bathroom was all in primrose yellow, with primrose yellow towels and soaps. 'Now then,' said Mrs Hochstadt. 'You are behaving like a silly child.'

Clarissa was wiping her eyes with the edge of her skirt. She raised a red, wet face to Mrs Hochstadt and wailed, 'I didn't start anything, she did.'

Mrs Hochstadt thumped her several times on the back with a view to calming and comforting her. This seemed the first requisite, since Clarissa was obviously very much upset.

'I haven't done her any harm,' Clarissa wailed from out of the hem of her skirt. 'I want us to be friends. Why must she be so nasty to me?'

Mrs Hochstadt went on thumping. She didn't want to say anything, because if she did she would appear to be taking sides and that, she felt, would undermine her authority.

'Whenever she can, she takes a dig at me. She says the cruellest things. Why, Frieda? I've always tried to be so nice to her.' And she looked up with such a puzzled, hurt look that Mrs Hochstadt felt she had to say something.

'We must make allowances for her. Etta is an unhappy woman.'

'Do you think I'm all that happy? But I don't go around deliberately hurting people's feelings.'

Perhaps there was a little truth and justice here, but Mrs Hochstadt, in pursuit of a greater good, shut her eyes and sighed. 'We must try and understand. Through understanding comes forgiveness and love.'

'It wasn't for my own ends I went to see Guppy. It was for the sake of the theatre. For an ideal. She can't understand that. She doesn't know what an ideal is. She's never understood anything except only self, self, self, that's all she's after.'

Mrs Hochstadt sighed and was about to say something when Clarissa cried out in pain:

'And he wasn't laughing at me! He was impressed with what I told him!'

'Of course. Etta didn't mean – '

'She did mean! Oh, you don't know her the way I do.' She got up from the rim of the bathtub and began to unfasten her blouse. She was breathing hard with strong feeling and looked very hot.

'India teaches us this one great lesson: only love, all-embracing love, must fill the heart,' said Mrs Hochstadt.

'Are you telling *me*?' Clarissa cried. 'Whose whole life is arranged on that principle?' She flung off her blouse and after that stepped out of her skirt and stood there, very bony and in the most unattractive underwear.

'Clarissa, what are you doing?'

'I'm going to have a bath.' She took up Mrs Kaul's soap and smelled it. It was lovely. So was the whole bathroom – quite irresistible, in fact, to someone like Clarissa who was feeling hot and upset and had no such pleasant bathing-place at home, let alone such soap and towels.

She turned on the shower and shouted above the rush of water: 'If only you knew how I've filled myself with love! Love and forgiveness and understanding! Always! All the way!'

Mrs Hochstadt had turned her back, for Clarissa was now quite naked. She said, 'Clarissa, will you promise me – ' But because of the water Clarissa couldn't hear.

In the room, Etta was poised and pleased with herself. Mr Jumperwala was recounting some experiences of his abroad and she was listening with such a show of interest that he felt encouraged to recall all sorts of curious and charming little incidents which had happened to him. He was smiling to himself with the pleasure of remembering.

'I was walking down – now let me test my memory: what was the name of the street?' and he snapped his fingers in the air and cried, 'Brewer Street!'; whereupon Mrs Kaul, who always enjoyed hearing and talking about places abroad, put in, 'Oh I remember Brewer Street – there is such a nice little shop there where you can get the most delicious chocolates, with cream fillings.' Neither of them noticed that Dr Hochstadt leaned forward and patted Etta's hand and told her in a low voice, 'You were very naughty, you know.'

She turned to him with dazzling innocence. 'Now what did I do?'

'She is very upset,' said Dr Hochstadt, nodding in the direction of the door behind which Clarissa had disappeared.

Etta did not comment; instead she turned all her attention to Mr Jumperwala again and, looking at him with green eyes stretched wide open and full of curiosity, said 'Then what happened?'

'Then,' said Mr Jumperwala, smiling with relish and crossing one neatly trousered leg over the other, while hitching up the crease, 'I raised my hand and stopped another cab and said, quite calmly, "Cabbie, to Knightsbridge please." ' He chuckled, and Mrs Kaul said 'I did a lot of my shopping in Knightsbridge,' and Etta clapped her hands lightly together and cried, 'Wonderful!' to Mr Jumperwala.

He hitched his trousers up a little farther, exposing tight suspendered socks, and swung his small foot. 'You must hear what happened to me in Paris.'

When he had finished, Etta laughed heartily and so did he, and while he was still laughing, she turned back to Dr Hochstadt. 'Don't give me such severe looks. What have I done?'

Dr Hochstadt continued to look at her shrewdly through rimless spectacles and puffed at his cigar. 'I leave you to your conscience,' he replied. She gave a low, sophisticated laugh and he too smiled, man of the world that he was. 'Promise me you'll be nice to her when she comes back.'

Mrs Kaul and Mr Jumperwala were discussing Paris. His favourite spot was the Latin Quarter, hers the Eiffel Tower. They both agreed that the Metro was easier to find one's way on than the London Tube. Both had stories to tell of how they had taken the wrong line on the London Tube.

Mrs Hochstadt came back from the bathroom. Her husband looked up at her inquiringly and she shrugged and said despairingly, 'She is having a bath.'

He took the cigar out of his mouth in surprise.

'I have asked her to promise to behave herself better.'

'And I have also tried with that one.' He indicated Etta, who was telling Mrs Kaul and Mr Jumperwala of an instance when *she* had lost her way on the London Tube, and she told it with so much spirit that both her listeners were quite enchanted.

She was still telling it when Clarissa came back. Clarissa was now looking and feeling clean and fresh, and her hair was wet and there were drops of cool water on her neck. She listened to Etta's story, and when it was finished, she said, 'I do like the way you tell things, Etta. You've got a real raconteur's gift.'

Mrs Hochstadt looked at her husband in triumph.

'Now that our little group is complete again,' said Mrs Kaul, 'we can go on with our discussion.' They did so, though there was not much left to discuss. All had agreed how desirable it would be to have a theatre, and how necessary for someone to finance it.

Etta was now taking a more positive attitude. Blowing smoke-rings casually into the air, she offered, 'I could have a word with Guppy to see if we can't get some of those ill-gotten gains away from him.'

Clarissa, very humble and good, said, 'That'd be lovely, Etta. You've got such a lot of influence with him.'

Now both the Hochstadts looked triumphant. Mrs Hochstadt tucked in her chin and adjusted the lace front let into her two-piece dress. 'How much can be achieved,' she said as she did so, 'when there is the friendly spirit.'

To her surprise, however, she found both Etta and Clarissa turning on her. Etta said, 'Really, Frieda, I don't think this is the time or place for your little homilies,' and Clarissa chimed in simultaneously with 'Anybody'd think you were our nanny.'

The Hochstadts exchanged some more looks. These were tolerant. They knew that the role of peacemaker was, by its very nature, a thankless one, but that only made them glory in it the more.

'So,' said Dr Hochstadt, full of good humour, 'now we can look forward to a big contribution from the big millionaire.'

Etta said haughtily, 'Guppy's *our* friend, Clarissa's and mine. I don't remember ever introducing him to you.'

Dr Hochstadt smiled in a pleasant way; so did his wife. Seeing everyone in such a good humour, Mr Jumperwala took out his address-book and, leafing through it, made a joke. 'Let me see now whether there are any millionaires in my acquaintance on whom we could work our charms.' He twinkled at Etta, but only Dr and Mrs Hochstadt thought it was an excellent humorous remark.

Judy was not a worrying person by nature, but one night she woke up dead afraid. So awful were her thoughts that she was frightened to be alone with them and had to wake up Bal. He had hardly got his eyes open before she told him, 'You'd better get a job.'

He was very tired and bleary, and certainly in no state to take her seriously. As a matter of fact, he thought she was talking in her sleep and limply patted her and mumbled, 'Don't have any bad dreams,' before falling asleep again.

So Judy had to go on worrying by herself. She thought, with more intensity than she had ever done before, of the future and of their children growing up and all the money that would be needed for their education; and how everything depended on her and her little job at the Cultural Dais. Supposing she were to lose it, as she had lost that other job? Or fall ill? Or get pregnant? Of course she had her savings

110

now, but even those could not be expected to last for ever. And after they were gone, then what? She groaned and was on the point of waking Bal again, but then thought better of it. She knew that, even if she could get him up and sufficiently alert to listen, he would never take her fears seriously. He would, of course, do his best to laugh, pet, coax, comfort her out of them – and would probably, through sheer charm and love, succeed in doing so – but she didn't want that. She wanted to be absolutely serious and realistic; these were the attitudes their present situation demanded, she felt, and Bal's (and her own) happy-go-lucky frivolity would no longer do.

Next day, an empty and idle one in the office, she confided at length in Sudhir, who listened sympathetically but did not finally have anything very constructive to say.

'Look, Judy. You've been all right for these ten years, isn't it? Then why not for another ten?'

She shook her head; and indeed, he knew himself that his argument was not good enough. So he talked some more, went on to assure her that everyone would like to have some kind of guarantee on the future, but that this was not easy, in fact not possible, to come by. Not for anyone, so why was she grumbling?

'But he's never had a proper job!' she cried suddenly in anguish. 'Never earned enough to keep a flea!'

Sudhir was silent. He knew how she felt, and that there was not really much point in trying to reassure her. He guessed that she had, these ten years, had to make do mostly with reassurances and promises of future satisfaction from ever-smiling Bal. Sudhir, therefore, did not try and tell her that everything would be all right, but only that everything had been all right, and that if she had got this far without mishap, then why not farther?

These arguments did not, however, seem to have much effect on her. Instead she was following a train of thought of her own which suddenly made her turn on him with suspicion. 'You're not thinking of leaving by any chance, are you?' And because he wasn't quick enough in answering – indeed, could distinctly be seen to hesitate – she cried, 'Oh you can't!'

Sudhir laughed. 'What, never?'

'Never,' she said, so firmly that it closed the subject.

But she reopened it herself after a few moments of evidently unpleasant brooding. 'If you weren't here, she'd have me out in no time, Mrs Kaul would.'

He wasn't sure that this dire prophecy was entirely unfounded. If

Mrs Kaul had some other protegée, she would not think much of dispensing with Judy – there had been one time – though he had never told Judy – when it had almost happened. Mrs Kaul had come to him and asked him whether he had found Judy entirely satisfactory as his secretary. He said yes, so she came out with it a bit further: there was another girl, much better qualified than Judy and, moreover, such a nice girl from such a nice home; her parents were personally known to Mrs Kaul. He understood that Mrs Kaul wished in some way to oblige these parents, and that did not make him any more amenable to listen to her. He pointed out that it was hardly possible to slide one person out of a job for no better reason than that you wished to slide another person into it; but here she could not follow him, for as far as she was concerned it was entirely possible. However, she tried one or two arguments more – such as that Judy had been in the job long enough and wasn't it time someone else had a chance – and ended up with the most cogent one of all: did he feel it was right to give employment to a foreigner when there were so many of our nice Indian girls looking for jobs?

'It'll be like that other place I had,' Judy said 'One fine day it was needed for someone else so out I went. And there wasn't a bean in the house.' And she added in quiet agony, 'Oh gosh.'

'You're alive, isn't it?' he said dryly.

'Only just. How I ran around looking for work – I went to see just about everybody, people I knew and people I didn't, and guess what was the worst? Not to let them see how much I needed a job.'

Sudhir knew this; he had done enough running around for work on his own account. He thought of poor Judy doing the same and felt more sorry than he cared to show.

'Of course I've got my savings now, that's something,' she said. 'But I'm not going to touch them, oh no, not if I can help it, not till the last. The day I leave this job, that day I'm going to start tramping around looking for another one. I'll have to. We need the money badly.'

He thought of that girl who had come to ask Mrs Kaul for her job back and had cried. 'But I *need* the money!' Judy said it quite differently, but it came to the same.

Sudhir thought grimly that he had got himself into a fine position, to have to stay in a job he disliked only so that Judy could keep hers.

It would not be true to say that Bal did not worry. But he worried on a higher level. He knew that the present state of their affairs was so entirely temporary that there was no need to waste any energy thinking about it. He was thus left entirely free to speculate on what was to come. That this would be to the highest degree satisfactory he never for one moment doubted, and the only questions to give him pause were ones of how and when. No one could say he was not practical, for he gave continual thought to these two questions and was for ever pondering ways and means of bringing them to a reply.

He looked forward impatiently to Kishan Kumar's next visit to Delhi. He had written two letters to him in Bombay, setting out some further ideas about the production unit, but he had not received any answer. Nor expected any: he knew Kishan Kumar did not care for correspondence, and his own efforts were directed not so much to any specific good as towards keeping the idea alive and in mind.

However, in this it seemed he was not successful, for when Kishan Kumar finally did come again – this time to play in a film stars' cricket match in aid of Flood Relief – he appeared to have forgotten all about his production unit. His friends, who had all been eager to start on the subject, looked at each other in consternation; they would have liked to refresh his memory, but he did not seem in a mood to listen to anyone except himself. They were all sitting under a striped umbrella on the hotel lawn. Other hotel guests sat under similarly striped umbrellas, but they seemed no more than extras hired to form a realistic background against which Kishan Kumar could be seen relaxing with his friends. He was leaning back in one wrought-iron chair with his foot raised to rest on another. He had on a pale blue sports shirt with pockets and darts and a hint of embroidery at the collar, cream-coloured tight trousers and Italian-style suède shoes – all of which were extremely becoming to him, as was the negligent air with which he wore them.

He told his friends of a party he had attended in Bombay. He spoke of the (illegal) liquor that had flowed and the famous film actors and actresses who had been there – he spoke of them casually and familiarly by their first names, often preceded by a patronizing 'good old' – and the antics they had all got up to. 'Boy oh boy, was that some party!' he declared and smiled with his splendid teeth and his eyes shone like stars. The others, listening to him, were so rapt, so carried away, that they too smiled and their eyes too shone, as if they had themselves participated at that grand party and had burst balloons and danced with actresses. Small wonder then that the production unit fell into the background and they could, for the moment, spare as little time or thought for it as Kishan Kumar himself.

And before they were able to get back to it, Kishan Kumar broke up the gathering by looking at his wrist-watch (which had a calendar and a compass built in) and announcing that they had better leave now because he had to go out. He was never very ceremonious about dismissing his friends. They filed out of the hotel gate sadly, for there was still so much left to say and they had not got round to saying any of it. They felt almost as if he had duped them, and it made them feel a bit ashamed, so that they avoided one another's eyes and wandered off in separate directions as soon as they had reached the corner.

Bal also felt ashamed at having allowed himself to be wooed away from his purpose, and after he had walked for a little way, he suddenly decided to go back. He couldn't just let things go, he had to talk to Kishan Kumar and come to some firm agreement with him. Everything depended on it.

Kishan Kumar was having a bath. Bal could hear him through the door, singing a song from his latest film while he splashed vigorously with water. Bal waited for him in the room, which was in luxurious disorder. A crocodile-skin suitcase lay half open on the floor disgorging a few silk shirts, and the clothes Kishan Kumar had just taken off lay scattered over several arm-chairs, and there was a half-finished drink and an open packet of cigarettes on the coffee-table. Bal shyly picked up the blue bush shirt Kishan Kumar had just discarded and held it in front of himself before the mirror. He found it suited him very well. He also slipped his feet into the Italian-style shoes, which were much too big for him but looked very handsome. Then he sat down by the coffee-table, and though the packet of cigarettes lay invitingly open and was, moreover, of a very expensive brand, he humbly took a crumpled packet out of his pocket and lit one of his own.

Kishan Kumar came out of the bathroom stark naked. Drops of water still glistened on his smooth, healthy, olive-coloured skin. He showed no surprise at Bal's presence and perhaps he was even pleased to have company (he always liked company). And he liked to be watched, the way Bal was now watching him, as he slowly, with loving luxurious gestures, never taking his eyes off his image in the mirror, began to dress.

Bal talked about the production unit. It was not clear whether Kishan Kumar's spellbound silence was due to Bal's eloquence or to the concentration required for the knotting of his tie, but whichever it was, Bal got plenty of time and opportunity to unfold his case. He was glad he had come back. From time to time Kishan Kumar gave him an encouraging nod and once he asked for a cigarette to be lit and stuck between his lips.

114

The finishing touches had been put to Kishan Kumar's toilette, as also to Bal's harangue. Now they faced one another in silence for a moment. 'It's a great idea,' Kishan Kumar said finally.

'You remember how we all talked about it the last time – '

'Oh yes, it'll be great.' He gazed at himself again in the mirror: 'How do I look?'

'Very nice,' Bal said and had the tact to leave a moment's respectful silence.

Kishan Kumar was pleased. He turned his head to see himself in profile and smoothed back the hair over one temple. 'I'm going to a reception in our honour by the Flood Relief Fund. There'll be some pretty big shots there.'

'When will we start?' Bal asked.

'What, you're coming too?'

'No, no – the unit – our unit – the Kishan Kumar Production Unit.'

'Oh that. Oh yeah, pretty soon, I guess. We'll talk about it.' He sprayed a little eau-de-cologne over himself.

'If we can start our first shooting schedule by December – '

'Sure,' Kishan Kumar said. He drained what was left of his drink. 'Tell them to get me a cab, will you.'

Bal telephoned down to the reception desk to order a taxi to be ready and waiting for Kishan Kumar. He enjoyed doing it, but at the same time he was worried and anxious to pin Kishan Kumar down to some definite commitment. He knew that an opportunity like this, when the two of them could be all alone and Bal could talk and plan to his heart's content, would not present itself again in a hurry.

'We must work everything out,' he said, quickly and desperately, for Kishan Kumar was already making ready to leave. 'Down to the smallest detail. You need a very efficient production manager.'

'You can be my production manager,' Kishan Kumar said generously.

Bal followed him down the corridor to the lift. He swallowed, and then asked – 'That role you said I was to play? The brother-in-law?'

'Of course that too,' Kishan Kumar said. He clapped Bal on the shoulder with a large friendly hand. 'Stick with me and you'll be okay, don't you worry.'

Bal felt tremendously happy. He followed Kishan Kumar into the lift and out of it and across the lobby. All the hotel servants they encountered had a very special salaam for Kishan Kumar and he a word for every one of them – 'How's the family, Joseph?' 'Still on the job, eh, David?'

The commissionaire opened the taxi door and slammed it shut after Kishan Kumar. The driver started the engine. Bal said, 'When are we meeting to discuss?'

Kishan Kumar was too busy acknowledging the salaams of the commissionaire to answer Bal. However, when the taxi started, he waved out of the window and called, 'Better come and see me in Bombay!'

Guppy was not in his suite in the hotel, but someone else was. Etta had never seen this girl before. She was a very young girl, and Etta wondered for a moment whether she could be Guppy's daughter. She was a large, strapping, very well-developed girl, and she wore a tight flowered silk kameez over a pink silk salwar. Her hair was cut and rippled thick and healthy to her shoulders. She wore rather too much make-up for her age. She was sitting on the divan, quite at home, reading a film magazine and drinking a frothy milk shake through a straw.

Etta stared at her with raised eyebrows and the girl stared back. The girl's stare held nothing except curiosity; she looked Etta up and down with looks that were slow and measured, not, it was clear, because she wanted to be offensive but simply because she was not very quick on the uptake and needed time to register and take everything in. The straw remained in her mouth and she continued to suck up her milk shake through it while she studied Etta. In face of this impersonal curiosity, Etta's ironic eyebrows were totally ineffective; and she soon lowered them and instead said, 'How d'you do,' in a cool, light, insolent voice.

The girl couldn't answer immediately because she was busy sucking the last bubbles of her milk shake up the straw. When this was accomplished, she answered Etta's query with 'I am very well,' showing herself to be a girl of breeding who knew how to counter a civil question with a civil answer.

Whatever further communication might have passed between them was cut short by the entrance of Guppy. A momentary expression of unease passed over his features as he paused in the doorway and saw the two of them together, but he soon mastered it and, stepping into the room with the decisiveness and, in spite of his heavy build, the quickness and lightness of the man of action, he spoke a curt sentence in Punjabi to the girl. She got up at once and, without any apparent hard feelings, shaking her hips not in a consciously provocative manner but only with what must have been her habitual gait, she left the room.

Guppy gave Etta a belated and therefore exaggeratedly hearty welcome. He rubbed his hands and laughed and said 'So you have come,' in a loud, jovial voice.

Etta sat down and crossed her slender legs, giving the impression of being quite relaxed. There were questions to be asked, but she shrewdly realized how much wiser it was not to ask them.

It was her very ease that made Guppy uneasy, her refusal to ask that made him want to answer. He went on rubbing his hands and laughing, and when still there was nothing from her, he came out with, 'Of course you have met my niece before?'

Etta continued to say nothing.

'She came to remind me for Sunday. Sunday there is a family function at my brother's house, she came to tell me. Her mother sent her, her mother said, "Be sure to remind your uncle, you know how forgetful he is." Yes, yes,' laughed Guppy, talking more quickly and more loudly just because there was no challenge and he knew he deserved one, 'you see what a bad reputation I have with my family.'

This little pleasantry too was allowed to pass, and instead Etta, who was now the acknowledged mistress of the situation, chose to change the subject. It was not clear whether she was being magnanimous or polite, but at any rate Guppy was grateful to her and so entered into this new subject with more enthusiasm than he might otherwise have shown.

The new subject was the theatre group and the possibility of Guppy's helping to finance it. Wary as he usually was where money was concerned, on this occasion he allowed himself to be quite expansive. He commended the scheme warmly and even went so far as to declare that it was the duty of private enterprise to interest itself in a project so noble and fine (he had only the vaguest notion of what it was all about, and even if he had been clearer, it was not something in which he could be expected to take any deep or abiding interest). And then he went even further, and committed himself to the promise that he would see what could be done.

Etta opened her bag and took out her comb. She drew it lightly through her hair. 'Are you going to see about it before you go or after you come back?'

Guppy realized at once that they had changed ground and were now back on to something uncomfortable. He opened a drawer and made out to be looking for something in it.

'I'm pinning you down,' Etta said with a smile. 'Once you get to your hoteliers' conference and all those glamorous places abroad, I know you're going to forget all about our poor little theatre group.'

'Oh no, no,' Guppy protested, and quoted virtuously: 'A promise is a promise.'

Still smiling, she said, 'And your other promise? What about that?'

He rummaged around in his drawer and murmured, under his breath but making it loud enough for her to hear how preoccupied he was, 'Where can I have put it?'

'I think you're trying to ditch your secretary, Gup.'

'Hm?' he inquired, busily searching.

'Well, I won't be ditched. I just won't, so there.' She was being awfully nice with him; mock-childish, mock-sulky, taking care to show how it was all meant as good fun. 'You *need* your secretary with you, Guppy, you know you do. You can't get on without me, and even if you could – well, I thimply won't let you go alone. I won't. Tho there.' She smiled and pouted, pouted, and smiled, making sunlight and shadow flit across her features for all the world to see.

Guppy slammed shut his drawer and took refuge in laughter and good humour instead. 'A very fine secretary who can't type or take notes and only smoke, smoke, smoke all day long!'

'Guppy!' she cried, making her lashes flutter to the point of parody. 'How you underestimate me!' She got up and went to him and clasped her hands lightly round his strong, thick neck. 'Don't you know that I'm a real devil with a pencil and a notebook and an absolute maestro on the keys? And efficient – my dear, I can't begin to tell you.' Her hands still round his neck, she looked into his face, balancing herself lightly on one foot, the other lifted in her eagerness off the ground. She looked at him coquettishly, smilingly, yet searchingly too, he saw.

He patted her on the hip and gave a laugh, though at the same time his eyes took on a slightly glazed, distant look. This meant, she knew, that he was beginning to think of something else. When private affairs began to bother or bore him – and this they did quickly, he was not really interested in private affairs – he abstracted himself from them and sank his thoughts comfortably back into his business problems.

But there she was still clinging round his neck, and when she saw that he was beginning to elude her, she renewed her efforts: 'You don't think I'd ever let you go by yourself, do you? You'd fall prey to God knows who in no time . . .' She laid her head against his chest and rubbed it to and fro in her most kittenish manner. 'A lovely great big male creature like you,' she said in a coaxing and obsequious voice. Yet at the same time she stood apart and very clearly saw herself clinging to him while he thought of something else and tried to disengage himself. But she held on tight. She didn't despise herself: it

118

wasn't for him she was doing it, she told herself, it was for the trip
abroad. She was handling him; she was being clever.

'There is someone waiting for me down in the office,' he said. He
spoke gently; he didn't want to hurt her feelings, and if he could
extricate himself without that, so much the better.

'No,' she said, 'I won't let you go. Not till you promise.'

He still laughed but his hands, trying to dislodge hers from the back
of his neck, became a little more determined.

And she too tightened her grip. 'Go on, say it: I, Guppy, promise to
take you, Etta – '

'I gave appointment for eleven,' Guppy said. He wasn't looking at
her but over her head and at the door through which he was resolved
to disappear ere long. And as he felt her grip tightening, so, almost
unconsciously, he tightened his.

' – and all your suitcases and all your hatboxes and transport you
straight to some lovely, lovely hotel in Cannes – '

He wasn't listening. He was thinking of some important matters
waiting for him down in the office and, determined to get there, he
used rather more of his strength than he would have done if he had
not been so preoccupied. Of course, with this he loosened her grip
quite easily and even made her tumble some distance away, so that
she lost her balance and would have fallen if she hadn't supported
herself on an arm-chair.

She was crouched over the arm-chair and hung on to it; one high-
heeled foot had turned over and her tight dress was wrinkled over her
hips. She looked awkward and undignified and she was glaring at him.

'Oh sorry,' he said; not much concerned, though, for obviously she
wasn't hurt and it was, after all, her own fault. 'I'm going down now.
If you are staying, please order anything you like – coffee, tea, anything.'

She straightened up. She smoothed her dress over her hips and
looked quite poised again. She was cool and disdainful. 'I suppose
you're planning to take your *niece* with you, are you?'

'My niece?' He had really forgotten. When he remembered, he said,
'Or you could order whisky, gin, beer, whatever you like. Be quite
comfortable while I'm gone.'

Jaykar lived with his son, a modest official in one of the Ministries,
in a remote new housing colony. The houses in this colony, which
were all identical and stretched row upon row, were in a weather-
beaten condition, their yellow plaster was peeling off, their ledges

119

were sagging and there were cracks in the cement-work. Yet they were new houses – indeed the whole colony was new, so new that there was not yet any adequate provision for electricity and water and both these services kept breaking down to the exasperation of the inhabitants who had in any case plenty of other annoyances, such as open drains and unlaid roads, to put up with. So everybody had plenty to grumble about, and they formed Residents' Associations and gave vent to their feelings in drawing up petitions and sending angry letters to the newspapers.

All this of course was meat and drink to Jaykar, who not only made the inefficiency of the official housing authorities a constant theme in *Second Thoughts*, but also played a leading part in the Residents' Association and drafted most of the petitions and many of the newspaper letters. His son, on the other hand, did not take part in any of these activities. He was a tall, plump, very timid man, who laboured under the constant apprehension that he might not be promoted in his job, or even, in his blacker moments, that he might be demoted, or, in the blackest of all, that he might be dismissed. So his life's policy was only to keep very quiet and out of harm's way and devote himself to his family – an attitude which was radically different from what his father's had always been. Yet they got on well together. The elder Jaykar was very gentle with his son, respected his timidity, never read him anything out of *Second Thoughts* and took a keen interest in his domestic affairs. This made for a pleasant relationship but not one which was really stimulating for the elder Jaykar; and he consequently turned a lot to Sudhir with whom he could express himself more freely.

He never exhorted his son to higher efforts and ambitions, but he did so constantly to Sudhir, whom he urged to leave his job, to go out and throw himself heart and soul into some great cause. Sudhir didn't like, at such moments, to ask what great cause, since obviously there were many: only it was not as easy to find them as it had been in Jaykar's day when there had been only one. Jaykar and his contemporaries had had to concentrate only on throwing the British out as quickly as possible, and had been able to postpone everything else till later. But now that later had come, and no one knew quite where to start and many started from different directions some of which turned out to be wrong.

One evening, though, Jaykar came out with a surprisingly concrete proposal. Sudhir, bored with reading and sitting alone in his hotel room, had come out on the bus to visit his friend. He came in by the bathroom door at the back which led straight into Jaykar's room; he always used this entrance, as did all of Jaykar's friends, and indeed Jaykar himself, so as not to disturb the son and his family. Jaykar was standing at his desk, which was like a lectern, for he could only work standing up. He motioned Sudhir to sit on the bed and went on writing with his steel-nibbed pen which he had to keep dipping into ink. His spectacles had slipped to the end of his nose and he was looking over the top of them, so there was really no point in his wearing them except perhaps that they gave him a very studious appearance. In some other room – the house was very small and the walls paper-thin – one of his granddaughters was having her music lesson. She intoned an evening raag in an unmusical but dutiful way. Jaykar wrote quickly but with flourish, and when he had finished, he snatched up the paper in haste as if he wanted to catch it hot from the anvil and read aloud to Sudhir:

'What our present state of affairs demands is not only a firm leadership of integrity and incorruptibility from above but also the same integrity and incorruptibility in the heart of every man – nay, let us say of every man, woman and child among these our teeming millions. This is not the time for self-seeking pursuits of private pleasure, for vainglorious attempts at personal aggrandisement, for invidious gestures of selfish vanity or vain selfishness! On the very contrary, it is the submerging of the personal in the great ocean of our concern for the common weal that must be our chief aim and ambition in these present pressing times . . .'

When he had finished reading, Jaykar flung the paper back on to his lectern with a grand, daring gesture as if he were flinging it out into the world to do its work there. Sudhir nodded appreciatively though he made no comment: all Jaykar's *Second Thoughts* statements were of too assertive a character to require comment.

The strange thing was that, in spite of the high-flown polemics in which he expressed himself in print, Jaykar's spoken pronouncements were always exceedingly down to earth. 'Now you see,' he said, indicating the sheet of paper which he had just read out in so fiery a manner, 'people will read this and they will nod and say yes, quite right, he is right. They will even be pleased that these words have been written because they feel that someone else's moral indignation will do in place of their own. They want to be scourged – it doesn't hurt them but makes them feel pure and good.'

He shook his head angrily and suddenly he struck his hand against the wood of the door. 'Look at it! Look at this rubbish!' Indeed it was a very poor quality wood which had already split in many places. 'The other day I had a talk with the contractor who built these quarters. I said to him, "My friend, I think you have filled your pockets very well at our expense." At first he tried to protest, to tell me that no no, he had used only first-class materials for everything, so much so that he was even out of pocket on this contract. It was a manner of speaking. Soon we were agreed that business morals nowadays were very low and from there we progressed to a discussion on the frailty and corruptibility of human nature. We had a very interesting talk together, and when he left me I think he felt pleased with himself for having cast such a searching look from such a lofty height over the moral field. I think that day he must have mixed in a little more sand than usual with his cement.'

Jaykar ended on a dry laugh and his eyes glittered. He was without his usual old white coat and wore only a vest over his white pyjama trousers, exposing his thin slack old neck muscles and his pitiful arms. But he looked, though frail in build and very wrinkled, somehow taut and straight and strong; an impression which was perhaps conveyed by his moral as much as by his physical qualities, and was in any case enhanced by his surroundings – that little room with nothing in it except a string cot to sleep on, the lectern to write on and two wooden shelves; a room as bare and clean as the life that was lived in it.

The granddaughter had finished her raag but started on it again immediately from the beginning. Jaykar shouted, 'Laxness, corruption, roguery everywhere!' Then he said in a quiet normal voice, 'It is time you left your cultural job.'

'I know,' said Sudhir.

Jaykar now became very kind and mild. He pointed out all the reasons why Sudhir must leave and go and do something else. They were all reasons Sudhir knew well for himself and, besides, the subject was one they had gone over together many times before. Usually they ended on nothing more than a hearty condemnation of Sudhir's job and of Sudhir himself for still being in it; but today Jaykar had a proposal.

A new Literacy Institute had been set up – not in Delhi, Bombay or Calcutta, but in a remote region of Madhya Pradesh. A friend of Jaykar's was in charge of it and, amid a host of difficulties, his chief one was to get anyone suitable to come and help him. What man of spirit, qualified to get work in more congenial places, would voluntarily bury himself in these desert regions to do nothing more spectacular than teach a lot of peasants to read and write? Jaykar asked this question as a rhetorical one, and looked challengingly at Sudhir while he was doing so.

Sudhir hesitated. He found he could say neither yes or no with any ease. It was true, he could see what a fine wholesome thing it would be for him, but there were also plenty of considerations to hold him back.

Besides the granddaughter's music lesson, there was also a clatter of pots from the kitchen and a boy was repeating his tables. Everything sounded very peaceful and domestic. But there was to be no peace for Sudhir. Jaykar glared at him as he sat on the bed and exhorted him to give up his soft town life and go out into the wilderness. As if it were Sudhir who was his son, and not the other one who went day after day, nine to five, to an office and was extra polite to his superiors lest something adverse might be written into his confidential report.

Bal was shocked that Judy, even after he had given her the fullest explanation, didn't understand the urgency of the situation. He usually found it easier to convince or at least persuade her. 'But I must go, I must,' he kept on saying.

'I've got to get to the office.' She was busy picking up some last-minute necessities and flinging them into her handbag.

'Wait,' he said urgently.

But she couldn't. She was already late. Calling good-bye to Bhuaji and Shanti (the children had left for school), she rushed out of the door let into the brick wall. Bal hesitated for an instant. He had not yet had his bath nor changed from the clothes in which he had slept all night. He was very particular about his appearance in public, but this time his anxiety overcame his meticulousness. He ran after her into the street, the tails of his crumpled shirt flying as he ran and his slippers slapping and flapping and making him stumble. 'Wait!' he called.

She stood still impatiently, allowing him to catch her up, and when he had done so, she said, 'I'm in a hurry,' and walked on with quick steps.

'He called me,' Bal said. 'He said, "Come to Bombay, we'll arrange everything there." I must go.'

'But 200 rupees!'

'How can I manage on less? Look, the fare alone, even though I shall go third class, will cost me sixty rupees return. And then I must have some money in Bombay – I have to eat and go to various places – '

'If he's all that keen to have you there, he'd better pay for you himself, your precious Kishan Kumar.'

'You don't understand,' Bal said in a despairing voice.

They had got to the bus-stop. There was a great crush of people there, and every time a bus came, they surged forward and the stronger got on and the weaker were left behind. Judy, who did this twice every day, coming and going in the rush hour, had a lot of practice at holding her position in the crowd while she waited for her right bus to come; but Bal, who had no practice at it whatsoever, was pushed around a lot and his feet were freely trodden upon. He became more and more annoyed, especially as he was already feeling uncomfortable and inferior and very conscious of the fact that he was unbathed, unshaven and dressed in crumpled clothes.

He told Judy crossly, 'Must you stand here when I have urgent things to talk with you?' And though he finished the sentence, she couldn't hear the end of it because just then the crowd surged again and she let herself be swept forward by it while he helplessly drifted back.

By the time they were reunited (for it was still not her right bus), he was very cross indeed. He hailed a taxi, which had temptingly slowed down at the stop and made Judy, in spite of her protests, get in. They were watched enviously by the rest of the crowd, all of whom had a bitter little thought about what it was to be rich and have money to spend on taxis.

'Do you know what this is going to cost?' Judy protested violently within.

He waved her aside impatiently; he was intent on only one subject and would not be deflected from it by her petty preoccupations.

'What is 200 rupees? It is hardly a fortune – '

'To me it is. And the five rupees this taxi is going to cost is a fortune too.'

He hated to see her taking up this hard, uncompromising attitude. At such times she seemed very English to him (her jaw seemed harder, her eyes bluer), whereas usually, when she was her normal self, he never thought of her as different, she suited him so well.

'Think for only one moment, Judy. So you are spending 200 rupees. All right, it is a big sum. But think what returns we shall be getting on this money!'

'What returns?'

He cried out as if in pain. After everything he had told and explained to her!

'All we'll be getting is promises from that precious Kishan Kumar of yours. If he's got the time to meet you when you're in Bombay, that is, you never can tell.'

Bal said in a quiet voice, full of dignity, 'He is my friend.'

Judy did not answer. Instead she looked out of the taxi window. She was beginning to enjoy this ride. It was so much better than standing, hot and crushed, in a bus.

'Why are you like this?' Bal was asking plaintively beside her. 'I'm trying so hard to advance in my profession and you want only to hold me back. A wife should give encouragement to her husband, not hold him back.'

The road was crowded with cyclists cycling to work and cars and buses and motor-cycle rickshaws, and there were long confused queues at all the bus-stops. Judy felt very select and secluded riding through it all in a taxi, and Bal beside her. The early sky was a pale whitish blue and the grass of the maidan before the Fort looked very green and the Fort itself a shining red. The morning air was still clear and fresh, in spite of all the traffic and the crowd. Judy, suddenly elated, gave Bal's hand a squeeze.

This gave him great encouragement. He cried out in a low, excited voice, 'Perhaps I won't come back from Bombay at all! We'll start our picture and then I'll send for you and the children and we'll all live there in Bombay! Will you like that?'

'What about Bhuaji?'

'She also, of course. We shall live very well, you'll see. I'll rent one of these flats for all of us, overlooking the sea and there will be a lift to go up and down by and a hall porter. You and I will go walking on the beach at night. In the afternoons children will go and play in the Hanging Gardens and they will have an Ayah to look after them and the Ayah will carry sandwiches for them in a basket in case they get hungry.' He stared in front of him, at the taxi driver's back, with the eyes of a visionary.

Judy didn't like to tell him just then that she still had no intention of giving him the 200 rupees on which all these glories were to be founded. She didn't want to part with the money; she couldn't. Her savings were sacred to her and represented much more than only money. And over and above that, she didn't want him to go to Bombay. She had no faith in Kishan Kumar's production unit; and she knew that once Bal was in Bombay, in the vicinity of film studios and stars and in the company of all the other people hanging and hoping around them, he would soon forget about his family and concentrate only on having a good time with his friends. It had happened, alas, before: about two years ago when he had a little job in Bombay and had stayed on and on long after it was finished, ignoring her letters and telegrams (he claimed afterwards never to have got them: which may have been true, for he had not had any fixed address in Bombay but had moved from friend to friend, sleeping now on the floor of someone's flat or the stairs of someone's house or even, on hot nights, out on the beach) till in the end his brother Mukand had to be sent to fetch him back.

'We shall have a lot of parties in our flat,' Bal was saying. 'Of course there is prohibition – but well, you'll see, there are many ways,' – and he gave an indulgent, clever smile. Bal didn't care for alcohol at all, but he regarded it as an indispensable adjunct to the kind of life he was looking forward to.

'Perhaps we shall also rent a shack on Juhu beach for the weekends; and in the summer you and the children can go up to Lonavla – it is a hill station where everyone goes to keep cool.' He had more ideas, but they had reached the Cultural Dais. Judy now for the first time looked apprehensively at the meter.

It was more than she could afford, but she was glad to pay. She had enjoyed the ride, and why not, once in a while? She was even smiling as she stood on the pavement, paying the driver. Bal still sat inside the taxi.

'Come on,' she said.

'I'm going home.' The pleased smile went from her face. 'I have to go home, Judy. Look, you can see, I haven't had my bath yet and my clothes, just see – ' He held up the end of his shirt and clicked his tongue at it.

'But not in a taxi!'

'How can I go by bus? I look so terrible, I would be so much ashamed.' He stretched out his hand for the money she was still holding. She hesitated for only a moment. It was the remains of a ten-rupee note which she had hoped would last till the end of the week. But she realized how unpleasant it would be for him to go home by bus – especially when he was already sitting so snugly in the taxi – and she placed the money in his palm. She was glad as soon as she had done so: it somehow made up for the 200 rupees she was not going to give him.

He waved and smiled as he was driven away.

'Oh you are spoiling me, aren't you,' Clarissa said as Shanti handed her a glass of pink-coloured sherbet and a few sweetmeats on a plate.

126

She smiled up at Shanti; whenever she came, she expressed great admiration for Shanti, and for Bhuaji too, and indeed for everything – the courtyard, the children, the brick wall – everything struck her as so fitting and right and genuinely Indian.

'I envy you,' she told Judy. 'To have married into such a wonderful, such a real good typical Indian family – what a sense of belonging that must give you!'

'What is she saying?' Shanti demanded eagerly.

'God bless your darling heart,' Clarissa told her. 'One day you and I must have a real long talk together. I'm sure there's such a lot I could learn from you, even though you aren't *educated* ' – here she made a wry face – 'in our silly Western sense. You've got wisdom and that's worth a thousand stupid so-called educations.'

Shanti looked at Judy in agitated curiosity. 'What? What is she saying?'

'She says you're very clever.'

Shanti threw the end of her sari over her face and dissolved with amusement behind it.

Clarissa, after giving her another warm smile, returned to the subject she had come to discuss. This was the theatre group; she felt very strongly about it. 'It's a wonderful scheme,' she told Judy, 'and I for one am not going to sit by and see everybody quietly forget about it.'

Judy wished they would. She felt uneasy now that so many people took an interest in the scheme, whereas Bal, who was responsible for it, seemed to have dropped it completely.

'This country needs a dramatic revival,' Clarissa said energetically, 'and unless someone pretty wide awake gives the whole thing a push, it's never going to come to anything. Action!' she cried and struck her knee with her fist in a buccaneer manner. 'And by gum, Judy, I'll see to it that there *is* some action. I'm going to be quite a bully. I know it's very unfeminine of me but that can't be helped. It just so happens I'm a very unfeminine kind of person.' She gave a bark of laughter. 'Probably that's why I never got married.'

Shanti asked Judy, 'What? What?'

'She says she never got married.'

'Poor thing, one can see.' And Shanti looked at the guest with her head laid to one side and a commiserating expression on her plump, homely face. When she caught Clarissa's eye, she gave her a tender smile which Clarissa returned; rapturously baring all her teeth. She felt very close to Shanti, even though they were unable to communicate with one another.

'Really I do, do so envy you, Judy,' she said. 'To live here among these simple people and speak their language and be just like them, I think it's wonderful.' Just then the rag-merchant passed, shouting in a hoarse voice for any old bottles, and old papers for sale, and stirring Clarissa to further enthusiasm. 'You're part of India here! You're right where its heart beats!'

'He comes every day,' Judy said. 'But he's a big cheat. You know last week he weighed all our papers wrong – '

'Oh I wish I had your opportunities, Judy! I try so hard to swallow my Western sophistication, to be simple again and in touch with the deep truths.' She sighed. 'It's not easy.'

Judy made no comment. It was not a problem which had ever really presented itself to her, so she did not feel qualified to discuss it.

'Of course,' Clarissa had to admit, since no one else came to her defence, 'I've succeeded to some extent. I think I may say that my values are spiritual and not material like that of other Westerners. Like Etta's, for instance.'

Judy's eyes lit up at that name and she asked eagerly, 'Oh how is she? I haven't seen her in ages.'

'A person like Etta has no right to be here at all. She simply doesn't grasp that India calls for spiritual adjustments. She carries on as if this were Europe all over again – thinking of nothing but dressing herself up and strolling down Chandni Chowk as if it were the Champs Elysées.' Clarissa gave a snort of disapproval but Judy cried out, 'She's a treat!' in delight.

Clarissa wiped her hands, which were sticky from the sweetmeats, on her skirt. As she did so, she told Judy firmly, 'She's frivolous. Spiritually frivolous.' Suddenly she leaned forward. 'Did you know she dyes her hair?'

'Oh no,' Judy protested, 'she's a natural – '

Clarissa threw back her head and laughed 'Hah!' out loud. But the next moment she remembered what she had come for and started on it with renewed energy, 'We've got to get going. We can't just sit by while something as vital as a country's theatre is strangled before it's even born.'

Judy, glancing down into her own lap to avoid Clarissa's challenging stare, murmured, 'I don't see what I can do.'

'Judy! Don't be so wet!'

'Wet?' Shanti, who knew a few words of English, inquired. Judy began to laugh, and to stop herself, buried her face in her arm which she bit.

'Even if you don't care for the larger issue, for the revival of the theatre in India, at least think of Bal. He's got to be given his chance, and how can he be if there isn't any theatre?'

'I think he prefers the films,' Judy murmured very low, so that there was a chance Clarissa wouldn't hear.

'What rubbish! Seems to me you don't know your own husband. Good heavens, of course he's first and foremost an artiste dedicated to the stage.' She jumped up with one of her clattering movements (which made it clear that, though she was thin, she weighed quite a lot) and trod heavily out of the room and into the courtyard where she stood, arms akimbo, looking round.

'I like it,' she declared. 'It's got character. I do think character in a place is so much more important than anything else, don't you? Now take a place like Etta's – that's got no character at all. No character, no atmosphere. Whose is that?' she asked, pointing to Bhuaji's little room which opened from the courtyard.

'Oh I might have known,' she said. She stuck her head into the room and looked round it, balancing herself on the threshold with one foot out behind her. 'It's so simple, a real little saint's room.' Indeed, Bhuaji's room had nothing in it except one trunk tied with string, a few cooking utensils in a corner and some holy pictures and statues on a little shelf; not even a bed, for Bhuaji slept on a mat which she rolled out on the floor at night.

Clarissa withdrew her head again and said brusquely, 'No spares, I suppose? I'm having trouble with my place again. That landlord is such a – well, I'm not going to say any dirty words in this lovely household so hold my tongue someone quick. He's been giving me trouble for years and now, if he really gets me out, I'll have to find somewhere to lay my ageing head, I suppose. Just for a short time,' she said appealingly, 'till I get fixed up.'

'What?' said Shanti. When Judy had translated, she said at once and without any hesitation, 'She can stay here if she wants.'

'Where?' Judy said.

'She can sleep anywhere – with you, with Bhuaji, with me upstairs, there is so much place.' She seemed surprised that the question needed thinking about.

'Of course,' said Clarissa in a firmly sensible voice, 'it'd be awfully useful if I were right here on the spot with you. Then we could work together for the theatre, shoulder to shoulder, you, Bal and I. We'd soon get the sparks flying! Let's have a dekko at the bathroom.'

They showed it to her and she stood looking at it, biting her lip in a thoughtful way. It was a rather primitive sort of bathroom.

*

Sometimes Bal and his friends were tired of hanging round the radio station or the coffee-houses. They longed for green trees and open spaces, and since there was nothing really urgent to hold them back, they never lost much time in fulfilling their longing. Those of them who had bicycles sat on them, with a friend or two at the back, while those without went by bus, and soon they all met in some pleasant green picnic spot away from the city. Here they grew very cheerful as they felt their spirits expand in a great surge of freedom, as if they had just been released from some dark, confining prison.

On a beautiful day, when it had rained not so long ago and everything though no longer wet was green and juicy, they lay on the grass at one such picnic spot, in between the tombs and the family parties rowdy with babies and transistor radios. They had brought nothing to eat along with them – these excursions were never planned – but the smell of the food which the family parties unpacked from their tiffin-carriers soon made them realize how hungry they were. Fortunately there were plenty of hawkers strolling around looking for customers like them and soon they were feasting on dried gram, nuts hot with chili powder and puffed rice, all served up with a twist of chutney on bits of newspaper. Then, pleasantly relaxed and full of romantic feeling, they lit cigarettes and sank down to lie on the grass. Some lay on their backs to look up into the foliage of trees and into the sky with the birds flying there slow and at ease, and others lay on their stomachs and made insects walk on blades of grass, or stared down the overgrown flight of ancient steps into the yellow fields beyond. Sometimes they talked, sometimes they yawned, sometimes they raised languid hands to chase equally languid flies from the tips of their ears or noses.

The Hochstadts' party was altogether a more energetic one. It was, of course, a fully organized affair for which plans had been taken firmly in hand many days before. Consequently it was now everything that a picnic should be and a monument to Mrs Hochstadt's good management. They sat comfortably on woollen rugs and supported themselves on foam rubber garden cushions; in the centre stood a big hamper wide open and overflowing with roasted chickens and smoked ham and hard-boiled eggs and fresh salad, all wrapped hygienically in greaseproof paper. The hosts wore special picnic clothes – Dr Hochstadt a brick-coloured bush shirt, carelessly open at the neck, and a cream-coloured panama hat with a black band round it; and Mrs Hochstadt, though in her usual two-piece, had for the occasion selected one which was discreetly gay with a pattern of navy-blue flowers set on a pearl-grey background, and she wore a white leather rose pinned to her lace front.

Their guests consisted of two or three students from Dr Hochstadt's economics class (the Hochstadts were aware of the enormous benefits, to student and teacher alike, to be derived from a free-and-easy, give-and-take relationship outside the classroom), who sat upright on the woollen rugs and listened to Dr Hochstadt holding forth, with expertise and fluency, on the present political situation. The other guest was Etta, who had not been included in the original scheme but whom Mrs Hochstadt had met by chance a day or two before and, finding her in low spirits, had persuaded her to join them for the sake of a change of air. Etta – so she herself kept insisting – had been *bullied* into coming along and had no intention of enjoying herself. She lay half reclined across the rug, making every effort to look languid and bored, and with her parasol propped up behind her to shield her from the irksome sun.

'The question remains,' said Dr Hochstadt, with a smile because this was a relaxed and quite informal discussion, 'is India ready yet for the democratic form of government?'

The students all looked intent (not only was he their teacher whom they respected but also, for the moment, their host whose food and drink they were enjoying), but Etta gave a great big yawn. Mrs Hochstadt rallied her gaily. 'Now then, sleepyhead!'

'I didn't want to come, Frieda. I told you. I hate picnics; they're *messy*.'

'What's this?' said Dr Hochstadt, breaking off his discourse. 'Mutiny in our ranks?'

All the students turned their heads to look at Etta and, taking their cue from Dr Hochstadt, they smiled.

Etta shut her eyes in weariness. She wished she hadn't come. She had only done so because she felt she couldn't bear to sit around in her flat any longer. She hadn't seen Guppy for weeks, neither had he telephoned.

Bal and his friends were discussing their future plans. Somehow it always happened that wherever they were – in the coffee-house, at the radio station, in someone's house – finally what they always got round to were their future plans. But though their subject might be the same, their tone differed according to the place in which they found themselves. They were all of them sensitive to atmosphere. Now that they were in these congenial surroundings, free of their everyday world and let loose among sky, grass and birds flying around, their plans took on wings and roamed far and free. Stirred by the beauties of nature, they recognized that everything in life was beautiful, and that if one only had faith, all one's hopes would, like the flowers, the trees, and the birds in their nests, inevitably come to ripeness and fruition. They talked to each other in gentle, dreamy voices, as they lay on the grass with their eyes half-closed and cigarette smoke curling upwards from their lips. Bal spoke of his forthcoming journey to Bombay, where Kishan Kumar was impatiently waiting for him to come and set everything in motion. The question of how to raise the money for this journey no longer troubled him; he recognized now how easy everything was in the world, and how God provided even for the tiniest insect that crawled over the tiniest blade of grass.

They talked for a while about Kishan Kumar and the production unit, but as it was a subject which had been dealt with very thoroughly on previous occasions, it was not as fascinating as it once had been; so they soon fell instead into a lively discussion of all they would do when they got to Bombay. There were many pleasures waiting for them. They spoke of wild film star parties, midnight excursions to deserted beaches, brilliant counter-measures against the prohibition laws, and sated themselves on these happy anticipations to such an extent that after a while a reaction set in.

Now they grew melancholy and all sank back on to the grass, to contemplate the high, blue sky and the yellow fields and the blackened monuments. In face of this Absolute, they recognized the transitoriness of all human pleasures and endeavours. Some of them sighed and some of them lit cigarettes and watched the smoke curl up into the high, clear air and dissolve and be no more. One of them quoted, 'O where are they now whose palaces glittered with thousand-coloured chandeliers? Silent in their graves: not a whisper.' Then they all sighed. There was pleasure in this melancholy. They realized they held the whole of this little world in the hollow of their hand and it was nothing. What were film studios? Midnight parties on beaches? Money, fame, Scotch whisky? What, even was Kishan Kumar? They knew the answer, and it filled them with a sense of peace and utter resignation.

Mrs Hochstadt took in good deep breaths of fresh air, heaving her contralto bosom up and down so that even the stiff leather rose trembled a little. 'In, out,' she chanted in time with her breathing, and then she encouraged the students and Dr Hochstadt himself to follow suit. They all filled their lungs – 'In, out!' 'In, out!' – except Etta, who remained reclining under her parasol and with her eyes closed as if in pain.

'Come on, Etta!' Mrs Hochstadt exhorted her. 'Drink up the good air, it is better than wine for us!'

Etta kept her eyes closed. 'You know perfectly well I'm an indoor plant, Frieda.'

'Deep breathing is very good for the complexion,' replied Mrs Hochstadt with a wink at Dr Franz: they knew from what angle their Etta was vulnerable.

But Etta, who was in a black, black mood, murmured, 'My complexion is past redemption.' She meant it; she felt old and greatly aware of the fact that the sun must be picking out, for the benefit of anyone who cared to look, each pouch, each wrinkle on her powdered face. Let them look, she felt; she couldn't care. There was no one now she had to please, and it seemed anyway she was past pleasing. Guppy seemed to think so. Her thoughts became hard and bitter, but just then Mrs Hockstadt temptingly held a hard-boiled egg under her nose.

'Well Etta, even if you won't look after your complexion, we mustn't allow you to starve, I think.' She had even peeled the egg and disposed of the peel in the special container she had brought with her.

Etta turned her face away. 'Please, Frieda. I haven't got a German digestion, you know.'

This insult Mrs Hochstadt swallowed with pleasure, together with the rejected egg. 'It's true,' she said humorously as she munched, 'my stomach is a good strong German one.'

Bal and his friends had enjoyed their short dip into the Absolute, but it was not long before they were forced to return to the necessities of this transitory life. A hawker passed, selling spicy vegetable cutlets the smell of which was so tempting that they became hungry again on the spot: only to find, however, that they had between them run out of everything except their bus money. The world, they realized, was still very much with them. With a sigh, then, they turned their conversation back to those matters which, in their higher moments, they recognized as shadow and illusion but which were still, alas, as far as they were concerned, solid substance. So thorough was their return to this reality that they spoke now no longer of production units in Bombay but of things nearer home and more in the offing, such as a possible radio broadcast or a programme of recitals in honour of the death anniversary of some Urdu poet.

Only Bal was impatient of these little plans. He cupped his hand over his head and held it there like a vice and cried, 'Think big! Think big! This is the secret of success!'

But the others were now in too gloomily realistic a mood to be inspired by his enthusiasm. They pointed out that their thoughts were always big but the commissions that came their way were nevertheless always small. They said that it was not lack of enterprise on their part, or of ambition, or of talent, but simply lack of the right contacts which nowadays were the only passports to success.

At that Bal became very excited. 'Contacts!' he cried. 'I have all, all the contacts that anyone can ever want!' And in his agitation he jumped up and stood over them, as if someone had challenged him, and his eyes roved round proudly and came to rest, between the tombs and the family parties, on the Hochstadts' group. He gave a cry of triumph: his words had been superbly vindicated, for even here, even in this far-away spot where one communed with God and Nature, there were highly influential people with whom, as he would soon prove to his friends, he was on the closest terms.

'Flies!' cried Etta in vexation and attempted to drive them away by waving her hand in various directions.

'We enjoy our picnic,' said Mrs Hochstadt, 'and so also the flies want to share with us.' She helped to chase them from Etta's naked white legs, laid across the rug, and did so to much better effect than Etta herself.

'They too are God's creatures and is there a God's creature that doesn't enjoy the picnic?' joked Dr Hochstadt.

'In China they have to a large extent eradicated the fly,' one of the students said.

This last remark – though it launched Dr Hochstadt on to a fascinating exposition on the differences between the economic systems of India and China – threw Etta into unutterable gloom. It seemed to her so terribly typical of the kind of company she was forced to keep these days and became, at the same time, a painful reminder of how different things had been in the past. Then she knew only the gayest and nicest people, and had at her disposal any time she wanted them – ah, such young men! Starting with her first husband, who had brought her out here to conquer and charm this virgin territory where lively blondes such as she were few and· far between enough to be at the highest premium. There had been a succession, which in the folly of her youth she had thought inexhaustible, of young Indians: all with this in common that they were, on the one hand, fascinated with and completely uncritical of the ways of blondes and, on the other, were all well-born, well-bred, charming, slender, athletic, with black eyes and black hair and strong white teeth for ever at the ready to flash at all her witty sayings. At that time all had been as wonderful as she had a right to expect; and yes – when India had appreciated her then she had been able, with a full and generous heart, to return the compliment.

'I can't stand it!' she suddenly cried, flapping at her own arms and legs. 'I will not live with flies!'

'Tchut, tchut, what a fuss,' said Mrs Hochstadt good-humouredly, and slap! her big square hand came down to kill a fly on Etta who gave a cry.

'So I think you will have to go to China,' twinkled Dr Hochstadt. 'No flies in China, remember.'

'Sometimes I feel that anywhere, just *any*where, would be better than this,' said Etta, glaring at the students who were watching her with kindly interest.

It was at that point that Bal, radiant with joy at having met such friends, came to greet them. He shook hands all round (as was befitting to their European status), even with the students, and smiled as he did so; a lock of hair had, in his excitement, fallen down into his face. The Hochstadts smiled with him and, though touched by his warmth and pleasure, a little bit at him to see him so worked up. Etta, however, only frowned more than she had already been doing and made it quite clear that as far as she was concerned the meeting was far from being as fortunate as Bal and the Hochstadts made it out to be.

Although Bal's primary motive in coming over had been to impress his friends, such was his natural fund of bonhomie that now he was actually with the Hochstadts – even though he did not know them all that well, and indeed they were no more to him than he to them – he was really overcome with pleasure, and the glow in his face and in his voice was absolutely genuine. He soon forgot about his friends and gladly accepted the Hochstadts' invitation to join their party; nor did he hold back when Mrs Hochstadt for his benefit reopened the picnic basket, the remains of which she had already neatly packed away (she had calculated that she and Franz could have a cold supper on it).

Bal's friends saw him sitting in the middle of that circle, eating and drinking with relish and holding conversation. They could not of course hear what he was saying, but they saw that he was saying it with animation.

He was, as a matter of fact, commenting on the beauty of the scene, on the pleasures of picnics and the joy of sharing the delights of Nature with friends. Everything had conspired to make him happy: he loved the mingled smell of jasmine and food in the air, the creepers, the tombs, the undefined ruins; his eyes roved happily round the countryside that lay green and gold and yellow in the sun and seemed as unlimited as his own hopes and prospects, and then came back to linger fondly on the faces of the Hochstadts and their party, who were all so kind to him and with whom he was so happy to be.

Dr Hochstadt gladly agreed with him that a picnic, always a delightful social event in itself, was rendered yet doubly so for being held in surroundings as propitious as these. What was it, asked Dr Hochstadt, that made the scene so pleasing to both mind and senses? Was it perhaps – and he ticked off each item on a thick white finger – the salubrious air? the vegetation? the animal life of birds, insects and monkeys? Or was it – and here he looked keenly round the circle, for he had reached the heart of his matter – was it perhaps most of all the sense of history, of deeds and thoughts and feelings past and gone, that emanated from the ruins which lay all around them?

Mrs Hochstadt, to show that she had grasped the point, nodded intelligently and so, taking their cue from her, did Bal and all the students. Only Etta couldn't have cared less and in a bored way she twirled her parasol, propped up open behind her, slowly round and round.

'Here is one of the fascinations that this ancient land holds for us from the West,' said Dr Hochstadt. 'Everywhere we look we see – yes the modern also, but behind it always, and not so much as shadow but as substance, the Past. And this Past of which these ancient stones and relics speak is not only history no, not only fact, but also woven in with it all the myths and beliefs of its so deeply religious people.'

Bal cried, 'How true!' – enthusiastically, though he could not really quite follow what Dr Hochstadt was attempting to say; but he saw that there was deep thinking in it, and this it was which stirred him. And, with equal pleasure, he listened to Dr Hochstadt's account of the origin and history of the place in which they now found themselves. Some of what he heard was familiar to him, such as, for instance, the names of certain kings, who had always been commemorated for him not so much through what they did or said or indeed who they were, as through streets and monuments called after them which he had known well and lived with since his childhood. And though he showed interest and pleasure in hearing everything Dr Hochstadt had to say, this detailed explanation (Dr Hochstadt had a fine grasp of history) did not in any way alter his own conception of the place, which was on the one hand, of something old and redolent of glories now crumbled to the edification of poets and philosophers, into dust; and,

136

on the other, of pleasant green surroundings where happy Sunday hours had been spent with his friends while hawkers catered to his needs with gram, betel and cigarettes.

When Bal cried out 'How true!' like that, Etta gave him a short, disgusted look which he was too engrossed to notice. After a while her eyes, almost against her will, strayed back to him and now she took him in whole: as he sat there, reclined against a foam rubber cushion, in one hand a leg of chicken, in the other a plastic cup full of Mrs Hochstadt's good coffee. His face looked young and open, with its broad forehead and firm chin and regular features, all framed by his curly hair which he wore too long; and his short body was set off to all its muscled advantage by the delicate transparent Lucknow shirt he wore. There was that in his expression, as he listened to Dr Hochstadt, which reminded Etta of her former young men, as they had listened to her: his lips slightly parted over his teeth and his large deep-black eyes, amid their silken jungle of lashes, luminous with a flattering interest, an eagerness not to miss anything, a complete, absorbed, self-negating concentration only on Dr Hochstadt. Just so had Etta's young men cared only for Etta.

She said, quite suddenly and brusquely and in the middle of Dr Hochstadt's account of some salient facts in the lives and reigns of the Tughlaqs: 'Where's Judy?'

Bal was too absorbed to hear; only some of the students looked at her. So she said it again, only this time louder and a lot ruder: 'Where's Judy, I said.'

Now they all heard. Dr Hochstadt, surprised, stopped talking, his mouth still open on the last word. Mrs Hochstadt, wondering uneasily whether Etta's black mood might be about to translate itself into something overtly aggressive, began to pack the remaining sandwiches back into the hamper; she made a lot of rustling noise with the greaseproof paper as if she hoped thereby to cover up anything unpleasant that might be said.

Bal too turned his head towards Etta and now his big black eyes were on her. 'Judy?' he said in a friendly voice. 'Yes, she is at home.' Then he looked back again expectantly at Dr Hochstadt, waiting for him to resume his discourse.

But before this could take place, Etta said dangerously, 'Why didn't you bring her?'

Bal looked at her again and repeated, inconsequentially but with a nice smile, 'She is at home.'

'Like a good Hindu wife,' Etta sneered in an offensive way – which, however, Bal did not recognize as such for he nodded and laughed and took it as a good joke.

'Oh it's something to laugh at, is it?' Etta slowly drawled. She could afford to take her time now, for she knew she had everyone's attention. She gave a lazy little twist to her parasol. 'You know, I wouldn't have thought so. I wouldn't have thought so at *all*.'

Bal looked puzzled now, though he still smiled a bit for he thought something pleasant and humorous was on the way of which he could not yet see the point but was ready to laugh at as heartily as anyone else the moment he did.

Mrs Hochstadt, however, who knew no joke was coming, looked up into the sky with a great display of anxiety and said, 'Oh dear dear, what do I see? Not rain clouds, I hope?'

'To bring a girl like Judy over here and then treat her as if she were one of *your* women – no,' said Etta and shook her head slowly and as if in wonder, 'although I do, I must admit, rather pride myself on my sense of humour, somehow, in this particular case, it absolutely fails me.'

Dr Hochstadt cleared his throat significantly a few times and looked at Etta with a severe professorial eye. But that only served to make her carry on the more blithely:

'In some circles, I dare say, it's the accepted thing for the husband to go out and enjoy himself and only come home to eat, sleep and make one or two more children.'

The students looked shy and abashed. They lowered their eyes. They were all unmarried boys and knew it was not right for them to hear such talk. Bal was also put out. The potent exploits of their married state was a subject on which he and his friends liked to tease one another, but he suspected that Etta was not teasing. He too lowered his eyes.

'Of course, no one,' she said, 'can accuse you of being a reactionary husband. You don't keep her locked up at home – oh no, you're a modern man with advanced ideas. You send her out to work.' She left a pleasant little pause.

Into this pause jumped Mrs Hochstadt. She heavily hoisted herself to her feet and said, 'Well children, it has been a lovely picnic I think, but all good things must come to an end.' She began to collect everything together and the students got up to help her. Bal too got up to help, though he still held his chicken leg in one hand and his plastic cup in the other.

Only Etta remained at ease under her parasol. She hadn't finished yet. 'Naturally, someone in the family has to go out to work and earn some money to feed those darling little mouths. And if she doesn't, then who will?' She looked up at Bal with amusement, smiling at him in such a friendly way. 'Not *you*, surely?'

He looked back at her. He was no longer puzzled. The expression of his eyes had changed completely and they were now two great black brooding clouds.

Dr Hochstadt laid his hand on Bal's arm. 'What a nice chat we all had together. Now we shouldn't keep you any longer from your friends or they will be very angry with us, I think!'

Bal shook off Dr Hochstadt's hand and kept on glaring at Etta, as she lounged on the rug. She seemed to him extremely old and ugly, though her hair was a bright blonde in the sun and her dress gay and flowered.

'She has insulted me!' he suddenly shouted. With a vehement gesture he flung away his chicken leg (Mrs Hochstadt, who hated to see litter, had to check an impulse to run after it and pick it up and put it in her special disposal box). He shouted again, 'I have been insulted!'

Etta, except for a light raising of her well-shaped eyebrows, remained unmoved. Lightning now flashed from the black clouds of Bal's eyes. He stood in front of her, short, broad, sturdy, his legs planted apart, all the muscles of his body tensed. He wanted to kick her with both his feet and after he had done that he wanted to catch her by the hair and drag her over the ground. There was no weak chivalry in him: already he had raised one foot.

'Please, please,' said Dr Hochstadt, interposing himself between Bal and Etta, his cigar in his mouth, looking as good-natured and easy about it as he could. He put up both his hands and held Bal's arms with them in a friendly gesture. 'It was all good fun only, you mustn't misunderstand.'

Bal said, 'She has insulted me.' His voice was loud and furious and other picnic parties took notice and began to draw near. Bal's friends too came hurrying over. Dr Hochstadt was still holding Bal from in front and the students came up from behind and laid timid hands on his shoulders which quivered in fury.

'First you pretend to be my friends and make me eat and drink with you, and then you insult me!'

'A misunderstanding,' Dr Hochstadt pleaded.

'There is no misunderstanding! I have understood everything. My honour has been insulted!' He swung round at the students and shouted, 'Don't touch me!' so that they fell back in confusion.

He pushed his way through them and went up to his friends, who at once formed a ring round him. He began to explain to them what had happened, talking loudly and fluently and with many gestures. They walked him away but were followed by other picnic parties, who crowded as close to them as they could in order to hear better as to the cause of this unusual disturbance.

From time to time they all looked back to cast curious, or indignant, looks at the Hochstadts' party, who were now very busy packing up their hamper and cushions and rugs.

4

Jaykar was in the office with Sudhir. He was talking to him about the new Literacy Institute, while Judy listened with growing horror. Finally she asked Sudhir, 'You're not really going, are you?' looking at him out of big, blue, frightened eyes.

He found it difficult to answer. But there was no need since Jaykar did it for him. 'Of course he is going!' said Jaykar. 'Did you think he was a person only to talk, talk and never do anything?'

Judy hesitated for a moment, so Sudhir said, 'Yes, that's what she does think.'

Judy was a bit nettled, especially since perhaps it was not altogther untrue. She turned her back on both of them and with a busy gesture inserted a new sheet of paper into her typewriter, though she had nothing to type.

'Or perhaps it is just my bad conscience,' Sudhir said with a smile at her.

'No!' cried Jaykar fiercely and he jumped up from his chair – forgetting that he had a few copies of *Second Thoughts* in his lap, which thereupon fell to the floor. He stooped to pick them up, fumbling a bit on the floor because he couldn't see very well, but when Sudhir tried to help him, he pushed him away. 'No,' he cried again when everything was recovered, 'don't talk about yourself in that way! I don't like to hear it. It is a very bad habit of our people – always to make much of their own faults even when these faults are not there at all but are only something that has been invented by interested foreigners in order to sum up the Indian character. As if the Indian character could be summed up!' He gave a malicious cackle. 'Well I think we are a bit too wily for that. Let them say one thing about us and the next moment they will find we are exactly the opposite – yes indeed,' – and he gleefully rubbed his hands – 'we are a slippery lot.'

Mrs Kaul came sweeping in just then, wearing a beautiful batik sari and smelling of French scent. She held her head high and turned it suspiciously from side to side and seemed to be sniffing the air. This was the way she always entered the office, as if she suspected something was going on which should not be and which it was her duty as Honorary Secretary to put a stop to.

'It is all right, madam,' said Jaykar, as soon as her shrewd eye rested on him, 'don't disturb yourself, I'm just going.' And he began to gather his papers and button up his frayed white coat in sarcastic haste, as if he were frightened to stay a minute longer.

Judy typed busily: she was glad now she had inserted that sheet of paper into her typewriter. She typed 'Gita Prithvi Bal Bal Prithvi Gita' over and over for several lines. At the same time she kept her ears cocked for any exchange that might take place between Jaykar and Mrs Kaul.

'All members of the public are welcome,' Mrs Kaul told Jaykar, but in such a way that it was clear some members were more welcome than others.

'I often drop in,' he assured her. 'I find great intellectual stimulation in these surroundings.' He was already on his way out but by the door he stopped with his finger raised in the air. 'I broadcast it far and wide that in my opinion, humble as it is, the greatest contribution to the cultural life of the capital has been made single-handed by the Cultural Dais.'

It struck her that he might not be as serious as he ought to be, but since he was not important enough for her to worry herself over his meanings or double meanings, she dismissed him from her mind as unceremoniously as from her presence, and turned to Sudhir.

'An expert on modern poetic drama is arriving from Switzerland. A lecture must be arranged.' But even she did not sound particularly enthusiastic any more.

After a while she gave a tiny sigh and did something to her smartly arranged hair. 'I think we must extend our activities,' she said and sounded wistful, as if the Dais was beginning to disappoint her.

'But we are already doing so much,' Sudhir told her. 'We have had a Japanese expert on the No plays, a Scandinavian expert on the language of design, a Russian on the Bolshoi ballet, an English expert on the French novel, a French expert on the English novel – and now we are to have a Swiss on the modern poetic drama – '

'I know,' said Mrs Kaul, but with another little sigh.

'And our teas,' said Sudhir. 'At which everyone meets and mingles freely and the juices of the intellect are made to flow.'

Mrs Kaul sat despondently on an office chair. It was all apparently not enough, or perhaps not what she had hoped for. She said in a pained voice, 'People are not very interested in purely intellectual matters.'

Sudhir raised his arms in a helpless gesture and let them fall again to his sides: he and Mrs Kaul, he thus suggested, had done their best and could not be held responsible for people's unformed tastes.

She nodded to show how much she agreed with him, but nevertheless ventured, 'We must start on something with a more popular appeal.' After a moment's thought she added, 'Popular but refined.'

Sudhir stood lost in apparent thought, on one foot, the other foot slowly scratching his calf as he pondered. He wore a very, very serious expression, biting his lip and frowning, as one who was revising all his ideas. Judy went on furiously typing – Gita Prithvi Bal Bal Prithvi Gita.

'I think our theatre scheme will attract a much larger public,' Mrs Kaul went on, with new heart in her. 'It is exactly what is needed at this stage. The committee is already formed and only yesterday I met the Deputy Finance Minister at a reception to the Governor of Orissa – oh these receptions! One after another, one after another.' She put back her head and laid two fingers on her weary eyelids, showing her utter exhaustion with the never-ending social round. While she was doing this, Sudhir took the opportunity to throw a paper pellet at industriously-typing Judy.

'The Deputy Minister and I,' said Mrs Kaul when she had sufficiently recovered, 'had a very nice chat. He was most sympathetic to our scheme and promised to see what could be done.'

Suddenly she was all energy again and stood up from her chair and walked round the office, straightening a calendar on the wall as she went and twitching the handspun curtain into place. 'We must get our first production ready as soon as possible. Then we shall have a first night, with a guest of honour – the Prime Minister, perhaps, or the Vice-President – and the proceeds will be given away to a deserving charity. Before the show there will be several speeches in which the work of the Cultural Dais will be laid before the public, and after the show young girls will garland the guest of honour and the artistes.' She was quite roused now and all her despondency shaken off. Sudhir had to admire her: she certainly had vision and enough energy and will power to bring it to reality.

'We shall have a great publicity campaign. We shall hire space to advertise our first production, and everywhere there will be big posters to say "Cultural Dais Presents".' She gave a laugh and said vivaciously, 'Presents what? Yes yes, that is now our first task. Take this down,' she told Judy and came and stood behind her, while Judy smartly ripped out the sheet of paper on which she had been typing and inserted a new one.

'Directors,' dictated Mrs Kaul. 'Playwrights. Actors.' Judy, very alert and straightbacked, waited with fingers poised over the keys. After some thought Mrs Kaul came up with 'Set Designers', and finally, 'Lighting Experts.'

'Now,' she said briskly before any more dictation could be expected of her, 'I want a team of such people to be got together. A meeting must be held as soon as possible.'

Sudhir told Judy, 'You had better tell Bal.'

'Some suitable play will be chosen and the production taken in hand at once.' She moved about the office, wafting scent, her sari rustling as she stepped out quickly, and clasping and unclasping her bejewelled hands. 'No delays, no delays,' she said, all tiptoe with excitement and energy. 'I want to have the date for our first night set as quickly as possible, for our guest of honour must be informed in good time. You have no idea what a busy schedule these people have – for them it is one engagement after another, from morning till night their time is never their own. We must all take our example from them: this is how a great country like ours is built. By hard work and sacrifice,' she pronounced and tucked her batik sari round her waist, ready for action.

But Bal said no. He was very sulky about it indeed. No, he would have nothing to do with this theatre movement; nothing to do with any of Judy's friends or acquaintances; nothing – not ever again.

Judy couldn't understand it at all. She had of course been told about what had happened at the picnic, but the narration had been too heated for her to be able to make much of it. Although she had been made to listen to a lot, and over a span of several days, she had not yet been able to piece together just exactly what had happened.

Bal's nostrils flared again, the way they did every time he remembered the wrong done to him. 'I don't want anything to do with their theatre. Let them leave me alone.'

'But it was you who wanted the theatre!'

'That was before they insulted me.'

'You keep saying that!' Judy cried. 'But I still don't get it –'

Bal snorted in anger and disgust.

'I don't!' she cried. 'For goodness' sake, don't you see it was just in fun! You got it all wrong.'

Bal had been sitting on the floor of their bedroom, trying to repair a doll of Gita's. When Judy said it was just in fun, he threw the doll down and got up and indignantly walked out. She ran after him into the courtyard. The servant was squatting by the tap, cleaning pots by rubbing them with ash.

'Honestly, they were just having a joke, that's all. Etta is like that. She's a big tease, but she doesn't mean anything.'

'I'm very sorry,' Bal said. 'You see, I don't understand the English sense of humour. Where are my shoes? Have they been cleaned? I'm going out.'

'You should hear the way she talks to me. You think I mind? Not a bit. She just makes me laugh, that's all.' And Judy did laugh, looking anxiously into Bal's face as she did so.

But it remained closed and forbidding. He said, 'I can't laugh when insults are offered to me. This is just not possible for me.'

'There you go again. Insults! How you talk, honestly.'

Bal stood in the doorway of Bhuaji's room. She was inside it, praying before her images, looking peaceful and happy.

'But what did she *say*?' Judy asked desperately.

He turned away from Bhuaji's room. Peace and prayer were not for him in his present mood. He called loudly to the servant, 'Get my shoes!' To Judy he said, 'She insulted me.'

'But how, how?'

'You and me, both of us. She said I make you work for me, that I can't earn enough to keep you – ' He clenched his fists in fury. 'Soon I'll show them! I'll show all of them!' And to the servant he shouted even louder, 'Are you getting my shoes or not?'

The servant began to grumble. He said look, here he was, cleaning pots, all the world could see he was cleaning pots. How many hands did a man have, how many feet?

'I'll get them,' Judy said and turned towards the bedroom.

'No!' cried Bal. 'Not you! I don't want you to fetch anything for me! Otherwise your friends will say that I'm not treating you properly, that I make you work for me – ' His voice went very high-pitched and ended on something like a sob.

Judy still wasn't sure just exactly what Etta had said, but whatever it was, she wished she hadn't. She herself could always appreciate Etta and take everything she said in the spirit in which she hoped it was meant. Bal was different. But when she tried to go close and comfort him, he pushed her away. He went into their bedroom and looked for his shoes under the bed.

'How often I have said I don't want you to go to any office! How I begged and begged you not to – '

'But I like it!' Judy exclaimed.

'You like it. But my position, this has never occurred to you, how it looks to others that I, your husband, allow you to go out to work, what a disgrace that is to me . . .' He was lying flat on his stomach, poking around under the bed with his arm extended as far as it would go.

'Etta never meant that at all. Of course she didn't. Good heavens, in England everybody goes out to work, all the married women and everyone – '

He pulled his arm out and sat bolt upright in indignation. 'This isn't England! Here do you see any of our ladies going out? Do you see my sister-in-law leaving her home to go and work among strangers? Do you think my brother would ever allow?'

'We've been over all that years ago,' Judy said, and they had.

'And I also won't allow! Why should you go there? So that people can come and insult me – '

'If you say insult once again, I'll scream.'

'And I also will scream! I'll scream loud and loud and loud! And I won't permit you to go out to your office, no, not ever again will I let you go there!'

She answered nothing to that and his brave words reverberated through the silent room. This gave him an opportunity to weigh them; which he obviously did, for he grew thoughtful and his mood changed.

He got up off the floor and came and sat next to her on the edge of the bed. 'Judy, let's go away.'

'Wherever to?'

'To Bombay – all of us together. We'll all go, we'll leave this place. What can I do here? A little bit of radio work sometimes, what more is there? We can't live on that. But in Bombay what opportunities I shall have!'

'Are you still thinking of your Kishan Kumar?'

'We shall start on our production unit, and then you will see! And all your friends will see too!'

'And supposing he's changed his mind and doesn't want to start it?'

'Of course he wants! You don't know how much it means to him. And he needs me so much – when he was here last he said Bal, please please come and be my production manager and also act a big role in my film. And I said yes Kishan, of course I shall do everything I can to help you. You see, I've promised him. He's relying on me completely. How can I disappoint him?' He took her hand and passionately squeezed it and gazed into her face with eager, loving eyes.

146

She looked down into her lap. She thought how they would all arrive in Bombay, with nowhere to stay and no money and nothing but Bal's vague prospects. She was afraid.

'And besides Kishan Kumar, there is so much. So many opportunities! How stupid I have been all these years, to sit here and wait and hope, when all the time all the opportunities were there, only waiting for me as I was waiting for them here. Now my eyes have been opened.'

Judy talked fast. She pointed out that he was wrong, that on the contrary his long-awaited opportunity had now at last come and there was Mrs Kaul eager and willing to start the theatre group he had so fervently wished for . . .

Before she could finish, he had jumped up and swept all she said aside with a grand, impatient swing of his arm: 'You can keep your Mrs Kaul-Paul! Let her make her own theatre!'

'But you wanted it, Bal, it was you who started the whole thing!'

'Yes, today she will call me and tomorrow she will say very, very sorry, there will be no theatre, instead we are having a charity fête. Don't I know these people? And still I should go and dance and sing at their whim!'

Judy felt that, in his anger and impatience, he had for once struck on a quite shrewd judgement. But she couldn't let him believe it, nor herself, for the theatre movement was now, she felt, the only thing that stood between their desolate arrival at a Bombay station, hers and Bal's and Gita and Prithvi's, each of them with a little bundle under the arm.

'She's ever so serious about it. She's already made a committee and spoken to some Minister or other – '

Bal, standing in front of her as she sat on the bed, rested his hands on either side of her and bent down towards her. He was full of energy and conviction, and she recognized that, in face of this, her own pleas, her own rather desperate hopes, sounded as weak as they were.

'Listen, Judy,' he said, his face close to hers as he bent over her, and his big passionate eyes eating her up, 'you don't know how it'll be in Bombay, everything that's waiting for us there. Please, please let us go, all of us together! Oh you will soon see and then you will bless me day and night for taking you there!'

She could not think of any adequate answer.

The Hochstadts had decided to forgive Etta. They had argued and

147

discussed with each other to and fro for many days, and though they had both been unanimous in their annoyance with Etta and their strong condemnation of her conduct, yet in the end their considerable store of forbearance and understanding asserted itself. They realized that the combination of Etta's character and her particular circumstances was so unfortunate that there was nothing for her friends to do but suspend their normal judgements and allow and forgive her as much as they could. They discussed her case fully and had many interesting things to say to each other on the subject of ageing beauties, on the one hand, and on the adaptations the Western consciousness has to make to the Orient, on the other. Dr Hochstadt had some fascinating comments on the latter subject in particular, he went right back to racial archetypes and quoted Jung, and held his wife spellbound.

It need not be thought, however, that Etta was in the least anxious as to the outcome of their debate. Quite on the contrary, she made it exceedingly clear from the beginning that she couldn't care less what they thought of her. On their way home from the picnic, she had been the only merry one in the party. They had been driven home in the station wagon, which had been specially hired for the outing, and everyone had been very quiet and glum, including the students who sat crammed together in the luggage space at the back. Only Etta, wearing a lilac gauze scarf to keep her hair from flying, hummed and sang and pointed out interesting sights on the way. They had dropped her off at her house first and she waved good-bye very gaily, her scarf fluttering in the wind. Since then she had made no attempt to get in touch with them, but kept proudly aloof as one who had no need to justify herself. Nevertheless the Hochstadts were now ready to recieve her, any time she cared to call, and to receive her in friendship and forgiveness.

It was not, however, Etta who came but Judy. They were less prepared for Judy and were embarrassed, for they guessed she had come to find out what had happened to Bal at the picnic. Their embarrassment made them shower her with attentions, they fussed around her and were so terribly cordial that she sat helplessly on their big stuffed sofa and did not know how to start on what she had come to say.

However, while Dr Hochstadt was showing her some extremely interesting old coins he had acquired and was explaining their origin and significance, she suddenly blurted out, still holding one of his coins and pretending to be looking at it, 'Now he says he doesn't want anything to do with the theatre group.'

148

Abrupt as this was, the Hochstadts immediately got the connection. They sighed, and Dr Hochstadt swept all his coins back into the cigar box in which he kept them and shut it.

'Etta is often very difficult for her friends,' said sad Mrs Hochstadt, and then kept a silence which was pregnant with indications of how much more she could say.

Judy, though she had come anxious to find out just exactly what had happened, suddenly decided that she didn't, after all, want to hear about it from the Hochstadts. There was no reasonable explanation for her decision. But she now concentrated only on talking about the theatre group.

'He says he wants to go to Bombay, in films.'

Dr Hochstadt leaned back in his chair. 'The film industry in India, though we can say it is highly developed from the commercial point of view, cannot yet be so called from the artistic viewpoint.'

'It is in the drama,' elaborated Mrs Hochstadt, 'that the fuller artistic expression must reveal itself. There we will find what is new, the work of young Indian playwrights moved by the contemporary predicament, and hand in hand with it also the revival of the great Sanskrit dramas of the past – '

'The *Shakuntala*, the *Mricchakatika*, the *Mudraraksasa*,' said Dr Hochstadt, pronouncing the Sanskrit with a great flourish, sharply enunciating each vowel and consonant and baring his teeth in the process.

'There lies India's glory!' cried Mrs Hochstadt, clapping her hands together and quite beside herself with enthusiasm.

Under these circumstances, Judy was ashamed to tell them that it was not the relative merits of cinema and drama as mediums of artistic expression that particularly exercised her, but rather their relative merits as sources of income.

She could, however, be more explicit with Sudhir and, as soon as she left the Hochstadts, she went up to see him in his hotel. There was nothing that could not perfectly well have waited till the next morning, when she would be seeing him in the office, but she felt anxious and, after her visit to the Hochstadts, frustrated and wanted to talk to someone who would get the point without her having to go into lengthy explanations. She was never very good at explaining herself.

His hotel was up a flight of stairs between a dentist's shop and a furniture maker's. The first landing ended on an open space round which the various rooms of the Royal Hotel were grouped. Some of the residents were sitting out in this open space, in their vests and dhotis, entertaining their friends; they were all young men and they all stared curiously at Judy. The doors of the rooms were open to let in whatever cool air there might be. Sudhir's was open too and she could see him and Jaykar sitting inside.

She didn't mind Jaykar being there. She liked him and felt she could say anything she wanted before him. So she went in all smiles to greet them both, but was taken aback to note that Sudhir was not very pleased to see her.

'What's the matter?' he said. He too like everyone else was in dhoti and vest, and he was leaning back on his bed with one foot propped up on a chair.

When he saw it was nothing urgent, he said, 'Couldn't you wait till tomorrow?' He seemed really quite annoyed.

Jaykar saw how crestfallen she was and pulled up a chair for her, and was as nice to her as he could be. But Sudhir went on frowning. 'Why do you come here?' he said, and he looked out of the door and saw all his fellow residents looking in with interest, and this made him angrier still and he kicked the door shut quite viciously.

Judy now wore the weak, placating smile of the unwelcome visitor. In an attempt to cheer her up, Jaykar picked up some photographs that lay scattered over the bed and showed them to her. They were excessively dull photographs. The prints were as depressing as the things they showed: which was of the interior of some strictly utilitarian brick structure without windows in which a few unintelligent-looking peasants could be seen sitting on the floor while a man was pointing to something he had written on a blackboard; and of the outside of the same brick structure (cleary donated in charity: here one could even make out the plaque which said by whom, and for what cause) and its surrounding countryside, which looked flat, stony and empty. The prints were under developed and that gave everything a sad, faded look and made one feel as if one knew the place well and had already spent many, many weary years there.

'Very nice,' Judy said, when she had looked and put them back on the bed.

Sudhir gave an unhumorous laugh. 'It's where he wants me to go.'

She snatched up the photographs again and gave them a much closer look.

Jaykar saw that these photographs, which his friend had sent to him with such pride, might perhaps create an unfavourable impression. So he took them away from her and said grandly, 'It is only a beginning, only a beginning.'

'But why should he – ?'

'Then what should he do?' Jaykar took her up energetically.

Judy kept quiet. She did not like to say that she thought he ought to – or rather, that she wanted him to – stay where he was.

'Get out!' Jaykar suddenly shouted, so that Judy had a little fright till she realized it was not meant as a literal command to herself in particular but a figurative one to many people in general. 'What is the use of sitting in this effete little empire of clerks and civil servants, when you should be out in the fields building, building, building from the foundations upwards?' He waved the photographs in the air.

'Bal wants to go away too,' Judy said. 'He wants us all to go with him.' She looked at Sudhir helplessly.

'He's got a job?' Sudhir asked.

She shook her head; her eyes were round and blue, she bit her lip and looked frightened.

'Very good,' Jaykar said. 'Let him go. People are not born only to sit safe and quiet in their own homes. What sort of life is that? And what can ever be achieved when our people behave like mice in holes?'

Sudhir said, 'But why does he want to go?'

She shrugged and looked unhappy. 'Just like that.'

This made Sudhir thoughtful. After a while he suddenly got up and flung open the door with unnecessary violence. 'Hot in here,' he muttered, and then he stood glaring at his fellow residents who were taking it easy out in the open.

'Oh, good Heavens no,' said Etta with a light laugh. She held her tweezers in her hand and was plucking her eyebrows.

'Just for a little while,' Clarissa pleaded.

'God preserve me,' said Etta with another laugh in the same manner.

Clarissa looked offended. She said, 'How mean and selfish you are.'

Etta leaned forward to the hand-mirror she had propped up in front of herself and did some very fine work to her eyebrows.

'Don't think I haven't got plenty of places to go to,' Clarissa said. 'Only I wanted to ask you first,' – she became tender – 'because I always think of you as my best, my very, very best, friend.'

Etta busied herself putting hand-mirror and tweezers away in their velvet-lined box. She was precise and quick in her movements, as always when she was engaged on arranging anything about herself or her surroundings (her languor was only her off-duty pose). She tidied the box away in her dressing-table drawer and then proceeded to filter some scent out of a big bottle into a little bottle. She looked busy and intent.

Clarissa complained, 'Why must you fuss about and do things when I'm talking to you?'

'Do go and sit in the other room. I'm not sure I like receiving guests in my bedroom.'

Clarissa plumped herself down firmly on the bed. And to make her point even plainer, she lay down flat with her shoes on. Etta turned round from the dressing-table and gave a pleasant little smile at this audacious challenge.

'Always posing,' Clarissa said. 'How I hate posers.'

'Poseurs.'

The room was filled with the smell of the very subtle perfume Etta was filtering. There was also the smell of a few fresh roses which she had by her bed. The curtains were drawn, so that even though it was the middle of the afternoon the room was in a sort of apricot-coloured dusk, very cool and soft and boudoir-like.

'Oh darn it, Etta, I'm fed up,' Clarissa said, and jumped up again from the bed; she was not a lounger by nature. 'I'm always having trouble with that place. Now they say I've got to quit within a month, can you imagine?'

'Why don't you go and see – ?' Etta mentioned the name of a very important personage indeed, who had on several previous such occasions extricated Clarissa out of her housing predicament.

'I've phoned goodness knows how many times and written letters and even been up to the house, but he's always been at a cabinet meeting or had someone with him or something. He's so rushed these days, you can't get near him.'

'Hm,' said Etta.

'I know what you're thinking! But you needn't think that. He's a very good friend of mine and when he says to me he's busy then, believe me, you can take it as gospel truth that he *is* busy.'

'Hm,' said Etta again.

'Sometimes I just want to *hit* you! And anyway I feel so mean bothering him about a personal problem, when, poor darling, he's carrying the burden of the whole country single-handed almost. No, it's not right. I suppose you wouldn't understand that sort of reticence. For you your own personal problems always come first, don't they?'

'That's right,' Etta sang out cheerfully, screwing the top back on to her scent bottle.

152

'Well, I'm sorry I'm just not made that way. Shall I answer it?' for the telephone was ringing in the next room and Clarissa loved answering telephones. She went in and lifted the receiver and said 'Hallo-ho?' in a mysterious voice.

Etta wondered whether it was, at last, Guppy. She thought, as she did many times a day, about how she would speak to him. Should she be cool and withdrawn? Or warm and welcoming? Or just normal, as if everything was as it had always been and they had been seeing each other every day? She began vigorously to brush her hair before the mirror so as to look her poised best over the telephone.

'It's so unfair,' Clarissa said on her return. 'I've been living there for years, not doing anyone any harm, and now – '

'Who is it?'

'Ha? Oh, wrong number.' She too sounded quite disappointed.

Etta flung down her hairbrush. 'I told you not to come into my bedroom!'

'What do you mean? I think you're going crazy.'

'Maybe I am, but all the same, you will please go into the other room. Or better still, go home. I have to have *some* privacy, damn it all.'

Clarissa gave her a withering look. Then, with dignity, she turned and walked off quietly into the other room. But once there, she discarded dignity and began to shout. She shouted about meanness, selfishness, impertinence. She got so angry, she took off one sandal and flung it against the wall.

'Get out!' Etta shouted back from the bedroom. 'Don't you ever dare come here again!'

'Just try and get me out! Just try!'

Etta sank down on to her bed. She held her head between her hands and moaned to herself, 'This is just too awful.'

'Of course it's awful!' shouted Clarissa, whose ears were sharply attuned to anything coming from the bedroom. 'I'm an awful person! You haven't any idea yet how awful I can be! But you'll see! You'll learn!' She flung her other sandal against the wall too.

There was a pause in which each listened to what the other might be doing. Then Etta came and stood in the doorway; she said in a calm, friendly voice: 'Clarissa dear, please don't make a nasty scene. You'll only give me a headache.'

Clarissa was standing in a fighting stance with her legs apart and her naked feet planted firm and flat. When Etta spoke like that, this stance seemed redundant but since she was already in it, she had to keep it up. She said defiantly, 'As long as you're mean to me, I'll make as many scenes as I like.'

'Oh *please*, Clarissa.' Etta lay down exhausted on her sofa and shut her eyes.

'Have you got a headache?'

'I think it's just coming on.'

Clarissa stooped to collect her sandals from where they had fallen. As she did so, she muttered now only half defiantly, the other half a bit apologetically: 'Well, you shouldn't upset me.'

'How did I upset you?' Etta asked in a patient, invalid voice. 'What did I say?'

There were by now so many grievances that Clarissa could not remember which was the one that had actually started her off. So she got back to what she had really come for:

'I can't think what earthly objection you could have to my staying here for a while. Good Lord, I'd have thought you'd be glad to help out a friend in trouble.'

Etta's reply to this was silent and to herself. For the moment, caution was the better part of her customary valour.

Holding her sandals in her hand, Clarissa plonked herself down on one of Etta's smart little chairs. 'What a mess it all is. Wherever will I find a new place to live?'

She seemed in such genuine distress that Etta began to feel sorry for her – the more so as she knew, or was determined, she could do nothing for her.

'Rents are impossible nowadays, with all those speculators about. And I need so little – just a corner somewhere!' She looked longingly round the room, but Etta wouldn't notice.

'I haven't got a fantastic income like you have, Etta.'

Etta smiled secretly, as she always did when her income was mentioned: no one, least of all Clarissa, had ever been told how much it was or just exactly where it came from.

'All I've got is that wretched little legacy my Great-Aunt Marie, God rest her soul, left me. And that's just nothing, not by present-day standards it isn't.' She threw down her sandals and slipped her feet back into them. 'Of course, my family don't care a damn. I've got all those beastly rich brothers, and sisters married to beastly rich stockbrokers or something, but of course it wouldn't ever enter their heads, oh no, that I might want a bit of assistance. Whenever I write and tell them for goodness' sake, how d'you expect me to live on £150 a year, even out here, all they can say is come back and we'll see what we can do. Come back, indeed! Not on their sweet lives. I suppose they want a free baby-sitter and nursemaid and general drudge about the place, that's what they want me back for. No thank you.'

She was taking pins out of her skimpy top-knot and then jabbing them back as viciously as if she were jabbing them into her brothers and sisters.

'I told them so. I wrote and said I'm not coming back there. I've rejected all Western values; I belong here now. Not that they'd understand. Honestly, Etta, you can't have any idea what my family are like. I mean, looking at me, you just couldn't believe it. They're the most conventional, dull, bourgeois, English *English* people you've ever met in your born days. God knows how I escaped being like that. We're like creatures from a different planet, absolutely. I really think I must have been Indian in my previous birth – in all my previous births – well, lots of people have told me so and it's true. I know it is. How's your head?'

'Better.'

'That's why I can't stand the English, but I do get on so awfully well with Indians. They feel I'm one of them, you see.'

Etta, who had had enough of caution by now, gave a rather rude laugh.

'Oh well, you wouldn't understand,' Clarissa said in a superior way which made it easy for her to be forgiving. 'You're like my family. But it's true, you know. There's a sort of vibration between these people and me – it's difficult to explain to someone like you – it's a sort of something that only very sensitive people can feel. Just to give you one small example: when I went to see Judy, her sister-in-law asked me, in fact she begged me to come and stay with them – '

'What? In that slum?'

'How rude you are. They've got a lovely little place and they're just the sort of family I adore. You really feel part of India when you're with people like that. It's home to me, spiritually and in every other way. Of course I've got lots of other people to stay with, I only have to say the word. I know Mrs Kaul'd love to have me and she's got the loveliest guest-room and bathroom, and the Kapurs and – oh just masses of people – '

'Then why bother about me?'

'I wanted to give you first chance.' She had another wistful look round the flat. But Etta's silence made it so very clear that the position she had taken up from the beginning would remain with her till the end that Clarissa found it expedient to try new ground.

155

'Do you think Guppy'd help?'

Etta was suddenly quite alert. She took her cigarette out of her mouth and looked at Clarissa.

'After all, he's got that whole huge massive hotel, surely he could find a tiny corner somewhere for tiny Clarissa? And I'd be so useful to him.'

'How?'

Clarissa hesitated – not that she wasn't absolutely convinced of her usefulness but it seemed to her so obvious as a general proposition that she hadn't bothered to give it particular thought. But of course, now that she put her mind to it, it didn't take her long to come up with a very convincing example: 'For one thing, I could be a sort of secretary to him.'

'He's got all the secretaries he needs.'

'Not that sort – you're so stupid sometimes, Etta, really. Sort of more of a social secretary. Or a liaison officer or something. With the theatre group, for instance.'

Etta looked very interested.

'He's going to sink a lot of money into that theatre group –'

'Oh?'

'Of course he is! We've both spoken to him about it and you know as well as I do he's dead keen on it.'

Etta nodded solemnly.

'And naturally, if he's going to invest all that money, he'll want to keep an eye on what's going on. But he hasn't got the time to pursue the thing, so he'll need someone to do it for him. And I'm quite willing – and able, I think I may well say.' She narrowed her eyes and gave Etta a suspicious, challenging look out of them.

'Of course,' Etta said.

'And in return for all that work and effort I'm going to put in for him, surely it's not too much to ask him to provide me one humble little room out of all those hundreds he's got in his hotel? I should think not!' She was already quite indignant, as if someone were denying her rightful claim.

Etta, however, had no intention of doing so. Instead she was so encouraging that Clarissa, giving her another shrewd look, said boldly, 'I think I'll go and have a talk to him about it.'

'Do,' Etta said. She got up and went over to her cocktail cabinet and mixed Clarissa a drink. As she gave it to her, she said, 'I think I'll come with you. To help convince him.'

Clarissa took the drink with one hand and with the other squeezed Etta's arm terribly hard, 'I'm sorry I shouted at you. It's my infernal temper – Mother used to call it my devil.' She gulped down her drink and on the last drop could not suppress a little sound of pleasure. 'I get too worked up over things, it's always been my trouble. And sometimes I just explode. But you know that I love you, don't you? In spite of everything I might say when my devil's got the upper hand, I do, do so love you. You know that, Etta, don't you?'

Etta said she did and refilled Clarissa's glass, and one for herself too. Clarissa stayed for the rest of the afternoon and they finished the bottle.

Mrs Kaul threw herself into her work heart and soul. Already their first production had been decided upon, though not without a good deal of arguing to and fro among the various committee members. Several people had suggested the *Mikado*, and Mr Jumperwala had been very keen on *My Fair Lady*, and some of the others favoured either the *Shakuntala* or the *Mricchakatika* (one member, a great purist, even wanted it performed in the original Sanskrit), and one very advanced committee member, a Mrs Desai who worked with the Handloom Board, suggested the *Caucasian Chalk Circle*. Finally, however, it transpired that one among their midst, who held a well-paid executive post in an international firm and was altogether a man of the highest culture, a perceptive critic and a charming essayist, had in his student days, some twenty-five years ago, made a translation into Hindi of Ibsen's *Doll's House* which had not yet been performed. This was obviously just what they had been looking for – something original yet at the same time an attested masterpiece, a world première which would serve to introduce West to East and East to West. Dr Hochstadt gave it as his opinion that the *Doll's House* was particularly suitable since the social conditions in Ibsen's time might to some extent be said to correspond to social conditions in present-day India, and he brought forward some very cogent arguments to prove his point, to which they all nodded and said how true. Anyway, everyone was very pleased, except perhaps Mr Jumperwala who still cast lingering looks at *My Fair Lady* and hummed his favourite tunes from it, to show them what they were all missing.

It now only remained to get the company together and the money to finance the whole project, and while Mrs Kaul herself took over the responsibility for the latter, she delegated the former entirely to Sudhir. It was a task he took on quite cheerfully, for he knew he had only to call on Bal in whose wake would come as large a troupe of actors and other aspiring stage people as anyone could wish for.

'It's just what he's been waiting for all these years,' Judy said miserably. 'And now he says he won't.'

Sudhir said, 'Nonsense.' But he wasn't convinced it was; in fact, he thought it was rather grand of Bal not to.

'You tell him!' Judy wailed. 'You don't know how I've argued with him and quarrelled and everything, but he won't listen! He just won't! All the time he's thinking of Bombay now and his awful Kishan Kumar and when you talk to him, you might as well be talking to someone who's already there in Bombay for all he hears.'

The Doctor came in, holding in his hands a broken door latch and on his face an expression of tragedy. 'This is how my property is treated by careless tenants!'

But they had no time for him. Sudhir asked Judy, 'And he wants you to go too?'

'All of us!'

Sudhir thought about the Literacy Institute; it seemed distinctly nearer. He turned to the Doctor. 'Will you be very lonely when we've all gone away?'

The Doctor looked scornful. 'Perhaps you think you can get a better place for such rent as you are paying here? Try, only try! I invite you to try anywhere in this town!'

'Oh no, don't worry, the Cultural Dais will be with you as long as culture still flourishes. I meant Judy, if she goes . . . And I . . .'

Judy said, 'Why you?'

'A Higher Purpose beckons.'

'Where are you two going?' the Doctor said.

'Our separate ways,' said Sudhir.

At that Judy became more downcast than ever. Everything was now – if not perfect, at least quite nearly so: the office with Sudhir in it and a regular income out of it, and a home which she liked, with Bhuaji and Shanti, and of course the children happy and well looked after. Whereas if they went, they went with and into nothing.

Sudhir also had a sinking feeling. Perhaps it was not so bad here after all; he had got used to the office, he liked Judy, he liked Jaykar, even the Doctor, all were familiar and comfortable. Nothing in the Literacy Institute would be either familiar or comfortable.

The Doctor, still holding his broken door handle, said with a superior air, 'Yes, for you it is easy – you can run here and there, today one place, tomorrow another and the day after God knows where. It is different,' he said and rose a bit on his toes and his stomach stuck out, 'for a man of property.'

158

Judy looked appealingly at Sudhir. 'You talk to Bal. Tell him about the theatre group – how grand it's going to be, tell him – oh you know what. Only so he'll stay and not want to go away. So we can all stay. Oh please.'

It was never difficult to locate Bal, for all that was needed was a quick survey of one or two of the more popular coffee-houses. Sudhir found him in the midst of a group of his usual friends, all of them drinking coffee and smoking cigarettes and having, to all appearances, a nice relaxing time. When he saw Sudhir, however, Bal at once jumped to his feet to welcome him with such fervour and excitement that he knocked over his chair.

All Bal's friends looked up expectantly at Sudhir. They liked to see a new face every now and again, and perhaps get a new angle on what was going on in the world.

'Let's go somewhere else,' Sudhir said; he did not relish talking in front of so many willing ears, for one thing, nor the smell and the lazy, smoky atmosphere, for another.

'Some coffee – perhaps a cold drink – something you must have!' cried Bal, hospitably sweeping his hand round the coffee-house as if it were all his and he was putting it all at Sudhir's disposal.

But Sudhir declined everything, even to sit down, so they parted from Bal's friends and walked out together. Bal suggested going to another coffee-house, but as this too was bound to be well filled with Bal's friends, Sudhir instead took him to sit in the near-by Jantar Mantar Park. It was very pleasant there, and Bal declared himself enchanted with everything, the palm trees, the flowers, the odd astronomical shapes of the Jantar Mantar jutting up in pale grey worn stone into the azure sky.

They sat on the grass under a tree and Sudhir at once launched into the subject he had come to discuss. Such directness embarrassed Bal – who would himself have spent a long time on some polite preliminaries and only very slowly and with seeming casualness have drawn into his proper subject – and he looked shy and lowered his head and plucked blades of grass.

'It was for you we started the whole thing,' Sudhir pointed out.

'I know, oh I know. And I am so grateful.' Bal squirmed with embarrassment. If he had had adequate warning he would have known how to put his case and explain everything to his own and Sudhir's satisfaction. But caught unawares like this, he floundered.

'No one asks you to be grateful. You are only asked to become a member of the group.'

'And how much I would like to. But just now – you see, there are circumstances – ' He trailed off and his attention strayed to two hoopoes pecking away at the grass.

'What circumstances?' Sudhir said.

Bal pointed at the hoopoes and said, 'What nice birds! What are they called?' He wasn't deliberately trying to change the subject, he was really interested. He spent little time outdoors, and when he did he was always charmed by all he saw.

'What circumstances?' Sudhir asked again.

'Yes,' said Bal, returning sadly to the conversation. 'You see, a friend of mine – Kishan Kumar, you must have heard of him? No? Oh he is a very famous actor, one of our leading stars.' Bal looked proud. 'And he is also very friendly to me. Kishan and I, we are so close, like brothers. Now he is starting a production unit and of course he needs me, again and again he has said Bal, please come to Bombay, please come. How can I refuse him?'

'What about Judy?'

'Of course she will come too. All of us are going.' He said this with a sort of quiet confidence, even matter-of-factness, which made it difficult to raise any protest.

Sudhir was silent for a while. Then he asked, 'You have somewhere to live there?'

Bal was not in the least troubled. He smiled: 'Oh, I have so many friends.'

'Yes, but for your wife and children – two children – '

'Of course, my friends will welcome them also,' Bal said with dignity. 'And it is only for a very short time. Then I shall take one of these new flats for them – you know, these big blocks of flats you have in Bombay, overlooking the sea. Judy will be very comfortable there,' he said with satisfaction, as if he had already installed her there.

Sudhir felt it was not his place to raise any objection. It was not as if he were a relative or had any rights over Bal and his family. And Bal was so confident, seemed so sure of himself, his plans, his future, that Sudhir felt at a disadvantage.

Nevertheless he tried again on the theatre group: 'It's quite an ambitious scheme. And of course you will be guaranteed a regular salary – '

Bal shook his head vehemently. 'For ten years – ten years! – I've been waiting here for something, and nothing has ever come. Now I'm going away. I'm going to take my own chance.'

'Yes, chance. But here it is more than chance, it is a certainty

160

He hardly dared say more. Mrs Kaul's activities and those of her committee could not, he felt himself, be the foundation of anything certain.

Bal was not listening very carefully. Probably his mind was made up so firmly that any listening he did was only out of politeness. For the rest, he gave himself over to enjoying his surroundings. Birds sang and cawed and butterflies played in the flower-bed. The grey of old stones and the green of grass and bushes and trees were all drenched in gold by the sun. The tops of feathery palm trees tickled against a sky which was still and blue as a lake with birds floating on it, high, high up, slow and lazy.

Bal lay on the grass with his arms spread and his eyes shut blissfully and he smiled. 'How silly we are. To sit around in the coffee-house when outside it is so lovely, Sudhir,' he said.

Sudhir grunted. He felt heavy and sullen and earthbound beside Bal. Bal seemed to him like one of those birds floating on the sky – drifting without thought or effort or fear, aerial and at ease.

'How stupid I have been all these years,' Bal said with a little smile at himself. 'I should have gone away long ago. What is the use of sitting and waiting only for success to come?'

Sudhir did not answer. He was unexpectedly reminded of Jaykar, who also disapproved of sitting and waiting.

Disturbed by Sudhir's silence, Bal sat up and leaned on one elbow and said, 'Don't you think so, Sudhir? Don't you think I'm right?' He was, however, so anxious for assent and confirmation that he could not wait for Sudhir to give them but had to do so himself. 'Of course!' he cried. 'It is so, I know! Yes, I have been very stupid.' He looked thoughtful for a moment, then he lowered his voice and said confidentially, 'And I think I was afraid also to leave my home and go away. You see, I was a coward, yes a real coward,' he said in a tone which was so condemnatory that it at once inspired him to be absolutely firm with himself. 'But not any more. From now on, you will see, I shall be quite a different person. And no one will ever dare to say to me again' – and his eyes blazed dangerously – 'that I can't support my own family. No one shall ever insult me like that again.'

Sudhir wondered who could have insulted Bal, but he did not get far in this speculation, for the next moment Bal's face cleared again and he spoke out joyously – 'In Bombay everything will be so different! Yes, a new life is beginning!' Then impulsively he turned to Sudhir, for he never liked anyone to be left out of anything: 'Why don't you also come with us? You can be our PRO – of course we shall need one in our production unit, it is a very important assignment.' Two butterflies, chasing each other and then interlocking wing upon wing, fluttered before his face, and he put up his hand as if he meant to catch them and laughed when they eluded him. 'Sudhir, what is the use of staying always in one place?' he urged.

Etta was not surprised to find the same girl again in Guppy's suite. She had almost expected her. The girl had taken off her shoes and was lying fast asleep on Guppy's sofa. Her scarf had slipped from her bosom and was trailed half across her stomach and half across the carpet. Her bosom, thus exposed, tight, full and young in her pale green silk shirt, rose up and down as she breathed. Her cheeks were a little flushed, her mouth a little open, a few locks of dark brown hair had escaped from their pins and curled around her plump face.

'Who is she?' Clarissa whispered.

Etta smiled, part smile, part sneer. 'His niece.'

'Well we'd better call him.' Clarissa strode over to the telephone and had herself connected with Guppy's office. 'Yu-hu!' she yodelled down the line. 'Three guesses!'

Whatever his feelings might have been about this unexpected visit, he had well mastered them by the time he arrived upstairs. He came in all welcome, large and genial and rubbing his hands in simulated pleasure. His eyes just flickered over the sleeping girl, but he kept on smiling. 'Please be comfortable, quite comfortable,' he invited them. 'What shall I order for you?'

'Gin and tonic,' Clarissa said promptly.

'Excellent, excellent, very good.' He made no move to ring for a bearer though. 'Well well, you have given me a nice surprise.'

'Yes, haven't we?' said Etta, looking at the girl.

He passed it over with ease. 'It is always nice to meet with old friends. There is an Urdu saying – it goes, well I can't quite remember but it says, yes well old friends are best friends, ha-ha-ha!' He rubbed his hands again. He seemed in excellent health as well as excellent spirits. Etta thought he had put on more weight – she had always warned him about that: he really was far too fond of his food – but he was one of those people who can carry almost any amount and yet remain, quick, active and light on their feet. He was dressed rather more flashily than he would have been under Etta's supervision, in suède shoes and a terylene shirt and a ring or two too many; his hair was thickly plastered with sweetly-smelling oil. Though by no means

162

young, he appeared full of physical vigour and a not incongruous match for the girl sleeping her healthy sleep on the sofa.

Etta gave another pointed look in that direction. 'Your niece appears to be sleeping.'

'Isn't she sweet?' Clarissa said, and she too looked, but in a far more kindly way. 'She's a lot like you, Guppy. Is she your brother's daughter or your sister's? You can see the family resemblance all right.' She shut one shrewd painter's eye and looked from the girl to Guppy and back again.

Etta laughed – genuinely, she was amused. Then she asked Guppy, with flippant good humour, 'What *has* she been doing to make her so tired?'

Guppy passed this over. Instead he returned to the theme of how glad he was to see them – though his cordiality was already a little cracked and gave indications of his desire to know why they had come, what they wanted, how long they were going to stay. One foot in its suède shoe tapped up and down on the carpet.

Etta sank luxuriously into his biggest arm-chair, lit a cigarette and exhaled her first puff of smoke with an audible sigh which expressed her pleasure and satisfaction at being there and her intention to stay a good long while.

'Of course, Guppy love,' Clarissa said, 'you do know that we're tremendously happy to see you again and that we'd run one hundred thousand miles just for the pleasure of meeting you, but this time, it's no use beating about the bush, we've come with a capital P Purpose.'

'You spoil the happiest occasions,' Etta said. 'Just when he was so glad to see us for our own sakes – '

'Well I'm very sorry, I'm just no hypocrite. It's not in my temperament.' She looked at him with frank eyes. 'Now then, Guppy, we've come for money.'

He had a visible shock.

'Stick 'em up!' said Clarissa, levelling two long forefingers at him. 'Your money or your life!' She gave a laugh and lowered her fingers. 'No seriously, Gup, it's about the theatre group.'

The girl slept through everything. Wonderful, thought Etta (who never slept without the help of pills and even then could be awakened by the dropping of a pin), the power of youth and health. She stared at the girl as if willing her to wake up, but of course was unsuccessful: the girl went on breathing in and out, blissfully, in and out, her breath delicately fluttering the wisps of escaped hair that curled around her face. Etta looked away again disdainfully, and with the same disdainful glance, looked round the room, at the fat, shiny sofa-sets and the satin lamps, which so often she had longed to change but which she now recognized as being eminently suited not only to Guppy's personality but to the girl's as well.

'Very nice,' Guppy was saying. Etta could see that he wasn't listening very much, but Clarissa was talking ceaselessly, holding herself spellbound with her own enthusiasm. She had soon unfolded all her plans to him and he was scratching his chin with his finger-nail as was his habit when he was being cagey, though he kept saying from time to time, 'Yes, very nice, very very nice.'

Suddenly the girl gave a cry in her sleep. Everyone looked at her and expected her to wake up, but instead she tossed her heavy body to the other side and, with her back to the room, continued sleeping. Her shirt had hitched itself up and was crumpled round her waist; large round buttocks clothed in green silk stared into the room. Guppy, Etta noted, seemed embarrassed.

'I could move in whenever you say,' Clarissa said. 'And of course the sooner we start our company the better all round.' She rubbed her hands. 'You'll find me a very active campaign manager.'

'Just now we are fully booked up,' Guppy murmured.

'Oh any little old cubby-hole would do.' She began to walk round Guppy's own suite, peering into the bedroom, the bathroom, even opening a few cupboard doors.

Etta snatched at the little privacy this afforded, and asked in a low voice, 'When are you leaving?'

But Guppy, who was evidently not in the least anxious to be private with her, answered quite loudly, 'In a week or two.' To Clarissa he said, 'But this is only the linen cupboard.'

'Lovely place you have,' she said, absently opening his wardrobe.

'So you're really going.' Etta stretched out one leg (a little too white and blue-veined, but still exceedingly shapely) from her short skirt. 'And going without me.' She smiled up at him, curving her mouth in a winning way. It did not escape her notice that, almost in spite of himself, he glanced down at that provocative leg.

He cleared his throat. 'It is a business trip.' He looked round as if for distraction or rescue.

'But I mean strictly business too.' Now she stretched out the other leg as well. She didn't know what it was she was still hoping for, but she felt herself to be desperate and ready to try, dare anything. 'I'll go and book my ticket, shall I? Shall I, Gup? Say yes.' She lisped on the last ('thay yeth') and looked up at him with big, appealing, loving eyes, but at the same time her fingers tensely twisted the handle of her bag to the point of ruining it.

'A really cosy nest,' said Clarissa, returning from her tour of inspection. She clapped Guppy on the back, making the thick flesh under the terylene shirt resound. 'Snug as a bug in a rug here, aren't you.'

He didn't know what she meant, but it was obviously a great relief to him to be able to laugh. He laughed excessively, even holding his sides, to the surprise and pleasure of Clarissa, who had not expected so overwhelming a response. Etta tried to light a new cigarette, but her lighter wouldn't work, it clicked and clicked in her slightly trembling hands.

At this point the girl slowly sat up on the sofa. She was warm and flushed with sleep. She looked at them all out of brown, liquid eyes which she slowly blinked once or twice. Her scarf was still trailed half across the sofa and half across the floor. Dazed and sleepy as she was, she groped for it, quickly to cover up her breasts which were very clearly in evidence through the tight silk shirt and on which, so lushly prominent were they, all eyes seemed to be fixed.

It was never any use talking about Bal to his elder brother Mukand. Mukand had given up on Bal years ago, so much so that, whenever Bal was mentioned, he would either pretend not to hear and go on reading his newspaper, or he would turn his face away and assume an expression of saintly resignation.

So Judy knew it would be no use to appeal to Mukand against Bal's decision to go away to Bombay. Mukand would want to know nothing about it, would have washed his hands of the affair before he had even touched it, though at the same time he would be, out of long habit, wearily resigned to be called upon to pull Bal out of any trouble he might with his new venture get himself into.

His wife's attitude was different. Shanti was enthusiastic about the whole idea the moment she heard about it – much to Judy's surprise and a little bit to her chagrin. She asked, 'Aren't you going to miss us?' put out to see Shanti glow and smile like that at the prospect of their departure.

Shanti had a round, middle-aged face, but her expressions were those of a young girl. As soon as Judy said that, her look of joy gave way to one of misery. 'Oh yes, it will be so dull and lonely here without you.' And then at once she changed back to joy again. 'But I'm so glad for you! It is so exciting! Bombay!' She smiled and looked dreamy and radiant. She had never travelled anywhere except, before her marriage, when she had twice visited a cousin in Dehra Doon.

Judy was amazed that Shanti could not see the terrible difficulties that she herself envisaged only too clearly. But Shanti was too enchanted by the prospect of a journey, a change of scene, for Judy and her family to be concerned with questions of where they were to live and what on.

She bent down to her youngest child, who was crawling round her feet. 'And when you grow big, you also will go to Bombay! And to Calcutta! To Dehra Doon, to Madras, to Aligarh – everywhere! To England also! Oh!' she cried and picked up the child and danced her up and down in her arms. The child's diaper had come off and she was stark naked under her little brown silk dress cut down from one of Shanti's old saris. She crowed with pleasure and put out fat little hands and grasped her mother's nose and touched her cheeks. Shanti laughed and looked into her child's face as if to read there traces of all the travel and adventures in store for her.

But Judy wanted only to stay where and how she was. It wasn't a very grand place, she knew – that broken old house behind the bazaar with its flaking damp-stained walls and its dangerous electric wiring – but she had grown used to it and fond of it.

Bal nowadays was full of energy. He got up earlier than usual, whistled and sang a lot and went out to more places than ever. He was always in a good mood. Once Judy overheard him telling the children about Bombay and how they would live in a beautiful flat with a lift to go up and down, and the sea and the sea-shells and jelly-fish and whales, and their Daddy acting big parts in big films. He held his audience spellbound, and Gita and Prithvi became prouder and prouder, and how Shanti's children begged to be taken too! And the only disturbing factor was Judy, who was in the bathroom but shouted from out of there, 'No one is going!' and furiously poured water over herself out of the bucket which served them as bath.

Bal tried to ignore this interruption, and continued to entertain his listeners with fascinating stories of Bombay in general and the film world in particular. But Judy came storming out of the bathroom, still dripping wet and her sari tucked round her in very haphazard fashion, and said, 'What are you telling them all that rot for!' Bal and the children looked up at her in pained surprise.

'We're not going!' she said and stamped one foot and her wet towel slipped from off her shoulders. She snatched it up again impatiently and proceeded towards the bedroom, shaking drops of water as she went. She banged the door hard behind her. The children and Bal looked at one another.

'We're *not* going?' Gita asked him reproachfully.

'Of course,' he said. 'Of course we are.' He stroked her hair, affectionately but a little absently, looking nervously towards the closed bedroom door.

'Tell more!' Prithvi said.

Bal tried, but failed, to recapture the earlier mood. Though he dwelt on the same interesting subject, the children soon sensed that his heart was not in it, their attention wandered and soon they were off in search of other diversion. Bal timidly entered the bedroom. Judy was lying flat on the bed.

'Why do you talk like that?' he asked her.

'Because it's true. We're not going.'

He was silent.

'We're not, we're not!'

'All right,' he said quietly. He went out. She followed him at once.

'I mean it!'

'All right,' he said again.

'What do you mean – all right?'

'All right, I will go on my own.'

He went into the sitting-room and sat down on a chair and picked up a film magazine that was lying there. He didn't have time to start reading it though.

'What, and leave us here? Not on your life!'

He patiently shut the magazine and laid it aside. She watched him narrowly, as if she suspected him of intending to rush up and out of the house and off to Bombay that very moment. But he only sat quietly and modestly on his chair.

'Say something!'

'What?' he said. 'What shall I say?'

She sank down on the sofa opposite him. How hard it was! One day they would get a real sofa, with springs.

'What do you want me to do?' he said, eyes sadly downcast.

'Stay here.' She wanted it so much, she felt, to stay here always. And one day they would have a proper sitting-room, buy proper furniture, not only a sofa but arm-chairs too and a little table with a glass top.

'And do what?' he said. 'Always the same – always running after something, hoping for something, and then it becomes nothing.'

This was perhaps the first time he had ever looked at his activities of the last ten years so squarely. Also it was probably the first time she had heard him speak of his life with any degree of bitterness. But she was at that moment too taken up with her own feelings to pay much attention to his. She was flooded with love for the shabby little room in which they sat and which was theirs. She looked with sentimental eyes at his two framed certificates and his photograph at the airport, and promised all three of them a grand future in silver frames.

'There is nothing here for me,' Bal said.

'The theatre group will be starting soon.'

'Don't talk to me of your theatre group! I want nothing to do with it. I want nothing to do with any of your precious friends.'

'Silly,' she said, quite affectionately. She would buy vases too and a lot of little ornaments. She was sorry for a moment that there was no mantelpiece in the room.

'Judy, but in Bombay – ah, you will see! How happy you will be there! And you will be so proud to speak of me to your friends and tell them now he is acting in this picture, now in that picture, he is earning lakhs and lakhs of rupees. Lakhs and lakhs!' he cried and laughed out loud and came over to her and embraced her with enthusiasm.

She pushed him away. Perhaps even a carpet on the floor, she thought; or at least a little rug.

Mrs Kaul did not slacken in her efforts. A woman of energy and ambition, once she had fastened on to a scheme she did not let go till she had pushed it through to its limits. Or rather, to *her* limits: for though she did manage, by persistence and ambition, to get a thing on to its feet, it somehow never grew or prospered to anything more than she and her friends could conceive of. Their ambitions were large but their conceptions – based as they were not so much on any profound inner need as on something heard or read about and found desirable – were so vague and weak that everything that came of them also tended to be vague and weak. That was what had happened with the Cultural Dais as well as with one or two previous schemes (such as a Discussion group and an International Music Circle): finally everything turned out disappointing, and then Mrs Kaul had to look for something new.

The theatre group came just in time to save her from the disappointment the Cultural Dais was turning out to be. She threw herself into it with enthusiasm. Once she summoned Sudhir urgently to her house and, when he got there, he found her in an elated state. She sat in her drawing-room, drinking tea out of a transparent china cup and told him with an air of triumph, 'We are making very good progress!'

'Oh?' said Sudhir, who had thought they weren't making any.

She dropped several lumps of sugar into her tea with a pair of silver tongs. 'I'm getting so many actors together. It is surprising how much talent there is.'

Sudhir wondered whether she had got on to Bal and his companions. He was surprised. He hadn't thought there was any direct road that could connect Mrs Kaul and Bal.

'It all happened yesterday at a dinner the Mahajans gave to the Swedish Ambassador.' She smiled. 'Mrs Mahajan confessed to me that in her College days she took a great interest in dramatics. Then we discovered there were so many other friends who had a lot of acting experience – Mrs Moitra, the wife of our Principal Secretary, had taken part in many fine performances while she was studying at Shantiniketan, and Mrs Labh Singh – the Major-General's wife – had taken a leading role in a regimental performance of *Arsenic and Old Lace* when they were stationed at Simla. And we all remembered that young Captain Lakshman was a leading light in the Army Headquarters Dramatic Group and – oh, we discovered so much talent!' she cried gaily, terribly pleased with herself, her friends and last night's party. Then she leaned forward and confided to Sudhir, 'It is best to keep it all as much as possible among people we know.'

Sudhir drew back instinctively as if wishing to dissociate himself completely from people one knew.

'One great advantage also, these people won't be greedy for money like those other actors, on the contrary, they will be very happy to give their services free of charge. They are all deeply interested in the advancement of the theatre movement in our country.'

Sudhir came to a sudden decision. 'I shall be leaving soon. I'm going to Madhya Pradesh.'

Mrs Kaul put down her tea-cup. She dabbed an embroidered napkin against her upper lip. 'I'm afraid it will be difficult for you to take leave just now. The burden of work will be very heavy while we are establishing our group.'

'I'm not taking leave,' Sudhir said brusquely. 'I'm leaving.'

Mrs Kaul accepted this in pained silence. She stared in front of her, at a Chinese silk hanging on the wall (brought back by Mr Kaul from a mission in Peking).

'I'm going to teach in a Literacy Institute. I think my level of culture doesn't really rise higher than to neo-literates.'

'Just at this time,' Mrs Kaul said in a voice trembling with reproach.

'But you don't need me! When you have Mrs Mahajan and Captain

– what was his name? who can all afford to donate their talents free of charge.'

'We have worked together side by side.' He noticed that she was really hurt, and it embarrassed him. 'And now, just when our biggest effort of all is beginning . . . I thought the work meant so much to you.'

Sudhir didn't even feel tempted to tell her just what it meant to him. He had often pleasurably anticipated the moment when he would be handing in his resignation and had never expected the occasion to turn out, the way it was now doing, in any way painful for him.

And then she was quite different. She cried out in a voice rich in real feeling, 'It means so much to me! Without this work, what is there in my life?'

He wished she would stop, but saw that there was little chance of that now. He took off his glasses and cleaned them and put them on, and then he took them off and cleaned them again. He knew exactly what she would say, and that was what she did say. Mr Kaul all day in his office, and always committees and meetings and not a moment to spare for her; and the children away at boarding-school (naturally, one wanted only the best for one's children) – who was there for her? Who needed her? She sat here in this big house, perhaps people envied her, but – ah, if they only knew, if they could only read into her heart.

She took a sip of tea for comfort, and when she had done so, she said, 'I'm like a bird in a gilded cage.' He realized by the way the phrase came out so patly that she had used it before and more than once, perhaps when she had sat like this in her drawing-room, drinking tea with some lady friend, and had suddenly been overcome by the feeling that life had not offered her everything it seemed once to have promised.

Etta phoned Guppy every day, and sometimes she went to see him. He was always cordial with her, both over the telephone and when they met, but at the same time brisk and preoccupied so that it was difficult to speak about anything very personal. Etta tried all sorts of angles, but he was too adroit for her. When she became serious, he contrived to call one of his staff and became involved in giving instructions. Once or twice the girl was there, and Guppy did not tell her to go away, and she sat there, lush and passive, pervading the room with her physical attributes, so that it was difficult to concentrate on anything but her.

These were bad days for Etta. She stayed at home most of the time, and sometimes she did not even bother to get dressed but lay on her unmade bed all day. She ate almost nothing but smoked an exorbitant number of cigarettes.

For the first time she disliked her flat, though she had taken so much trouble with it and had made it as chic and modern as she still knew how. Now it was stale with cigarette smoke, untidy and dusty, closed in like a cage. Yet it was a cage that was necessary to her and out of which she would not break even if she could: for outside lay the dusty landscape, the hot sun, the vultures, the hovels and shacks and the people in rags that lived there till some dirty disease carried them off.

She lay on her bed and smoked and thought about Europe. It was infinitely distant and infinitely desirable. But she was afraid of it too. Here at least she had her personality: she was Etta, whom people knew and admired for being blonde and vivacious and smart. In Europe there were many blondes, and there they might more easily notice that she was not as young or as vivacious as she once had been; and they might not think her smart at all. She no longer knew the way they dressed there, or the way they talked, or the fashionable foods they ate and drinks they drank, the books they had read, the conversations they had held with one another, while she was out here.

Yet if she could have gone with Guppy, it would have been all right. She would have been rich, protected, staying in the best hotels. She would have carried everything off beautifully and been treated with deference by waiters, taxi-drivers, hairdressers and shop assistants. But on her own there would be nothing like that. Instead she would be arriving with her smart suitcases and there would be nowhere to go, no one to meet her, no one to know who she was. She could not face it: to break through such a barrier of indifference would take more strength and youth than she had had for a good number of years. She longed for Europe, it was true, and would do anything to get there, but she could no longer tackle it on her own.

Once Judy came to see her. Etta raised her head from her pillow, took in Judy wearing a sari and her hair in a bun, groaned 'You look awful,' and then wearily sank back again.

Judy tried to hide it, but she was shocked by Etta's appearance. She had never seen her like this. Etta's face looked sunken and the skin stretched tight over the fine bone structure; there was something about her eyes and forehead which made it seem as if she had been suffering from a severe headache for a long time. She looked strained and – though Judy hardly liked to think it even to herself – old.

'Why've you come?' Etta asked with her eyes shut. 'Don't you know I've had a fearful row with your precious what's-his-name? Where's your wifely loyalty?'

Judy hadn't meant to bring up this subject at all, and now that it had been, she wanted only to pass it over. She didn't feel she had any quarrel with Etta. She was sorry, of course, that she and Bal should have had such a scene but wasn't inclined to blame either of them. It was all, she was sure, some awful misunderstanding. Bal and Etta were unfortunately two people made to misunderstand one another.

'He wants to take us to Bombay,' she said. She got ready to tell Etta the whole story but Etta cried, 'I don't want to hear! I'm just not interested!'

Judy did not insist. She got up and walked round the flat. She noticed that everything looked different. There was a layer of dust and ashtrays were full to overflowing. The windows were all shut and the curtains drawn over them.

'Where's your servant?' Judy asked. She suspected that Etta had dismissed him – she changed servants frequently – and hadn't got a new one yet. She wanted to offer to tidy up a bit, and perhaps get Etta something to eat; it seemed to her that Etta was sick, and she was sad to see her so alone.

'Oh he's around somewhere,' Etta said. 'I've told him not to come in here – I can't stand him around, I simply cannot. He smells so.' After a moment she added, 'They all smell.' She hated servants. They perspired and wore dirty clothes and were stupid and dishonest.

Judy hesitantly picked up one of the full ashtrays. 'Shall I –'

'No! Put it down! Don't touch anything! Don't *fuss*!'

Judy quickly put it down again. She stood by Etta's bedside, awkwardly fiddling with the loose end of her sari. She felt she ought to do something but didn't know what. 'Are you sick?' she said at last, in a cracked, uncertain voice.

'Yes I am. Sick, sick, sick. Sick to the depths of my soul.'

'Oh dear.' This mild comment was not made to be ironic, but it was the only one that rose readily to Judy's lips. After it had crossed them she stood and bit them.

Etta painfully screwed her face into an expression of disgust. 'Your sympathy overwhelms me.' Then she turned her face to the wall. 'Oh go away,' she said.

Judy stood there twiddling her sari a while longer. Etta didn't stir, pretending to be asleep. 'I'll be going then,' Judy offered. This brought no response. 'Good-bye,' Judy said, standing still.

172

She waited in vain. So she left the bedroom and went into the next room to reach the main door. She walked reluctantly. She had already opened the door and was about to close it quietly behind her when the summons she had been waiting for came. At once she was back by Etta's bedside. 'Did you call?'

Etta said wearily: 'I'll probably be going away soon.'

'Oh, Etta.'

That seemed to sting her. She sat up. Her blonde hair, which now looked very brittle and false, slipped down over her face and she pushed it back impatiently. 'You think I'm here for ever? You think I'm going to let myself *rot* in this – this – '

'Hole,' Judy tactfully suggested.

'Hell!' Etta emended with violence. 'No, thank you, I rather flatter myself I've been reserved for a better fate. I'm packing up. I'm getting out.' She swung herself off the bed as if she meant to there and then. She paced the room angrily, her arms folded, holding a cigarette between the fingers of one veined, nervous hand. She was wearing her nylon apricot-coloured negligée, but it was somewhat crushed. She had no fresh make-up on and traces of the old had remained on her face, making it look discoloured; her lips were thin and very pale and her eyes dim. It pained Judy to find her so unglamorous.

'It may be all right for you here,' Etta said. 'God knows why, but you don't seem to care how you live or where or with what sort of people. But I care! Passionately!' She took a long pull from her cigarette and filled her lungs with smoke in a deep, passionate breath. 'I've wasted quite enough of my life here. Now it's time for me to get back where I belong. To a civilized place.' She looked Judy up and down as she stood there in her crumpled cotton sari. 'The trouble with you is you've forgotten what it's like to be civilized. To wear decent clothes – go to theatres – concerts – drink wine with meals – ' She brought up her clasped hands to her forehead and shut her eyes and seemed rapt beyond speech with longing and desire.

Judy saw that Etta was moved by strong feelings, so she sympathized with her. But for herself she had none of these feelings. The things Etta spoke of were familiar to Judy only from the magazines and the pictures, and she had no hopes that they would ever enter into her own circumstances. Her Western world was only little semi-detacheds with smoking fires and frozen pipes and carefully drawn curtains bought at two and eleven a yard at the sales.

When Etta had recovered sufficiently, she at once renewed her attack on Judy. 'I don't know how, but somehow or other you've

173

managed to fool yourself you actually *like* being here.' And quickly she forestalled the protest which Judy in any case wasn't going to make. 'Don't try and fool me, though! Making a virtue out of necessity may be a favourite English pastime, but no one asks you to pretend you find it a pleasurable exercise. My dear child, I wasn't born yesterday. I can *see* what's happening to you. Look at you, just look at you!' – and this was said so peremptorily that Judy really looked at herself in the mirror, but saw nothing very extraordinary.

Suddenly Etta came up behind her and pulled the pins out of her hair. Judy's hair, which she did up in a plain bun (in order to look like everybody else – Shanti, Bhuaji and all the neighbouring women) came falling down over her shoulders. It was fair, very fine hair. And with another tug Etta pulled off the sari, so that it dropped off and lay in a pool round Judy's feet. There was Judy in her sari-petticoat and the short blouse, looking young and vigorous and pleasing, with her apple breasts, her bright eyes and her fair hair framing her face.

Judy blushed. Her face – too pale after ten years in India – was suddenly the fresh pink it had been intended for. At that moment Etta, who, fearing perspiration, human dirt, alien flesh, usually hated touching anyone, put an arm around her and said, 'Come on, we'll go together, you and I – we'll take a place somewhere, in England, France, Italy, anywhere you like, and we'll have a good time! Shall we, Judy, shall we?'

Judy was embarrassed. First, by Etta touching her, which was unexpected and then too by something desperate in Etta's tone which she could not understand. To hide her embarrassment, she stooped to pick up her sari and tuck it back into her petticoat-string.

Etta turned away from her. She stubbed out her cigarette and lit a new one. After a time she said, 'Catch me going anywhere with you!' – and she laughed in a dry, hard way. Judy uneasily laughed with her.

Jaykar was delighted when Sudhir decided to go. He wrote a paragraph in *Second Thoughts*, specially in his honour, which went as follows:

'Now is the time it behoves our Youth to leave their cushioned chairs, gird up their loins and stride out into those areas of our vast land where the trumpet of Progress has not yet sounded its first triumphant notes. What is this Progress of which we speak with proud and eloquent tongues? Is it a mere toy to be bundled up and praised and cherished in the speeches we make to one another in our comfortable corners? Nay, rather is it a banner to be lifted by the strong arms

174

of our Youth and carried into the fields, the huts, the villages, the deserts and the jungles! Let each man raise his banner and advance! Forward into our Future!'

He read this out to them in a ringing voice, and when he had finished Sudhir cried 'Wah!' in applause. Sudhir was in a light-hearted mood and had been ever since he had decided to go. He tried to fire Judy into joining his applause, but she wouldn't. Her mood was not in the least light-hearted.

The Doctor had been, as usual, much impressed by Jaykar's eloquence, but now that the effect of its rolling waves had passed off, he had time to ponder its sense. He scratched his head dubiously, and after he had scratched it, he shook it; he evidently could not agree with what he had heard.

'A rolling stone gathers no moss,' he finally quoted and compressed his lips together with a wise air.

Jaykar became angry. He accused the Doctor of being a reactionary, a fogy, a brick-bat stuck in the wheels of progress. He pointed out how the Doctor's philosophy was an encouragement to gather moss not only on the body, but also on the mind, the heart and the soul.

But Judy thought how pleasant it would be to gather moss. Her parents had never rolled and had gathered a lot of it – perhaps she was, after all, more like them than had hitherto appeared.

She and Bal had many quarrels nowadays. She had only one argument against him, which was not so much an argument as a principle and consisted mainly of, 'I won't go.' She was thus at a disadvantage to Bal, who had many, and marshalled them with tireless skill and fervour, beginning with a blooming picture of the life of ease and luxury that awaited her in Bombay and ending, when all else had failed and she would listen to neither appeals nor promises, with an exhortation to the precept of Sita. Had Sita said 'I won't go' to Rama? Had she, or had she not, followed him into exile, into the jungle, into whatever places and hardships fate might lead them? And all this without hesitation or demur, following with sweet devotion and of her own free assent the path of wifely duty.

Judy turned often to Bhuaji. She felt she wanted an ally so badly, but was disappointed over and over again in Bhuaji's complete – not refusal, but sheer inability to see her point of view. Judy spelled it all out for her: didn't they have to have some security, she and the children, at least the knowledge that something was waiting for them at the other end? Instead of packing up and leaving everything on the

175

strength of nothing more solid than Bal's optimism? It was so ridiculous, so unreasonable, it could not be expected of anyone; she
talked herself into a state of righteous indignation, which was aggra-
vated by the lack of response. Bhuaji evidently tried to be sympathetic, but she did not get indignant along with Judy. Instead she
said, 'Life takes us here and there,' and turned up the palm of one
hand in a gesture of resignation.

One day, though, she said, 'If you want, I'll come too.'

'Come where?'

'With you. To Bombay.'

Judy stared at her for a moment, then dismissed her with, 'Talk
sense.'

'No no,' Bhuaji said, eager as a child, 'really I'll come.'

'Come to what? We got nowhere to stay, we got nothing there.'

'Never mind. It will be all right.' Then she said, almost pleadingly,
'Take me with you. We shall manage.'

Judy felt no gratitude. On the contrary, she was critical of Bhuaji,
who appeared to her as irresponsible as Bal. In comparison with the
two of them Judy felt herself to be very adult and sensible, and very
English. English people didn't behave like that, they didn't on the
whim of the moment give up everything they had and go wandering
off in search of no one knew what. That might be all right for people
like Bhuaji and Bal and all those holy men in orange robes one saw
roaming about. But it was not all right for anyone English and sensible; not all right for Judy. She was determined to hold on tight to
what she had, like her mother, like her Aunt Agnes, like all those
other stubborn dwellers in little houses among whom she had grown
up and who, she now decided, were her kind.

Clarissa was extremely indignant. 'Wait till I come back, he says!
Three months!'

Etta appeared totally uninterested. She lay on her bed, smoking, in
her negligée; the ashtrays overflowed; the curtains were drawn; the
room had evidently been neither dusted nor aired for many days.

'I certainly can't wait three months. I've got to clear out of my
place by next week. Whatever shall I do?'

Etta's lack of interest became quite dramatic.

'And after all he promised ... Naturally, when a man makes all
those promises, you rely on him. I do, anyway. I've got faith in
human nature, that's my trouble. He could have told us he was going
away!'

'He did,' Etta muttered.

'Instead of making all those promises and then running off. What did you say?'

Etta didn't say it again. She slipped down on her pillow and turned her face to the wall.

'You ill or something? Why don't you get up? And it isn't only me! It's the whole theatre group he's leaving in the lurch. And just when we've really got things going. Why didn't you come to the meeting on Wednesday?'

'Oh leave me alone, please do.'

'Certainly not. You agreed to sit on the theatre committee and now you can't simply forget about it, just because you're not in the mood. Everybody kept asking where you were. Mr Jumperwala must have asked at least four times.'

She went over to the window and roughly pulled back the curtain. Harsh daylight fell into the room. Etta sat up in bed, one arm shielding her eyes. 'Don't do that!'

'I'm only opening the windows a bit. It's so stuffy in here.'

'No!'

Clarissa shrugged and pulled the curtain shut again. She didn't want to make an issue of it; there were other things on her mind.

'Naturally, I told them at the meeting all about how Guppy was going to make a big contribution and practically support the whole thing. Everyone was so pleased. And now he's gone and walked out on us.'

'He's gone?'

'His plane left this morning. His niece went with him too. He's taking her for higher studies abroad.'

Etta's face was still turned to the wall. She lay absolutely still. There was no sign that Clarissa's information made any impression on her at all; indeed, she did not appear to be listening. But Clarissa was too full of her own indignation to be put out by or even to notice any lack of response.

'Why do people behave like that?' Clarissa asked. 'Making big promises and then, when the time comes to do something, they're off. There's Sudhir too. Now that we're all ready, with such nice actors Mrs Kaul's found who're all going to work for nothing, now he says he's leaving. Found another job or something. People are so mean. But of course the meanest of all is your Guppy. Honestly, Etta, the whole thing makes me so depressed, I can't tell you. I want to believe in people – I *do* believe in them – but then to be let down like that, oh

177

it's so unfair. I think I'm going to cry.' She took out a big handkerchief, which had already seen some service, and trumpeted her nose into it.

'I'm not crying for myself. I'm not that kind of selfish person. What I'm crying for is human nature. Why are people like that, Etta? Surely one must have some principles, some sense of right and wrong. But wherever you look, all you see is selfishness and dishonesty. It's so beastly. Isn't it, Etta? Etta?' she inquired and there was a listening pause and then she cried, 'Etta!' and next moment she was kneeling by the side of the bed, with her arms around Etta. 'You're crying. You're crying too.'

'Nonsense,' Etta said, turning her head away.

'I *saw*!' She tightened her hold and laid her head affectionately on Etta's stomach.

Etta struggled to get free and, at the same time, to prevent any more tears from falling.

Judy was tired of quarrelling with Bal and went out for a walk with the children. They went to the old Moghul park which was always very busy in the evenings. There were teams of volley-ball players, and many children, and at least three prayer meetings. Bhuaji was at one of the prayer meetings. She sat with a lot of other old people on the ground, while a pandit recited to them out of Tulsidas' *Ramayana*. He interspersed his recitation with commentaries and sometimes broke into song.

Gita and Prithvi soon found friends to play with, while Judy sat on the grass a little way off and waited for Bhuaji. There was actually not much grass, for most of it had been trodden down and died for lack of water. It was a big park, and the municipality did not have enough money to keep it up; but people enjoyed themselves in it all the same. They came in the evenings out of their crowded houses in crowded lanes and found tranquillity under the big old trees that had been planted by the Moghuls. There was also a lake, and on the edge of the lake was a pavilion in which a Moghul princess was said to have had secret trysts with her lover (both came to a bad end). Now bats lived in the pavilion and students sat in it to do the studying they could not do in their noisy homes.

Judy liked being here. It was busy and crowded and yet at the same time peaceful. This was a paradox she discovered over and over again, wherever she went. One left the house and everywhere it was full of people, so much going on: little shops in which women bargained, men played cards on a bed pulled out into the street, students studied under a lamp post, holy men cried Ram Ram tapping with a long staff and rattling a tin, and film songs came out of a radio: yet always, above everything, the sky was large and beautiful, and one had only to look up and it was peaceful. She looked up now and found the sky, in its first dawn of night, a smooth soft surface of pale silver. The old trees were black silhouettes and you could see each leaf quite still and very delicate against the silver.

She couldn't ever remember having looked up at the sky in England. She must have done, but she couldn't remember. There had been nothing memorable: nothing had spoken. So one locked oneself up at home, all warm and cosy, and looked at the television and grew lonelier and lonelier till it was unbearable and then one found a hook in the lavatory. Judy could not imagine ever being that lonely here. In the end, there was always the sky. Who spoke from the sky here? Why did it seem to her that someone spoke? She must be going batty.

She smiled, sitting by herself, and thought of Bal. She was sorry they quarrelled so much nowadays, though she liked him even when she was quarrelling with him. The last words he had said to her before she left for the park were, 'You don't believe in me, but when you see me acclaimed by millions, then you will know!' He had been standing in the courtyard, one foot raised up on a string cot, his arm shot out to point at her dramatically. She could still see his brilliant eyes in his dark face and the way his nostrils had flared as he flung her that challenge and the proud movement of the head with which he had tossed back his hair. He was like a film hero already.

Bal had so much confidence – not in himself perhaps so much as in his fate. He trusted. Whereas Judy only wanted to be safe where she was. But when she thought now of her home to which she clung so, with the furniture that wasn't furniture but mostly old tins and trunks, it didn't seem so very desirable. Not even when, in her mind's eye, she transformed the old tins and trunks into sofa-sets with springs. These too seemed a trivial cause to tie one down in a world which was so wide, encompassed by a sky out of which perhaps someone spoke.

Why should she be afraid to go out into that world? Bal wasn't. He had nothing waiting for him in Bombay any more than she had, but still he was ready to go, full of hope.

Bhuaji's prayer group had all burst into song. They sang rather raggedly, some ahead and some trailing behind, but with fervour.

Judy too could find a job in Bombay. Yes, it would mean running around, the way she had had to here, and waiting about in people's offices and being told 'no' many times over, but even that would not be so bad. She had done it before, she could do it again. Anyway, even if she stayed here, she would probably not be able to keep her job; and, without Sudhir there, she wouldn't want to much either.

How happy Bal would be if she were to return home now, and say all right, let's go! When Bal was happy, he laughed and laughed, he played and sang, he hugged the children till they screamed. If he had money in his pockets, he would spend it all on some special treat, rushing out to buy fruits and sweets and toys and coming back with his arms full and his eyes shining. Afterwards he would make love to her all night and only go to sleep when it was time for everyone else to get up, a smile still on his face.

Bhuaji's prayer meeting came to an end. It always came to an end in the same way, with a final song which everyone knew and sang lustily in cracked old voices. Then, after a few polite inquiries concerning each other's ailments and daughters-in-law, they dispersed. Judy collected the children and walked home with Bhuaji, who was in a very good mood. Bhuaji was mostly in a good mood, but after a prayer meeting she was especially so. She walked vigorously, waddling from side to side, and smiled to herself like one who has just eaten an exceptionally fine meal.

Gita was in front, with Prithvi, and Bhuaji looked at her admiringly and remarked, 'How tall our girl is growing.'

Judy also looked. Gita had long, thin, brown legs and her frock had grown too short. She was nine now; a few more years and she would be out of frocks. Judy had heard many tales about how young girls have to be guarded in India and she did not think she could manage by herself. She needed Bhuaji, who knew about these matters.

And she needed her for so much else besides. Judy looked down at her and asked, 'Are you really coming with us?' but she felt shy (it seemed too much to ask of anyone) and spoke too softly, so that Bhuaji, still smiling and sunk in her own pleasant thoughts, failed to hear her.

They came to the betel-seller's little hut and here Bhuaji stopped to buy aniseed for the children (she had a theory that it was good for their digestions). She told the betel-seller, 'Soon we shall all be going away to Bombay.'

'Take me with you,' he pleaded. 'I want to meet Waheeda Rehman.'

'You and your film stars,' she said. The walls of his tiny shop were

180

plastered with pictures of actors and actresses in languishing attitudes torn out of the screen weeklies; only the centre portion was reserved for a gilded picture of the god Ganesh, decorated with a little garland of jasmine.

When they walked on, he called after them, 'At least send me her picture with autograph!'

Judy said 'You've got so many friends here, you know everybody. There we'll all be strangers.'

Bhuaji shook her head, as if this were too silly an argument for her to reply to.

Judy didn't say any more. But next day she went to the bank and drew out all her savings: 725 rupees. That day Bal was very happy.

The Hochstadts had gone to bed early. They lay side by side in the big double bed, both of them propped up from the back by fat pillows; Dr Hochstadt was reading aloud to Mrs Hochstadt from the works of Coomaraswamy. She listened with her hands folded before her, her big head, neat in a hair-net, inclined slightly towards him the better to hear and concentrate. He stopped at any particularly interesting passage they came to and commented on it, and sometimes they had a little discussion on it in which Mrs Hochstadt also expressed her opinions – though, of course, she was always ready to modify them in accordance with his. Mrs Hochstadt prided herself on her intelligence, but she was happy and even proud to cede to her Franz's superior one.

While they were thus pleasurably and beneficially employed, the telephone rang. They were surprised, for it was almost ten o'clock and they could not think who might want to reach them at so unorthodox an hour. Mrs Hochstadt got out of bed, and so startled was she by the unexpected and insistent ringing, that she went straight into the next room to answer without giving herself time to wear her wrap or slippers. Shortly after she had lifted the receiver, Dr Hochstadt heard her gasp and now it was his turn to leap out of bed and rush into the next room.

'We are coming at once,' she said and put down the receiver. She looked at Dr Hochstadt with a shocked expression: 'It was Etta. She says she has taken too many sleeping pills.'

His face at once took on the same expression as hers. Suddenly they looked like twins, both of them round-eyed, round-mouthed, in their identical nightgowns out of which protruded identical thick, naked, white feet: two bulky twin angels from a German print with a peculiar air of childlike innocence about them.

But once dressed, they became their own decisive selves again. They were soon in a taxi and it was not till then, till they were on their way, that they allowed themselves to comment on the occurrence. Even then, not much comment was required, for they knew themselves to be perfectly in agreement. After the first shock, they were in full command of both their faculties and the situation. They did not panic, for they were shrewd enough to know that Etta had not taken very many pills. Probably she had intended – at least had pretended to herself that she intended – to finish the bottle, but by the time she had swallowed a not too fearful number, she had bethought herself of the Hochstadts and had picked up the telephone. It was not unlikely that she had bethought herself of the Hochstadts before she even started swallowing, and the only factor she had been imprecise about had been just exactly at what stage to call them.

They guessed all that, but did not resent it. They knew that for Etta they were the bourgeois whom it was her pleasure to astonish; that she regarded them as solid, good, dull people to be often made fun of and shocked whenever possible. But because they were solid, good and dull, she needed them and relied on them: they were content with that. As long as they were here, they would play that role in Etta's life, and after they had gone back to England, they would send her letters written in a humorous style but full of sound precepts and advice. Nothing she said or did could ever alienate them, for they were people of the world and understood her and took pride in that understanding.

Thus they rode in their taxi, purposeful, resolutely bent on the rescue to which they had been called, and though they had been got out of bed and nightgown, they expressed their feelings in nothing further than the headshakes the strong may be allowed to expend over the weak.

Sudhir's fellow passengers were all asleep. There was a dim nightlight in the compartment and he could see them sprawled in uncomfortable attitudes amid bundles and baskets on their benches; arms were flung out, here a head drooped, there a leg dangled, and every now and again they groaned or cried out as they heaved themselves into new positions. And while they thus fitfully slept, the train clove wide awake through the darkness and took them farther and farther away from where they had started. Sudhir found this process of being removed, whether he liked it or not, so exhilarating that he could not sleep. He was not thinking of where he was being taken, but was glad to be taken somewhere. He was not thinking of what he had left behind either.

When the train stopped at a small station, he got off. The air outside was very different from what it was in the crowded sleeping compartment. A little breeze, laden with smell of dust, blew through the warm night. A few people ran about, swinging hurricane lamps and calling to each other in voices that pricked as feebly into the large surrounding silence as their lamps did into the darkness. The station seemed a very small one, with a low building which could just be made out in silhouette and looked as if it had been propped up in cardboard against the ocean of flat empty land that stretched, as far and wide as one could conceive, all around it. The sky had no stars or moon, but a tattered silver veil of clouds shifted and sailed across it.

Some new passengers were getting on. They were two well-dressed women, jingling with jewellery, their silk saris drawn modestly over their heads, and they were being seen off by an elderly but vigorous and well set-up man with a white moustache. He gave orders in a commanding voice for the bestowal of the luggage, and then spoke to his two charges in a much lower but very urgent voice, as if he were trying to impress something on their minds, while they nodded to show they had understood and gave golden little jingles with their bracelets. Sudhir stood very near to them and looked at them curiously. They were unexpected passengers at this forlorn little station, and he wondered where they could have come from, out of those dusty desert tracts that lay beyond the station and seemed to speak of nothing but jackals and cacti.

When he was sitting once more in his carriage, and the train speeding ahead, he found himself curiously excited over the unexpected appearance of those two dainty, well-dressed women. Although the unexpected was nothing new to him: he had been born and lived all his life in India, and knew that one could never be sure what sudden thrill might not spring out of even the most unpromising soil. He remembered how once he had wandered through an abandoned slum colony, where the pitiful shreds of pitiful lives lay scattered over the cracked and filthy earth and an old woman dug hopelessly in a heap of ashes, and suddenly it was sunset and the sky blazing with the most splendid, the most royal of colours and everything – the old woman, and the ashes, the rags, the broken bricks, the split old bicycle tyres – everything burst into glory.

His fellow passengers slept, they heaved, they groaned, they cried out in their sleep. When they were awake, they were very talkative, and had already exchanged the most intimate details of their personal lives. There was one very lively woman, with dancing black eyes and winning little ways, who made it her business to draw everyone out.

She had made Sudhir divulge the circumstances of his life to the compartment in general, and when she had finished with him, she started on a morose old moneylender who kept muttering to himself in a corner. By means of skilled little flatteries and coaxings and teasings she had succeeded in making him respond: but instead of retailing the details of his life – which, in any case, were probably exceedingly monotonous, consisting of nothing further than a sour counting and recounting of his profits with occasional heartbreaks over losses – he confided his ambition, no, more, his yearning to go to Tiruvannamalai, where Sri Ramana Maharshi had lived and died, and to stay there, within the aura of departed holiness, for what was left of his poor, sinful days. And this note he had struck found a response in the others, so that soon several of them were divulging their secret longings – starting with the talkative woman, who could not have a child but wanted one so badly that she spent all her time going from one place of pilgrimage to another, praying and offering and offering and praying, wandering all over the country, quite unafraid and ac- companied by no sturdier bulwark than this old great-aunt of hers they saw nodding over a basket of provisions which she hugged tight on her lap, who was herself a childless widow and had been left totally deaf by an attack of smallpox.

These revelations, and others that followed them, had not par- ticularly stirred Sudhir at the time. He had listened only because he was trapped and there was nothing better to do; and he had, as a matter of fact, even felt a movement of distaste against these out- pourings in which he saw too many obvious sentiments expressed in obvious (though of course grand) phrases. But now at night, when he alone was awake among sleepers, he recalled those conversations with intense pleasure and recognized in them a manifestation of all the variety and unexpectedness of the fertile lives that sprang out of this soil, which was in itself so various and unexpected and was now desert and now flourishing fields and now the flattest plains and now the highest and highest most holy of mountains.

He thought about all the discussions he and Jaykar and other friends were for ever having about India, and indeed how everyone always talked about it, incessantly, compulsively, and yet never said anything that was in the least conclusive or that could not be instantly and authoritatively contradicted. But it seemed to him now, shut in with an assortment of strangers and travelling through a landscape which was too dark to be seen and could therefore be only guessed at, that perhaps the paradox was not a paradox after all or, if it was, was one that pleasurably resolved itself for the sake of him who accepted it and rejoiced in it and gave himself over to it, the way a lover might.

Etta's flat was dusted, airy and smart again. She lay on her bed, in her best negligée, her hair newly blonde and her face made up bravely. She had cut down on smoking.

'Of course you know you're here only for the time being,' she said. 'Till I'm all right again.' She said this at least three times a day.

'Sh,' Clarissa replied. 'Quiet now.' She patted Etta's pillows, making them more uncomfortable; she was an earnest but a clumsy nurse.

The bell rang and Mr Jumperwala came in with a big bunch of flowers done up in white tissue and tied with a blue satin ribbon. He came every day and every day with an identical bunch of flowers.

He tiptoed into the bedroom. 'And how's our invalid today?' Coyly he laid the flowers by her side.

'Oh Jumpey, aren't they gorgeous. Did you make them yourself?'

He had a hearty laugh. He found her wit irresistible. He sat by the bed, on a little white chair with an apricot-coloured silk seat. 'You remind me of my friend Baxter. He was the same, a joke for every occasion. Jolly we called him. Jolly Baxter.' He shifted the chair closer to her pillows. 'Did I ever tell you of the time we all went boating at Maidenhead?'

'Not too much excitement,' Clarissa warned from the doorway.

'Oh go away,' Etta said. 'Let Jumpey tell his tale.' She turned green eyes on him, with glamorous green lids.

Clarissa went out on to the terrace. All her possessions were piled up there, her old bags and suitcases and canvases and a few pieces of derelict furniture. None of it looked worth keeping but she regarded the pile fondly and then looked up at the sky and hoped it wouldn't rain. Certainly, before any rain was expected, she must move everything into the rooms. It would be a bit of a tight squeeze, and Etta was so awfully fussy, but it had to be done. She could stuff quite a lot under Etta's bed and some more under the divan and on top of the wardrobes.

'. . . so he said "ere alf a mo" – in cockney, you know, the cockneys don't pronounce their hs – "ere alf a mo, that there is our hoar," he said. He had put h, you see, in front of oar in the cockney way, and of course that made it – do forgive me – a naughty word too.' He looked at her with naughty eyes and then lowered them bashfully and allowed himself a little titter. 'Jolly was such a witty chap, so amusing.'

'Awfully,' said Etta, flattering him with all her attention – so that she didn't notice Clarissa coming in, carrying some canvases tied up in tattered brown paper.

'He was a wonderful sportsman too. A real all-rounder.'

'What *are* you doing?' Etta asked, as Clarissa poked around under the bed.

Clarissa straightened up, wiping the dust off her hands and looking rather pleased: she had stowed her canvases away very successfully and found there was room for lots more under there. 'Now then,' she cried heartily, 'who's for a lovely drink?'

'Just a cup of tea,' Mr Jumperwala said. 'You know me: a strict t-e-a-totaller.' He smiled. So did Etta.

'Spoil-sport,' teased Clarissa.

'Yes, my English friends were always very cross with me on that score. "Dusky," they'd say – they called me Dusky, you know – "Dusky, one day we're going to drown you in a butt of malmsey like the Duke of Clarence." It appears there was some Duke – the English aristocracy have always been most eccentric.'

Etta didn't let up on her listening smile, but at the same time she told Clarissa, 'The curtain's not drawn properly.' Through a chink she could see a bit of too blue sky and the black wings of some birds of prey flashing against it.

'Lady Fusspot,' chided Clarissa, but with obliging good-humour she tugged the curtains together and closed the chink. Etta relaxed: now everything was as it should be. The room was dim and apricot-coloured; her jars and lipsticks glittered on the white rosewood dressing-table; the flowers Mr Jumperwala had brought still lay, elegant in paper and ribbon, across the bed. She picked them up and, rustling the paper apart, idly smelled them while Mr Jumperwala told her some amusing anecodotes about the English aristocracy. In the next room Clarissa was clinking with glasses and bottles; she had also put on a record and Piaf was singing *La Vie En Rose*.

All Bal's friends came and they made a big crowd on the platform and were an annoyance to porters, other passengers, conductors and men pushing mail-bags. But they were in a very merry mood and had brought quantities of sweets and fruits as gifts for the journey and clowned and joked with Bal. Judy sat quietly inside the compartment, with Bhuaji and the children. There were some other people in the compartment, who stared at them and at the goings on outside on the platform, in amazement. Bhuaji soon got into conversation with

186

them, and gladly answered all questions as to who they were, where they came from and where they were going.

Apart from their bedding, and their baskets of provisions for the way, they did not have much luggage. It was amazing, as Judy had found when they were packing up, how few possessions worth taking they had accumulated in their ten years. The only item of which they had anything like a profusion was children's toys, and these were mostly broken so that Gita and Prithvi, in a surge of farewell sentiment, had distributed them among their cousins and friends. There was no furniture, the kitchen utensils all belonged to Shanti and, as Bal pointed out, they wouldn't need their winter quilts in Bombay. So the only relics of ten years of home and housekeeping turned out to be the framed photograph of Bal at the airport and his two framed certificates. They didn't have very many clothes either – except Bal, and he gave a good many of his away because he said he could get nicer ones in Bombay.

Although his friends had brought many gifts for the journey, Bal could not resist the hawkers who plied up and down the platform, and he was soon buying everything within sight and thrusting magazines, plastic toys and packets of dried fruits into the compartment. Judy cried out to him to stop, but he was too excited to take any notice. He also treated his friends to cups of hot tea and spicy potato cakes freshly fried by a man squatting over a brazier he had set up on the platform.

Bal's friends teased him and said they hoped that this was only a small foretaste of all the treats he would provide for them when he came back. He laid both his hands on his chest and solemnly swore that he would give them a party the like of which they had never seen even in their dreams. He flung his hands from his chest and now used them to pluck promises out of the air – liquor, he promised, oven-baked chickens, musicians, poets, dancers – everything, everything the heart could desire. His friends soon entered into the right spirit and contributed their own ideas for this forthcoming party to celebrate Bal's fame and fortune. They grew more and more imaginative, and soon they had drawn close together, their arms slung round one another's shoulders, and were whispering among each other: suddenly to burst apart again in an explosion of loud laughter, and they slapped each other on the back in appreciation of their own daring and exuberance, while porters in tattered red shirts with mountains of luggage on their heads and shoulders shouted and wheedled a way through.

Someone had brought a camera, and Bhuaji, Judy and the children were brought out of the compartment again and arranged on the steps of the train: at the top, Bhuaji, smiling uncertainly from under her sari; on the step beneath her, Judy, blonde and scowling a bit, saying hurry up now, and beneath her, the two children, posing with earnest faces; and on the first step, holding on to the rail with one hand, the other akimbo on his waist, was Bal – his face in profile, head slightly tilted backward, feet at an angle in a resolute stance.

'Now please smile!' the photographer invited them, peering in a professional manner through his box camera. All the friends smiled in unison, but of the group being photographed, only Bhuaji obliged. The others remained solemn – even Bal, who wished to be commemorated on this occasion as a man seriously facing a serious future and so took care to present to the camera a profile that was, like a soldier's or an explorer's, stern and keen in its expression.

Just as the camera clicked, Prithvi began to cry because he was afraid the train would start and they would be thrown off the steps and left behind.

Dr and Mrs Hochstadt had just come back from the world première of Ibsen's *Doll's House* in Hindi. Socially, it had been a memorable occasion. There had been flowers, flashlights, wonderful silk saris, new hair-dos and the Prime Minister as guest of honour. There had also been many speeches: by the Prime Minister, one or two ordinary Ministers, by Mrs Kaul and the Norwegian Ambassador (who had seen the occasion as one more link in the chain of friendship that so closely bound the peoples of India to those of Norway).

About the artistic success of the venture the Hochstadts tended to have their reservations. Of course, fair as always, they had to admit that they didn't know the language and so probably missed a lot of very fine nuances. But they could not help feeling that the production as a whole lacked that certain élan which makes for a really satisfying evening at the theatre. Mrs Mahajan, who had taken the part of Nora, had several times forgotten her lines, which had not unnaturally flustered her and rendered her unable to understand the prompter though he spoke loud enough for most of the audience to hear him quite clearly. Captain Lakshman, as Torvald Helmer, had delivered all his lines with his right hand raised in the air: which might, the Hochstadts didn't know, be an Indian dramatic convention, but they rather felt it made, as far as the present production was concerned, for a certain stiffness. There had also been one or two technical hitches, such as the curtain not closing promptly enough at the end of an act, which had tended to undermine the dramatic impact of the last lines spoken and had left actors and audience staring at one another in some embarrassment; and the electrician, a large Sikh in striped underpants, had made his presence a little too conspicuous by casually strolling on to the stage – in pursuance, it was true, of his duties, but unfortunately in the middle of a scene – fiddling about with a refractory light and, his task achieved, casually strolling off again.

But these were petty details, and the Hochstadts had, after mature reflection, no difficulty in rising above them: which left them free to contemplate the larger issues and applaud, with all their hearts, the courage and daring of the enterprise. Here was a true attempt, on the one hand, to revive the theatre and rekindle in the people a love of that great art which they had lost but which had once, in ancient days, been so triumphantly theirs; and, on the other, to weld this ancient heritage to what had since been achieved in countries of the West and so bring about a synthesis not only of old and new but also – and what could be culturally more fertile? – of East and West.

To such an enterprise the Hochstadts could not but give their most wholehearted assent. And, further, they saw in it a reflection of the spirit of India as a whole – of that new India, which strove to bring itself in line with the most highly developed technical achievements of the twentieth century and yet retain its own culture: its art, its religion, its philosophy (and where in India, as Dr Hochstadt so aptly remarked to his wife, can one draw a dividing line between these three manifestations of the human spirit?) which had ever been, and would ever be, an inspiration to all the world.

The Hochstadts felt truly privileged to have been given the opportunity to witness the renaissance of this old, yet newly born, country at such close quarters; and if, in their own small way, they had been able to lend a hand here and there, to point perhaps, however tentatively, a path, that was not something on which they prided themselves but, quite on the contrary, simply considered it their own good fortune. Now their stay in India was drawing to a close. Another few months and Dr Hochstadt's assignment would be at an end, and it would be time to return to the normal course of their duties. In a way they were not sorry: all good things must come to an end, and they were beginning to miss the cosy flat in St John's Wood (at present let out to an exchange professor of tropical medicine) and several other features of their normal settled lives.

But what a store-house of memories they would be taking with them! How greatly they felt themselves enriched by their contact with this fabled land!